# Tied in Knots: Get Knotted!

## A REVERSE HAREM OMEGAVERSE

### EVE NEWTON

**Tied in Knots**
**Get Knotted! Omegaverse**
**By Eve Newton**
Copyright © Eve Newton, 2022

# Preface

Dear Reader,

## SEX DOLL!
### And Berk is a word!

Did I get your attention? Yeah? Excellent!

This book is British. Very, very British. From arsehole and berk, to wazzock, wanker and quid, you will find all the wonderful slang and idioms and SPELLINGS, that we British use.

Also, a quick note on some possible trigger warnings. There is mention of domestic violence (not seen), a hunt and abduction (seen).

If you know the scene which Faith makes reference to in Chapter 27, YASSS! If you don't, you can check out the iconic blow-up doll scene from Only Fools and Horses here: https://evenewton.com/latest-updates

Enjoy and let me know if you also feel a bit sorry for Gertie ;-)

Love
Eve

## Chapter One

Faith

*Three Months Ago*

"You're gorgeous," he pants in my ear as he pounds into me, slamming me up against the door of the dingy, dimly lit, small toilet cubicle in this dive bar in East London.

"You too," I murmur, wondering when the fun part starts for me.

"You feel so good."

"Mmm."

Sure, this beta between my legs is super cute with his brown hair and chocolate eyes, but so far, he's not doing it for me. I only accepted his offer to buy me a drink because my arsehole older brother, an alpha through and through, ditched me when some pretty omega decided he was worth going after. I'm pissed off and lonely here and I have no idea how to get back to my brother's place.

Wrapping my legs around him tighter, I plant a kiss on his lips, twisting my tongue around his to try and bring my arousal to the surface. He is a good kisser, and it works. I gasp, going damper round his cock.

He groans and grips my hips tighter, fucking me until an orgasm ripples through my body and he comes straight afterwards with what sounds like a relieved grunt. And I mean that in the sense that he is relieved I finally came all over his cock, so he could come too.

As far as one-nighters go, this leaves a lot to be desired, but it passed some time and I feel less angry at my brother. Not that I would have confronted him about it anyway. I hate confrontation. I would rather just let it go, but hold on to the grudge until doomsday. I'm a people pleaser to my core. I hate that about myself, but I don't have a choice in the matter. It's part of my survival instinct. The rebel inside me is dying to come out, but I just can't let her. A low form of contrariness is about all I can release when the situation calls for it. I hate being told what to do, but I do it because I hate the confrontation more. I just mutter to myself about how much I dislike everything and leave it at that.

I unwrap one leg and place my dainty high heeled shoe on the floor before I steady myself enough to uncurl my other leg. Shoving my dress back down, I bend down to retrieve my knickers from the floor of the cubicle. Gingerly placing them in my tiny bag and not back on, I snap the bag shut, ready to leave.

"Can I see you again?" he asks, doing up his pants.

I shake my head, looking down.

"Why not?" he cajoles, tipping my chin up so I can look into his face.

I don't. I avert my eyes. "I'm just visiting."

He scoffs in my face, as I half-expected him to. "Sure you are. If you don't want to see me again, just say so. It wasn't that good anyway."

The rage that bubbles up inside me makes me quiver, but I don't say anything.

With a noise of disgust, he roughly lets go of my chin, and pushes past me to open the cubicle door and storm out.

"Not that good," I mutter under my breath. "You never had it so good. Prick."

I follow him out of the cubicle, hearing the door to the ladies slam shut. Glaring at myself in the mirror, I sigh. Fluffing out my light blonde hair, I then wash my hands and take a step back.

Reaching into my bag, edging the knickers out of the way, I find my birth control and take it, choking it back without water. There is no way I can go home accidentally knocked up if I fall into the one percent category of omegas who get pregnant without ever having a heat. I mean, come on...if it was going to happen to anyone, it would be me. If it did, my stepdad would kill me. He is a nasty piece of work and so much of me wishes I could stay here with my older brother, but my first heat is coming up in a few months, and there is no way I can be away from home, as horrible as it is. I have to return and double my efforts to find a nice pack to mate with like all my friends already have. I feel like the last omega spinster on the shelf, scrapping about for a pack and willing to take sloppy seconds. This would never have happened if my dad was still alive. Pete, my stepdad, doesn't give a flying fuck. He just wants to keep me around to use me as a slave.

Tears pricking my eyes, I turn to leave, shoving open the door and making my way across the noisy, crowded bar, darting around strangers so I don't touch them, grateful to see Derek, my arsehole brother, sitting at the table I'd vacated a few minutes ago with the unnamed beta.

He growls when he sees me and stands up abruptly, knocking back the chair. He grabs my arm and hauls me out of the bar and onto the wet street, the gloomy rain pouring down in the dark night. I shiver as the freezing cold December air hits my bare arms in this skimpy white dress, the rain drops adding to the icy fingers of the wind as it skitters across my skin.

"Where were you?" he asks.

"In the bathroom."

He breathes in deeply and I cringe.

His disgusted look matches that of the beta and shame fills me, but I try to push it aside. I'm an omega ready to bond and mate and have babies. There isn't anything anyone can do about that, not that I'd want them to. It's my ticket out of my family home and to a place where I will be taken care of, if not cherished.

"You're going back home tonight," Derek states. "I'll drop you off at the station."

"What about all my stuff?" I complain.

"You can get it next time you visit. Sharon is waiting in the car for me, and I don't exactly want my little sister around when I take her home."

"Oh, great," I mumble, seeing I have no choice. "Just great."

Ten minutes later, I'm on the last train home, my face pressed to the glass as I wave goodbye to the big city, my stomach tied in knots. I shed a tear to be going home where tomorrow things will be hard and humiliating and humbling.

*Please let me find a pack soon. Please, please, please.*

## Chapter Two

Sebastian

It is nearing midnight when our beta, Matt strolls into the country manor, on the huge St. James's estate which we call home. As soon as the door closes, I freeze and inhale deeply.

*That scent.*

It has my dick going stiff, my knot throbbing at the base. I haven't even stood up yet from the leather chair behind the large mahogany desk that sits across the far corner of the room, on the ground level of this two-story house.

"Matt," I call out, rising and going to the door. "Matt!"

He is heading up the sweeping staircase, looking dishevelled like he just got a fucking good shag. He turns and heads closer to me, taking the stairs quickly.

"What is it, Seb?" he asks.

"Where were you?" The urge to grab him and hold him closer to me so I can breathe that scent into my lungs, into my *soul* almost overwhelms me.

"East London pub called the Hand and Dagger. Why? Something up?" He narrows his eyes at me, running a hand through his hair. He is a couple of inches shorter than me, not as well-defined, but a good-looking lad.

Breathing in through my mouth so I don't jump on him and scare him half to death, I narrow my eyes. "You hook up with someone?"

He gives me a smug, self-satisfied look that grates on my last nerve. "Oh, yeah. Hot, little blonde omega. Railed her in the bathroom and she came all over my dick like a good girl."

The urge to smash him in the face with my fist overcomes me and I have to clench it at my side to prevent me from breaking his nose. But the need to get a jab in overcomes me anyway. "Guess she was blind drunk to allow *you* anywhere near her."

Matt's eyes narrow in irritation. He is itching to throw a punch, but he wouldn't dare. "Well, sorry we can't all be like you, Seb. Besides, not all omegas like tall, dark and whatever the fuck your face is."

"Oh, ouch," I drawl, rolling my light blue eyes in a show of nonchalance which I strictly do not feel.

The scent of that omega is driving me into a state where it is about to throw me into a rut all on its own. I need to find her. I don't know why or how; all I know is that my primal instinct is driving it.

I make the mistake of drawing in a breath through my nose, and I growl deep and low as the scent hits my senses. She smells like strawberries on a hot summer's day with honey dripped sparingly over them and a dash of whipped cream.

"Seb?" Xander calls out, running down the elaborate, thick carpeted hallway, to skid to a stop underneath the chandelier where Matt and I are standing. The glint of the crystals is sparkling against the gilt of the stair banister, distracting me momentarily from my alpha pack brother.

Drawing my gaze back to Xander, I watch as he sniffs wildly at Matt, his face uncomfortably close to the beta, his hands stroking Matt's chest as if he is trying to collect the omega's scent, making him squirm. Out of the four alphas who live in this house, Xander is the least restrained. As the prime alpha, it is my job to keep him in line and it is sometimes a full-time job.

"Who is she? Where is she?" Xander pants, shoving his blonde hair out of his eyes, where it had fallen all mussed up from his sprint down the long, tapestried hallway from the informal sitting room.

Matt gives him a shove and steps back. "What the fuck, man?" he growls. "Get your face away from me."

Grabbing onto Xander, I yank him back from the fight that is about to go down. Catching my eye, I see Benjamin leaning over the balcony at the top of the stairs, being overlooked by the full-length portrait of the first ever alpha of the St. James pack. Our pack. Instinctively, I know if I turn my head slightly to the left, I'll see Harvey loitering. Just to prove to myself that I know, I do it and feel smug when I see the huge, red-headed alpha hanging back slightly, almost afraid to come closer out of fear of what he will do.

I clear my throat. "Well, it seems we have a bit of a dilemma on our hands here. Matt, any chance you could pass along this delectable omega's name." It's worded as a question, but it's not a fucking question. It is a demand, and one he will give in to if he knows what's good for him. Our pack is a few weeks away from making a decision on a suitable omega. We have it narrowed down to three candidates, all of whom pale in comparison to this unseen, nameless creature that is driving our senses wild.

"Don't know it," he grunts.

"You fucked her without getting her name?" I ask, the scorn in my tone making his cheeks go red with annoyance.

"Wasn't time. She threw herself at me after I bought her a drink," he boasts, trying to save face from my derision.

"Indeed," I murmur. "Anything else you can tell us? Anything at all?"

Matt shakes his head. "She blew me off. Cunt."

Without warning, without thought, I reach out and clamp my hand around Matt's throat, squeezing tightly, a deep, possessive growl escaping my lips.

He chokes, his hands scrabbling at mine to get free.

There is no chance. I could break his neck with just the right amount of pressure.

Ben's steady voice drifts down the stairs. "Sebastian. Let him go. He doesn't have the capacity to understand why this is so important."

It's an insult and Matt takes it badly, scowling furiously, but I let him go. I'm reasonable enough to know that none of this matters to Matt. He is a beta. He can smell her scent, but it doesn't affect him the way it affects us. It's not as potent, as alluring, as sinfully delicious as it is to us.

"Then we retrace all of your steps. Find someone who knows her and knows where we can find her." I take in the other three alphas with a wicked smile. "Gentleman, we just approved our omega. Now all we need to do, is find her."

## Chapter Three

Faith

Three months after I visited Derek, I wake up to the irritating voice of my stepfather droning above me.

"The dishes, Faith. The sink is fucking full. Get up, you lazy cow and get the kitchen cleaned up."

"If you want it done so bad, do it yourself," I mumble into my pillow, still half asleep.

The silence that follows, wakes me up.

I gulp.

*Did I say that out loud?*

It becomes clear that I did, when Pete yanks the duvet cover off my cold body and grabs my arm, hauling me to my feet. I shiver in my soft, white cotton pjs. It's freezing in this house in the middle of winter. Pete is too skint to put the heating on, so we all have to suffer.

"Get your fat arse downstairs now, girl before I tan it for

you," he growls right in my face, his spit spraying onto my cheeks.

I resist the urge to gag. He is ugly and overweight, but he is still an alpha, even if he is the runt of all alphas. He could kill me with his bare hands if he wanted. Lord knows my mother gets the brunt of his fists on a regular basis.

Lowering his eyes, he sees me submit and he lets me go. I duck around him agilely and scamper off down the stairs, bursting into the kitchen to see my mother about to do the dishes.

"No, Mum. Go sit down," I murmur, guiding her away from the sink.

She gives me a wan smile, her dirty blonde hair scraped back into a ponytail and her blue eyes, just like mine, tired and sad.

I hate this. I hate Pete for being such a dick. I hate Derek for leaving us with him. I hate my dad for dying...

Tears prick my eyes and I turn to the overflowing sink in the cold, dark kitchen, removing all the dishes so that I can rinse them off first before I wash them. Guilt creeps out of the darkest depths and takes hold of my soul, forcing the tears to break free and roll down my cheeks. I bite my lip hard to stop myself from making a sound. Mum would only feel worse if she knew how much I cried, how much I hate this tiny three bedroomed terrace house with badly decorated, paper thin walls and ragged carpet that has more holes in it than a slice of Swiss cheese.

"I'm sorry, Dad," I mouth silently. "I love you and I wish you were here."

I miss him so much it aches. He was a wonderful man, a true alpha. We lived in a big house with beautiful gardens in a posh part of town. Derek and I wanted for nothing, but Dad always made sure we earned our treats. We did our chores, but we were happy to help out. It was what families do. Here, I'm just a slave. Someone for Pete to boss about and wash his disgusting, skid-marked Y-fronts. Retching slightly at the thought of the laundry that also needs dealing with, I bite the inside of my lip to prevent the ugly sob that wants to escape.

"Anne!" Pete's annoying whine filters down the stairs.

The downstairs area of this house is open plan, which offers little privacy or quiet. You can hear everyone's conversations from all over. Not that I have anyone to really talk to. There's only my cousin, Rayne. She's about a year younger than me and my dad's brother's daughter. We used to be closer before Dad died, but now we live about half an hour's drive away and even with phones and texts, we don't keep in touch as much as we used to. All the other friends I had, stopped calling when we moved about five years ago, and I heard from Rayne that they're all mated and happy. The new friends I made here aren't the best calibre of person you have ever met. I prefer my own company most of the time, but they'll do for the days when I get really lonely, and the loser guys are okay for a quick shag when it becomes too much for me to deal with. I was so excited to visit Derek in his new flat in London. It's about a hundred miles from here and it seemed so adventurous of me to visit him alone. Hooking up with that beta was literally the highlight of that short trip, which just goes to show you how let down I felt by my brother. Kicking me out and sending me back to this dump three days early without all my stuff was mean and even though he has since apologised a thousand times, he can go get stuck on his own knot for all I care.

"Anne!" Pete bellows as my battered and bruised mother is taking her time going to him up the stairs to their bedroom.

His tone is different. He's excited about something. Not that I'll be told what's so thrilling as to change his mood from the dour pig he is to someone who cracks a smile.

Done with the rinsing off, I shove the plug in the sink and

squirt in a minute dose of washing up liquid. If I use too much, I'm called wasteful and ungrateful. However, I'm forbidden to go out into the real world and get a job to help pay for things around here. I would in a heartbeat if I was allowed. It's a flaming miracle I was allowed to visit Derek without a chaperone. Turning on the hot water and swirling it around and around to create as many bubbles as I can, finding a small, pathetic joy in seeing them, I hear my mum squeal in delight.

Turning to the stairs, I frown. What in the world would make my mother so happy when she is the most miserable woman I have come across? Nothing makes her smile anymore. I think the last time I saw a genuine smile on her face was the day she married Pete, six years ago, and it all went downhill from there.

Morosely, I turn back to my chore and scrub the dishes clean before I dry them off and put them away. Then I set to work wiping down the counters and the small round piece of wood that serves as a dining table. My feet are freezing on the cracked black and white linoleum floor, not having had time to put my slippers on.

Squeezing out the dishcloths, I leave them to dry and rubbing my arms against the chill, I head back upstairs to hopefully have a warm shower if there is still any hot water left.

*"Are you sure? Absolutely sure?"*

I hear my mum's voice and I pause at the top of the stairs.

*"Yes!"* Pete exclaims. *"They said they'd take her off our hands for twenty grand. Twenty grand, Anne. I could finally claw back a bit of standing in this community with that. Rent a better house, buy a bigger car, some nice clothes. A membership to the golf club..."*

Tilting my head, fear hitting me as I hear their words, my hands start to shake.

*Take her off our hands.*

'Her' has to be me. They are *selling* me for twenty grand to who knows which pack.

*"They're not very nice though," mum whispers loudly. "They have a bad reputation around town."*

*"Who cares? An unmated omega is a commodity, and we can cash in on her. All she does is sit around here on her arse all day, anyway. She's going and that's that."*

My heart fills with a searing hurt that brings a whimper to my lips. The tears that I silently shed earlier are back, threatening to fall once more. I brush them aside and make a rash decision. I cannot stay here and be *sold* like some sort of possession. Especially to a pack that sounds terrible and unsafe. As quietly as I can, I sneak into my bedroom and get dressed in my comfiest blue jeans, warm socks, a baggy t-shirt and hoodie. I grab my backpack and shove as much into it as I can, which isn't a lot. Just a couple of pairs of knickers, a spare bra, some joggers and tees, a few toiletries from my dresser. Snatching up my warmest coat from the back of my wardrobe, even though it has a big hole in the right pocket, I pick up my phone and slip my trainers onto my feet. Knowing that I will have to make it to Derek's and hope he will take me in until I can figure out my next move, I poke my head around my bedroom door. When all is quiet, I creep out into the hallway and make it to the top of the stairs before Pete's voice cracks out like a whip.

"Where the fuck do you think you're going?"

## Chapter Four

Benjamin

Glaring at Xander from across his bedroom, which is decked out in bright colours and is too 'fun' for my sophisticated tastes, I ask, "Why am I here?"

"Seb wanted you here to make sure I don't do something stupid," he replies, dragging something out from underneath his bed that looks like a body bag. He hefts it onto the super king-size bed with the ocean patterned cover on it and unzips the bag.

I roll my eyes and sigh when he pulls out a life size sex doll that has blonde hair and smallish tits. It is exactly how Matt described the omega he shagged three months ago, which we haven't been able to find hide nor hair of.

"Really?" I snap.

"What?" Xander asks, stroking her hair lovingly. "She was expensive. She's made from high quality TPE. Made to order, with three holes."

I groan. "Jesus. And what am I supposed to do exactly? Join in?" The thought makes me feel a bit ill.

"No, you need to stay here while I get over my rut. Seb said so." He starts to strip off his baggy shorts and tee.

"Why?" I complain, but sit down anyway on his desk chair and roll as far away from the bed as I can. "If Seb doesn't want you doing something stupid, why isn't he here?"

"He's locked himself away in the wine cellar. You know how he gets during his rut."

Gritting my teeth, I concede that it is probably for the best.

Xander strokes the doll before he applies a liberal dose of lube to his fingers and proceeds to, presumably, imitate slick from an omega by sliding his fingers inside the doll. It's like a traffic accident. Gross, but you can't look away.

Once she is prepared to his satisfaction, he takes his rock-hard cock and slides it into the doll with a loud groan.

"Oh, fuck, yes."

*Oh, fuck, no.*

Placing my hand over my eyes so I can't see him rogering the doll, unfortunately I *can* still hear him.

"Oh, Gertie, you're so wet, oh, yes, baby. Uhn, uhn." He speeds up his thrusts.

"Gertie?" I deign to ask against my will, peering out through my fingers.

"Dirty Gertie," he pants, clutching at the doll's hips. Its tits bounce a little bit enticingly, and I'm mesmerized by them for a moment before Xander notices me looking.

"Pretty perfect, isn't she?"

I draw my eyes away, but drop my hand. "Hmm."

"Well, she'll do until we can finally find Strawberries." He growls as he says the nickname we've given her, for lack of anything better. "I'd offer her up, but you've got your little playthings coming over later, right?"

I shake my head. "No, not this time." *Not ever again.*

"Oh?" He pounds and pounds, having the stamina of the strong alpha he is.

He might not be able to keep his baser instincts to himself, but he can hold onto an orgasm when he wants to.

"It feels like a betrayal," I say softly, hoping he won't hear me over his grunting.

He does though. "I know what you mean." He indicates the doll.

I give him a look that says I understand and won't joke about it anymore. He's doing what he needs to do. Much like I will have to in a little while.

Although what that is without the hot omega playmates to occupy my time, I have no idea.

"You can have a go with Gertie when I'm finished," Xander says, interrupting my thoughts.

I actually think about it for a second before I shake my head. I don't think I'm that desperate.

Yet.

Xander concentrates all of his efforts on banging the doll into submission. Moments later, he lets out a low growl as he knots the doll and shoots his load into it. He collapses face first onto it before he turns his head to stare at me, resting his cheek on its face. "You sure? She's fucking good."

"I'm sure," I assure him and stand up.

"Hey, where are you going? You're supposed to stay with me."

"I'll be back in a little while. I doubt you're going to go anywhere or do anything with a sex doll stuck on your knot, for fuck's sake."

"Good point," he agrees. "Be back in ten minutes. It'll start to go down then."

"Ten minutes," I repeat and slip out of his bedroom to march down the hallway of the first floor of the manor house until I reach my own room, three doors down.

Aiming straight for the bathroom, I shut the door and lock it, turning to glare at myself in the mirror over the cream marble basin. Dressed in a crisp white shirt and navy trousers, I look good. I have made sure to be impeccably dressed since the night Matt came home with the scent of our omega all over him, just in case we find her.

We haven't.

Three long months and nothing. We have searched everywhere. Combed the entire city and have now extended our search outwards. It is upsetting and frustrating and I understand why Sebastian has taken himself off for the night. He has been more aggressive than usual, which is saying something. We have all felt the lack of her being here, even though we have never even met her or know her name, her scent is enough. We know we want her, and we *will* find her and make her ours, no matter what it takes.

I fix my already perfect, short brown hair and lean forward to stare into my hazel eyes. They are tinged with just a bit of blue this evening. I am the personification of restraint, elegance and sophistication, but don't let the exterior fool you. Inside lurks a beast just as possessive and obsessive as Sebastian and just as psychotic as Xander.

I just know how to hide it better.

Bending down to open the cupboard under the basin, I pull out the blue t-shirt that Matt was wearing the night he screwed our omega. Something which is not talked about anymore or we would probably tear him to shreds. Their encounter is best forgotten, but I can't forget. I won't. Not when I have her fading scent on his piece of clothing that I snatched out of his laundry basket before the maid, or one of the other men, got to it.

Holding it to my face, I breathe in deeply, closing my eyes and picturing her slicking all over my cock.

My muffled groan is louder than I wanted, but I don't

care. I unzip my pants and pull my stiff cock out. The illegal suppressants I've been taking have stopped my rut this time. I haven't told the other men about it because Sebastian would skin me alive. They are dangerous and could potentially neuter me, but until we find our omega, I don't want to rut. It's as simple as that. I rub the t-shirt over my cock, picking up the faint scent of her to carry around on my member so that no other female comes near me.

Stashing my dick back in my pants and replacing the t-shirt under the basin. I check my Rolex. Unlocking the bathroom door, I hasten back to Xander's room, just in time to see him pull the sex doll off his knot and fling it across the room, where it hits the far wall and slumps to the thick carpeted floor. He dives for the door with a feral growl.

Luckily, I'm standing in his way and his drop is nothing a hard fist to the face won't cure.

I knock him out with one strike, and he slumps to the floor unconscious, just like his sex doll.

Sitting back in my chair, I eye up the doll, wondering what it would be like to slide my dick into it, but with a sigh, I turn back to keep my eye on Xander, for as long as his blackout psychosis lasts.

## Chapter Five

Faith

I freeze at the top of the stairs. The threadbare carpet under my feet is slippery and the floorboards squeak. I should've tried harder to remember where the squeaks are.

"Do you think you're going somewhere?" Pete spits out, approaching me quickly.

Using my instincts only, and with no thought whatsoever, I turn back to the stairs and bolt. The backpack on my back jiggles from side to side and I take the stairs two at a time. It throws me off balance. Pete is thundering down after me, knowing I'm about to run where he can never find me to sell me.

He reaches out for me.

Grabs me.

Turning and yanking my arm out of his grip, I teeter on the step and lose my balance. Terrified of both falling down the stairs and being captured by Pete, I scream.

My first reaction to save myself is, to flail around until I find something to grab.

My hand connects with something solid.

Pete's arm.

Eyes wide with terror when his evil smile swims into view, I try to pull my arm back, still balancing precariously on the edge of the step.

The weight of the backpack gets too much, and I can't hold myself upright any longer.

My foot slips on the tatty carpet and I tumble, banging my knee on the wall, my head on the handrail and twisting my ankle as I plummet to the bottom of the stairs.

Pete lets go of me to save himself, but it's too late.

With a yell, he follows me, crashing down the stairs, not as prepared as I was to fall. I brace myself for impact and hit the floor at the bottom of the stairs with a loud moan of pain that shoots through my ankle and my head, disorienting me momentarily.

Pete lands near me and I scrabble away as his head slams against the floor and lolls to the side.

Breathing in deeply, I look up and see my mom at the top of the stairs, her hands clutched in front of her, a look of sheer surprise mingled with terror on her face.

Did she push him?

Us?

"Go, Faith. Quickly."

Blinking rapidly, I launch myself over to Pete and snatch his wallet from his back pocket where he keeps it, so I don't steal from him. With trembling hands, I open it and pull out the two twenty-pound notes. I drop it and get to my feet, my head swimming from the crack it got on the way down. I feel a lump on the back of my head as I reach up to tenderly rub it and hobble with my sore ankle towards the front door.

Yanking it open, I see daylight, I see my escape.

Stepping across the threshold, I hear Pete growl, "Get back here, bitch!"

I don't look back.

I just run.

Well, a hobbling run while trying to stuff the money into my jeans pocket for safe keeping.

With the backpack hitting me in the back as my feet hit the ground, almost winding me, I keep going. My heart is hammering in my chest, my breath is coming in harsh, lung-burning pants. I'm not that fit. I'm not that strong, but I'm free and that will keep me moving even if my body tries to give out.

I won't be sold like a slave. The indignity of it makes my cheeks flame with humiliation. How could they do that to me? Knowing I'm so close to my twenty-first birthday and my first heat makes it even worse. I wouldn't have even had time to get used to the alphas, or even know them before they took my body and mated with me, implanting a baby inside me to grow and raise.

Chancing a look back after I've been running through the neighbourhood streets, weaving in and out of the roads to throw him off my trail, I don't see anyone following me. That doesn't mean I'm safe. He could just be hiding, or maybe he will suddenly appear in front of me somehow. That thought makes me spin my head back to face the front. Gasping for breath, I finally see a bus pulling up at a stop. Almost crying with relief, I pick up my pace and run as fast as I can with a twisted ankle.

I see the open doors. I see the steps leading up to the bus driver.

He looks over at me, and with a smug smile, he pulls away before I can climb aboard.

Skidding to a stop, I yell after him, "You fucker! I'm in danger!"

But he doesn't stop. He keeps trundling along sitting in his swill of self-righteous power.

"Bastard," I rasp, my throat burning, my mouth so dry, I bet it feels like the desert.

Glancing around in panic, I can't see Pete anywhere, and now that I've stopped, I can't keep going. My ankle feels like it is on fire and my head is swimming. My vision is blurring, and I can't breathe.

"Fuck. Fuck," I pant and start to stagger along to the next bus stop. I can't linger.

The sun is shining in my eyes, making them sting. Raising my hand up to shade my eyes, I keep going.

"Please, please, please," I whisper as I push myself more than I ever have physically. I want to curl up into a ball and die while crying.

When I see the next bus stop, there is a shelter with a metal bench running along the inside.

I can't.

I mustn't.

I have to.

Sinking onto it gratefully, with a low moan, I slump my shoulders, hunching them with my backpack still on. I hope the next bus will be along shortly.

With something going my way, a bus pulls up a few moments later.

Hauling my battered body to my feet, I lurch for the doors as they swing open and grab onto the railing to help me up.

The female beta bus driver gives me a smile. "Where to?"

I almost weep with gratitude. "As close to the train station as you can get me."

Glancing over my shoulder in a panic that Pete is going to show up and drag me off the bus while I'm standing here vulnerable and afraid, her gaze sweeps over me.

"As it happens, I'm going right by," she says steadily and shuts the doors behind me. "Take a seat," she adds, looking back at the road and sets off.

"Thank you," I whisper in relief and sway over to the nearest seat. I sit down and stare out of the window, just in time to see Pete running after the bus, his arms waving, his face full of rage with blood pouring into his eyes.

Averting my gaze, I look straight ahead, numb, scared and alone.

## Chapter Six

Faith

I reach for my phone and send a text to Derek, telling him to pick me up at the station and then I switch it off. I don't know if Pete has the ability to track my whereabouts, but on the off chance he can, I won't give him the opportunity.

A few minutes later, the bus driver stops at a red light and turns to face me. "You can get off here, hun. The station is just to the left."

I stand up immediately and say, "Thank you so much."

She gives me a knowing smile and opens the doors for me. I slip off and hastily make my way down the cobbled road, hunching my shoulders and keeping my head down. Entering the train station, I pull out the money I stole from Pete and buy a one-way ticket to London. The next train leaves in ten minutes and stops a million times, but I don't care. I will sit on it and wait until it gets to London. Deciding to wait until we are in the arse end of nowhere to switch my phone back on to text Derek the time I'll be coming in, I sit in a corner where I can see the entrance to the station, counting the seconds methodically until the train pulls up. I rise on shaking legs, not believing that I'm about to get on this train and escape my life. Surely Pete will be lurking, ready to snatch me before I can board.

But I make it onto the train. I sit down, placing my backpack on the blue seat next to me, so that hopefully no one will want to sit in that seat. Tapping my foot impatiently, staring between the doors and the window, I breathe out in relief when the door slams shut and the train rattles along the tracks, slower than the direct train, but I don't care. It will get me where I'm going and that's all I'm bothered about.

I chew my lip nervously, my hands clutched in front of me, I wait three stops down the line before I pull out my phone and turn it on. There are a dozen messages, all from Pete threatening me, calling me names and promising me he will find me. I delete them all, disappointed that Derek hasn't replied to my message yet. I fire off another one with my arrival time and then switch the phone off again. I really hope he gets it before I turn up with no place to go. I don't even know if he will take me in. He callously threw me back on the train three months ago without a thought to me or my safety that late at night. Not to mention he left me there with Pete the prick in the first place. I don't blame him for leaving, but the least he could've done was take me with him.

"Arsehole," I mutter, and then go back to tapping my foot and chewing my lip.

* * *

After about an hour, I start to relax enough to sit back in my seat and unclench my fists. Pete isn't on this train, and I doubt very much now that he will be waiting for me at the next station. He has no way to get there and no way to know where I would be. I sincerely hope, anyway. He isn't a tech whizz by any stretch, so him tracking my phone is a long shot. But better safe than sorry. Now that I'm out, I'm not going back.

I spare a fleeting thought to my mum and the abuse she will endure with me gone, but I shake my head. I can't let that force me to go back.

I am the *worst*.

The worst daughter.

The worst person in the world to put myself above my own mother, but I just can't go back and be sold to a horrible pack who will do fuck knows what with me.

We pull up into the last station before London and I sit up again, glancing cautiously out of the window, pulling my hood up even higher in case Pete is lurking, but nothing. Just a bunch of rowdy teens heading into the big city.

I sit back again and lower my eyes, tucking my chin into my neck as they pass me, hoping and praying they don't stop to talk to me or harass me.

They don't.

They don't even see me.

* * *

My stomach twists into a knot when we finally pull up to my destination. I wait for everyone else to get off the train and then I stand up and grab my backpack. Slinging it onto my back, I step carefully down from the carriage and scan the platform for Derek, feeling the ache in my ankle.

"Dammit," I mutter when I don't see him. "Where are you?"

I risk switching my phone on and checking my messages. More from Pete. None from Derek.

"Fuck." What am I going to do now? Somehow, I'm going to have to make my way to his small flat in East London by myself, with no idea where I'm going and hardly enough money to catch a bus, let alone a taxi.

Glancing from side to side, begging for Derek to suddenly show up, I know I have to move. I can't hang around waiting in case Pete arrives. He isn't the stupidest man on the planet. He will know there's only one place I'll go. It's just me outrunning him until I can get to my brother. The weather is colder here, the sky darker. Almost foreboding. It's going to rain. If I don't get inside soon, I'm going to get soaked.

Moving forward, but looking back over my shoulder, I bump into someone. It makes me jump. My heart hammers in my chest.

I swing my head to face front and see that it's not Pete.

"Sorry," I murmur and lower my eyes, sensing an alpha.

My breath coming rapidly from my fear, I shiver.

His scent.

It's all woodsy and like fresh rain.

I look up at him.

He is staring down at me with bright blue eyes.

His nostrils flare.

His eyes darken.

The expression on his face terrifies me.

He grips my upper arms. "You," he growls.

"I'm sorry, I don't know you," I stammer and pull my arms back, stumbling backwards.

I crash into another alpha who has snuck up behind me.

"Get off me!" I hiss when he grips my shoulders.

He is hot, really hot, with his hazel eyes. To be fair, they both are but what the fuck?

They are pawing at me as if I'm some sort of toy.

"It's her," Hazel eyes says, breathing in deeply.

My alarm bells ring.

Pete must've sent them.

"No!" I shout, trying to make a scene so someone will help me.

No one does.

They are all oblivious, going about their days, not even looking in my direction.

I have to save myself.

Panic setting in, making my heart hammer, I hear them growl. They know what I am, and I don't mean a sitting duck to their advances.

An unmated omega.

I duck out of Hazel eye's grip and run. I don't care where I'm going now, I just know I have to get away from them, sore ankle or not.

"You can't outrun us, Strawberries," Blue eyes calls after me.

Panting, scared out of my wits, I look back to see them following me and two more have joined them.

They are coming after me like predators and I'm their prey.

They are hunting me.

# Chapter Seven

Sebastian

I surge forward.

There is no way on this green earth I'm allowing her to escape. We have searched for *three* months, non-stop. The one fucking day we take off to visit the Inter-pack parliament in Hertfordshire by train, we find her...

And let her go.

We never travel by train. We have drivers or drive. This was a last-minute decision when the Range Rover broke down.

Fate?

Destiny?

Kismet?

Whatever the fuck word you believe in, this is it.

"Fuck's sake," I thunder, bursting out of the entrance of the train station to hundreds of people milling about. My eyes scan the crowds, but she's gone.

I take the time to pause.

Standing on the pavement and closing my eyes, shutting out the entire world, I focus on that scent. *Her* scent.

Inhaling deeply, I catch it. The aroma of strawberries and honey is unmistakable.

I open my eyes and gesture to the left. "That way."

As one, we lunge forward, but this isn't going to work.

"Wait."

"Not a chance," Xander growls, his green eyes flashing dangerously.

"Hear me out. If we all go straight after her, we stand a good chance of losing her. We need to create a net and close in on her from all sides. Xander, you follow behind her, Ben, to the right. Harvey, work your way around to approach from the front and I will go to the left. Once you catch her scent at the point where your dick goes hard, close in on her. Drive her towards the centre of the net. Got it?"

They nod their compliance.

"Xander. Go fetch."

Snarling, he sets off, shoving people out of the way and causing a bit of a stink, but he doesn't give a flying fuck.

Neither do I at the moment.

I gesture for Ben and Harvey to get going, and then I take a moment to calm my hammering heart. The sky has darkened even more. It is going to pour down. The chill in the air makes me stuff my hands in the pockets of my black cashmere coat.

I duck my head, focusing on the lingering scent in the air and follow it, but creating a wide berth to the left. I ignore the crowds around me, ducking in and out of the irritating people in my way, not touching them where possible. I really don't like strangers and it's worse when they touch me. If I initiate contact, then that's fine, but if someone lays a hand on me without my consent, it sends my stomach into an aching ball of anxiety, which turns into aggression. The other guys don't know about it. They just think I'm controlling. Which I am, don't get it wrong. But there is a *reason* for it.

Frowning when the wind picks up and blows the wrong

way, I lose the faint scent that I was following. Crossing over the road; I need to get closer. I contemplate her reaction to seeing me and Ben. She was scared shitless. I suppose it makes sense, we did pounce on her the second we caught her scent, but I get the feeling she was scared before that. I wonder what caused her to be so afraid.

I don't think about it too long, though, as the strawberry aroma suddenly gets stronger again. Very strong.

My gaze scans the throng eagerly. She is within a short distance of me. I am prepared this time for her to bolt. She will not get away from me twice.

My frustration grows as I can't see her amongst all these people. She is too short for the taller men and women around her. She is hiding in plain sight.

"Dammit."

I march on trying to keep on the left of the scent, but it's too difficult. Weaving in and out of the pedestrians in the middle of London, trying to find someone is like trying to find a needle in a haystack.

Then, I see her.

Her blue hood is pulled up over her light blonde hair, which I caught a glimpse of when she struggled with me, along with those cornflower blue eyes. She is even more gorgeous than I'd hoped. Small and curvy, she is everything that I desire in an omega, and I want to get my hands on her so desperately, my palms start to itch.

Now shoving people aside to get to her, she sees me.

Our eyes meet.

Her gaze is terrified.

Mine is determined.

She whimpers and slips away before I can reach her.

"Move!" I roar at the group of youngsters taking up the entire pavement and trailing along like they have all fucking day.

I ignore their pissed off shouts as I barge past them rudely.

"Fuck!" I shout out, when I lose her again. "How? How are you escaping me?"

She isn't going to make this easy.

But there again, who said easy was the preferred option?

Having her slip through my fingers again has brought out the true alpha in me. The one that deals solely in primal instinct. The one that Xander allows to rule, but I try to control for the good of the pack.

It flicks a switch in me.

Before I wanted to reach her, explain, and while she has no choice in returning to the Manor with us, I wanted her to want it. Now, I don't give a fuck. I will hunt her to the ends of the earth and take her by force with no words, hoping that her fear overwhelms her. Her fear will allow us to find her more easily. She is our prey, and nothing will stop us from hunting her down and taking her.

"You want a chase, Strawberries, you've got one."

# Chapter Eight

Faith

*Just keep moving.*

There is nothing else for it. They've split up. I've spotted the two who grabbed me, but at separate times. I only caught a quick glance at the other two when I looked back over my shoulder, but I think I can recognise them. I hope so, anyway.

Pete must've sent them. There's no other explanation.

I can't even stop to think about how absurd that really is. But it's the only thing I can think of, and over my dead body am I being dragged back there to be sold like a slave to do God knows what, with God knows who.

No, thank you.

Ducking up an alley, the rain starts to fall. It's not just any rain either. It's a torrential downpour and I'm soaked within seconds. My coat is plastered to me, wet through. Wiping the raindrops from my face like tears, I try not to give in to the fear, the vulnerability this chase has cast over me.

It's not fair.

I have always tried to be good. I haven't done anything to deserve this.

My breath hitches and just as I'm about to crawl into a corner and cry my eyes out, I spot a door to a dingy pub. I aim for it. As I approach, a man stumbles out, drunk and wobbling all over. He pulls out a cigarette and lights it. His eyes are unfocused as I brush past him, scraping my backpack on the doorframe, causing me to stumble as I enter the pub. He blows a stream of smoke at me, and I wince.

It's busy inside, which surprises me. For a crappy, old-fashioned pub, it is packed to the rafters.

I dodge the swaying, beer drinking men and wine swilling women. When a loud, pretty bad rendition of *The Wild Rover* erupts from the crowd over the jukebox, I figure this is an Irish wake of some kind. It brings hot tears to my eyes, to be reminded of my dad. He wanted me to learn about his Irish heritage, but I couldn't be bothered at the time. Now, I wish I had.

I avoid eye contact, keeping my head low as I make my way into the ladies' toilets. Shoving open the door and letting it swing shut behind me, it blocks out the rowdy noise from the pub and I sigh in relief. I crinkle my nose up at the smell, but then ignore it.

Pushing back my hood, I look at my reflection in the dirty, cracked mirror under the bare yellow bulb and cringe.

Slipping into a cubicle and sliding the loose bolt across, I lean against the door and pull my phone out to see if Derek has messaged.

Nothing.

I ring him, but it only goes to voicemail.

I try again, and then a third time.

"Shit, Derek. Answer the phone, you fucker," I whisper and then slam my lips shut as the door opens and the noise from the pub spills in. Moving quietly away from the door, my heart hammering, my palms sweating, I barely breathe when the door of the cubicle next to me crashes against the dividing wall.

Clutching my phone, I wait for my door to be kicked in, but I hear someone peeing instead and it nearly makes me wet myself in relief.

Drawing in shallow breaths, I try to formulate a plan. What the fuck do I do?

The toilet flushes.

Another crash of the door as it opens.

Water running and turning off.

Then the loud music and shouting from the pub, which fades away as the door closes again.

I can't stay in here indefinitely. They will find me and turf me out at closing, but it's a start while I figure out my next move. Hopefully, Derek will get his shit together and ring me back soon.

I remove my backpack and hang it on the wobbly hook on the back of the door. Then I take my wet coat off and hang that over the top of it to try to dry it off a bit. Wishing I had some food and water, I climb on the seat of the loo, and seeing as it doesn't have a lid, I park my arse on the cistern, my feet either side of the cheap, black plastic seat.

Moments later, the door opens again and my blood thunders in my ears, but it's only someone wanting to barf in the toilet next to me.

Pulling a face as I listen to them heave up the entire contents of their stomach, I'm grateful they at least flush the bog, so I'm not trapped in here with a toilet full of vomit.

They stagger back out after running the tap and I'm alone again.

All alone, terrified, hungry, thirsty and awaiting my doom as the minutes tick by until the landlady throws me out.

* * *

I'm left relatively alone after that. Only two more visits, one by a bloke who seems to have drunk enough to sink a ship. I rest my head against the wall and soon feel my eyes closing.

I jolt awake, hearing the wind whipping outside and the rain smattering against the tiny, murky pane of the window above the toilet I'm still sitting on.

I hear the door open, but this time it's quieter. The rowdiness from before is gone, but it's still early enough for the pub to be open. I glance at my phone and see that it's nowhere near closing time. There is *still* no message from Derek, so I turn it off and climb stiffly off the toilet.

"You okay in here?" a female voice calls out.

"Yeah," I croak out, the fear making my throat thick. I have no plan. I can only hope the men have given up and started to search further afield, at the very least.

I slowly put my coat back on and shiver as I replace my backpack. My stomach growls as I open the door.

The friendly-looking landlady gives me a smile. "You sure? You've been in here a while."

Should've known I'd been spotted, even in that crowd. "Yeah, just felt a bit off."

She nods. "Do you want to ring a taxi?"

I shake my head. I've got to go back out there and figure something out. I can't afford a taxi, anyway.

I'm guessing Derek must be away because there's still nothing on his phone. I wish I'd paid more attention on how to get to his place, maybe I could've figured out the bus route.

She gives me an encouraging smile and shoves something at me. It's a towel. My coat is still drenched so the desire to wrap it around me is all-consuming, but I will look like an idiot. I can only guess she gave it to me in lieu of a blanket. But fuck it. It's dry and warm, soft and cosy, and I'll take it. With a smile of thanks, I take it and ram it into my backpack, even though I can barely zip it back up.

As I open the door and peer out into the cold, dark night, my hand resting lightly on the frame, I step out into the dingy alley, in the rain, in my still-damp coat, with my eyes down. Cramming my hands into my coat pockets, I slip away into the dark night and decide that my best option is to make my way to the nearest park to hole up for the night under a bush, where no one will be able to find me.

# Chapter Nine

Xander

Lost.

Completely lost.

This fucking downpour has masked her scent and it is driving me to distraction. I want to hunt her, find her, bite her and mate with her until the knot on my cock bursts. I want her slick all over me, I want to taste it. I want to see if it tastes like strawberries.

I slam my fist into the wall of the nearest building, ignoring the looks of the few passers-by who've stumbled out of a pub down a small side street.

Glaring at them, I suddenly freeze.

Inhaling deeply, my head snaps to the side.

There's that scent.

It is fixed into my senses as if it was one of my own.

With a flash of speed, I zing to the door of the old pub as if I'm attached to it with an elastic band. My nose pressed up against the edge of it, I breathe in deeply, my eyes closed, my dick going hard.

"Found you," I growl and practically yank the door off its hinges before I lunge inside, my head flicking left and right, trying to latch onto her.

"Looking for someone?" the landlady asks.

"Short, cute blonde. Has she been in here?"

She looks to the left and then shakes her head.

*Lies!*

I know she was here.

I can *smell* her.

"Hmm," I murmur, the slight red haze of rage descending around me.

This beta bitch is trying to keep me from my omega and that doesn't sit well with me. I want to crush, destroy, kill...

A heavy hand lands on my shoulder.

I shake it off. "Fuck off, Ben. She knows something."

"She isn't here," Ben replies, gripping my shoulder again more firmly, hurting me even as he drags me back out of the pub and into the dingy alley, where Sebastian and Harvey are also standing, drenched, cold and fed the fuck up.

"She was here not that long ago," I say, turning back to the door and stroking it gently, the urge to cause pain disappearing as the scent consumes me and soothes my soul.

"But she's gone again," Ben adds.

"This rain has completely fucked us over," Sebastian growls, infuriated.

He should be. He had his hands on her and then let her get away. Him and Ben. What the fuck were they thinking?

"Let's think about this logically," Harvey says, his slight Scottish burr, quiet and lilting. "She was already running scared when we saw her on the platform. That much was obvious. You two scared her even more. She has no money, or she'd have just caught a taxi, even a bus, but she didn't. She ran, on foot, away from us. I don't blame her, for fuck's sake. She is an omega, so let's think like one. She will be looking for somewhere safe to hole up. If she has nowhere else to go, I say we start with the nearest park."

I can't fault his logic. But that's Harvey all over. The logical one. The quiet, serene, happy-go-lucky one.

"Agreed," Sebastian snarls, his eyes slightly wild.

He is beyond pissed. But it's nice to see that he has the ability to lose control like the rest of us. Always so strait-laced, I like seeing him come undone. It makes me feel like less of a fuck-up. He and Ben are so perfect, so in control. Harvey barely has feathers to get ruffled, but me? I'm the wildcard. I know, and I know they know it too. Ben plays guard dog, fuck, my face still hurts from when he took me out a few weeks ago. The feeling of failure floods me like a swamp of primordial ooze. It drags me under, makes me go dizzy. The fear of being overwhelmed with any kind of emotion other than anger or menace messes with my brain. It goes into overload and right now, I'm about to crash and burn.

"Hunt her, find her, bite her, mate her," I murmur.

Sebastian's hand clamps around my throat, drawing my wandering eyes to his. "Hunt her and find her only. The rest will come. You touch her before I do, and you will wish you'd made a better choice."

I lower my eyes. "Understood."

When he is in a mood like this, even I know not to push him.

He lets me go and turns on his heel. "Same plan applies. Surround her and close in."

He stalks off in the direction of the nearest park.

I press my face to the door frame again before I follow. I need to keep her scent in my nostrils to keep me calm. This alone shows how my brain isn't wired like the others. Her scent sends them into a frenzy. To me, it's the opposite. I want to curl up with her wrapped around me.

I crave it.

Gertie is a welcome distraction to keep my dick from exploding with sexual frustration until we find our omega, but it's pointless trying to pretend it really helps.

Setting off after Sebastian, I start to run. I overtake him, my feet pounding on the pavement, splashing through puddles on the uneven surface, wetting my black boots and soaking the hem of the fancy trousers Seb made me wear for the Inter-pack Parliament meeting.

As I race into the park, I pause and close my eyes. The strawberry scent hits me square on.

"She's here," I murmur when Sebastian pulls up next to me.

He nods once as Ben and Harvey join us. "Cast the net and close in. She *does not* get away this time," he growls.

The rest of the alphas disperse, and I carry on moving forward in a straight line.

I frown when the scent goes faint, but turning my head to the left, I pick it up again stronger. Two paces and then it fades again. This time I pick it up to the right.

"For fuck's sake," I snarl. "She's zigzagging."

I follow her trail for a few more zigs and a couple more zags, and then I spot her blonde head.

Her face turns towards me and our eyes lock over a large bush that is practically as tall as she is.

Her eyes go wide, filling with terror, visible under the park light.

She turns and ducks out of my sight.

"Oh no," I murmur, leaping forward. "Not this time. You are mine."

# Chapter Ten

Faith

*No!*

I duck behind the bush I was checking out to see if it was a good fit for sleeping under for the night, my hands trembling. I bite my bottom lip, and then my fight or flight kicks in. I cannot fight them, so I have to run.

Again.

I dart forward over the wet grass, slipping and turning my already tender ankle. Not making a sound, though, I carry on running through the park knowing I need to get out from under the lights and into the darkness.

I'm so tired. My lungs are burning with the effort, my heart is slamming against my ribs. My blood is roaring in my ears, almost deafening me. Tears prick my eyes as I surge forward, risking looking back over my shoulder to see where my hunter is.

I don't see him.

Feeling relieved at the slight respite, I don't slow down, but pick up the pace.

Shock and pain reverberate through me as I suddenly crash into a brick wall.

"Oof!" I cry, turning my head to face forward, wondering where the fucking wall came from, when it grows hands and grabs my upper arms.

"Get off me!" I hiss, realising that the wall is in fact a large man, and by large, I mean, my head comes up to his chest and I have to tilt my head back to look up into his face. Squirming like a hellcat to release myself from his iron grip, I somehow manage to get free from the reasonably cute man with dark red hair who smells oddly like marshmallows, by kicking him in the groin. It doesn't connect, but it's close enough. I don't care about fighting fair. I'm fighting for my life.

I launch my body to the right to get as far away from him as I can while I steady myself on my feet, but I see another one, the dark haired one from the train station, standing in my path.

"You are not escaping me this time," he growls. His voice is deep, low, kind of sexy, if I wasn't scared stiff.

"I'm not going back!" I yell at him and duck under his outstretched hands, surprising him.

"You are a slippery little thing, aren't you?" he snarls, using the momentum of him falling forward to turn and right himself.

"I'm not going back to that prick!" I scream. "You will have to drag my dead body back to him!"

Running as fast as I can, which isn't as fast as I'd like. I'm exhausted, afraid, panicking, not to mention hungry and thirsty, and heading in the opposite direction. The blonde one who spotted me a few minutes ago is there, grabbing my arm roughly and bringing me to a dead halt. I reach out and scratch the skin of his hand that is clutching my arm.

He hisses, his eyes narrowed in fury.

"Please!" I beg, suddenly losing all the fight. "Please don't take me back." I start to sob and draw in a breath that hitches when I inhale his scent. He smells like the ocean.

"Back where?" he yells at me, as I start to struggle again, but this time, I'm picked up from behind and hauled off my feet.

"No! No! Help! Someone help me!" I shout, but there is no one there to help me.

The marshmallow scent hits me again, only making me sob harder.

"Stop, lass," the great big Scot who has me in his paws like a doll, says to me as I strike out with my hands and feet, hearing the thump of shoe on skin. "Fuck, you're a hellion!" he snaps, but it doesn't sound irritated, more amused.

"I'm not going back to that prick!" I yell again, this time right in his ear as he swings me over his shoulder, fireman style, making me go dizzy with the motion and feel a bit sick. He rests one hand on my arse and the other bunches in the back of both legs of my jeans, in an effort to stop me from kicking him.

He is strong.

And so, so tall. Six-five, maybe?

I can see the ground from all the way up here, slung over his shoulder like a sack of spuds, and I stop struggling. If he drops me from this height, I'll break when I hit the ground.

"Is she secure?" dark-hair, woodsy-rain-scent thunders.

"She's not going anywhere, are you petal?" Marshmallows asks.

"You fuck!" I shriek like a banshee, wiggling around again, but all it does is make him laugh. Probably because my arse is jiggling around near his face, while my hands claw at his back. I'm upside down and this is not good.

"Jesus Christ," a really posh voice sighs.

I glance towards it and see it's Hazel eyes from the station. He sounds like Hugh Grant.

"It's a good thing you are worth it," he adds, coming up to me and bending down to look at me, his face upside down next to mine.

"Please don't send me back," I sulk, knowing I'm beat. Four alphas is not a fight I can win.

"Back where?" Woodsy-rain asks.

I blink and slam my lips shut.

*Back where?*

I get the sinking feeling that Pete didn't send them, and if that's the case, I'm about to be abducted off the street by four weirdos. I'd take going back to Pete any day when the reality of my current, undignified situation hits me.

With my arse stuck up in the air, Marshmallows starts walking forward and in my panicked state, all I can think is *please don't fart in his face.*

I would die.

Literally die.

Maybe that's preferable, though.

"Can you put her down?" Woodsy-rain asks. "This doesn't look good."

"Are you going to run?" Marshmallows asks. "We aren't taking you back to any prick. You're ours now, petal."

I stay silent.

He heaves me back over his shoulder and with his arms wrapped tightly around me, I slide down his rock-hard body. It sends the omega inside me into a wild frenzy. My hands resting on his broad chest, I look guilelessly up into his face, almost enjoying the feel of his massive arms around me.

Too bad, he doesn't know me, or how high my survival instinct runs.

Bringing my knee up straight into his groin, he lets out a pained grunt as I definitely connect this time, and lets me go with a curse.

"See ya, knobheads," I say before I dart off, escaping them once more for sweet freedom.

It lasts all of two seconds.

Woodsy-rain takes a giant step forward and clamps his hand around my wrist so tightly, I think he's going to break it.

I cry out and contort my body, so he doesn't snap my arm in two.

"You are not going anywhere, Strawberries," he says, in a voice so low and dark, I shiver. "You have fucked us about all fucking day, and I'm about at the end of my rope with this."

He reaches up and loosens his tie with his free hand, pulling it over his head and then wrestling my wrists together. He binds them tightly in front of me with the tie, keeping hold of the leash end while his gaze bores into mine, heated and angry. He flicks open the top button of his expensive white cotton shirt, exposing the smooth skin of his neck.

To my surprise, and his, a deep purr escapes my throat, telling him and the rest of them, exactly what I think about that.

## Chapter Eleven

Faith

Silence descends all around us.

I realise my faux pas instantly and press my lips together.

It's too late though.

Woodsy-rain heard me and it affected him in ways that he is currently trying to squash, judging by the tormented look on his face.

He growls, low and fierce. It sends a chill down my spine. I lower my eyes, ready to do his bidding when he drags me to him by the leash of his dark blue silk tie.

I stumble forward.

Reaching out with my hands to stop myself from falling, I clutch at his shirt awkwardly as his free hand goes under my elbow to steady me.

I look up into his dark eyes. I think they're blue, but it's hard to tell in the dark park, only semi-lit by the intermittent old Victorian lamp posts scattered about.

He glares back at me, his mouth a firm line of aggravated annoyance.

I breathe out softly at the same time as he inhales. His eyes close, but snap back open in the next instant. He lifts the tie up, bringing my hands closer to his mouth. He grabs the fingers of my right hand and pulls back, bending my fingers backward.

"Ah," I cry out softly when he lowers his mouth to the sensitive skin on the inside of my wrist.

He presses his lips over my pulse and then he opens up and bites down sharply, giving me a mark that claims me, but not in the way that makes me his mate.

No, he has decided he now owns me.

"Seb," Marshmallows wheezes after the kneeing I gave him. "Don't."

'Seb's' eyes flash with danger and he releases me from his bite, pushing me back slightly.

"It's to keep her safe until we get her home," he murmurs, eyes never leaving mine.

"Safe?" I spit out, my fire suddenly reappearing after it was temporarily banked by the hot, growly alpha bod I'm still nestled up against. I take a giant step back. "Let me go!" I yell as loudly as I can, but no one even bats an eye.

"Let's go," Seb states and stalks past me, yanking me along with the tie, making me stagger behind him until Hazel-eyes rights me with a hand under my elbow and whose scent I can now pick up.

It makes my knees weak.

Summer rain.

A totally different animal to woodsy rain.

This is completely undignified, and the survival instinct kicks in again and I start to struggle.

"Nope," Marshmallows says. "We have you, we are not losing you again."

He sweeps me off my feet, cradling me like a child and marches off, apparently his boo-boo balls all better now.

Seb lets the tie go and smirks as I wiggle about, trying to get free. But my captor is like a giant with all the strength of one, so yeah, I'm not going anywhere unless I bite him. Sadly, the only place close enough to my mouth is his neck and that isn't happening. Not in a month of Sundays.

There's nothing left for it, but to be hauled away like a prisoner and stuffed into the back of a waiting black Mercedes, which appeared at the curb side, the second we hit the pavement.

"Please let me go," I whisper to Marshmallows.

"Can't do that, petal," he says with a soft smile, squashing into the back seat with me, while Ocean-breeze slips in on the other side.

I glare at him, but he ignores me and starts sniffing my hair, tangling his fingers into the wet mess.

I let out a soft sob as the other two alphas get in the front, Summer-rain replacing the driver who gets out to, I don't know...walk home?

Wherever home is.

"Why do you want me?" I weep, the tears flowing freely now. "I just want to go home."

Well, that's a lie, but they don't know that.

"Don't, Strawberries, I can smell the lies on you," Ocean-breeze murmurs in my ear.

I cringe.

Not from being caught out so much, but because now I think I stink like a liar, and a fearful one at that.

He nuzzles my neck, but Marshmallows slaps his face away with a low growl. "Hands off."

"We've been searching for you for a very long time," Seb states but leaves it at that.

"Why?" I cry. "What did I do?"

He turns to look at me with those hard eyes and I sink back into the seat. "You fucked the wrong man, Strawberries," he grits out and then faces forward again and no more words are spoken, from anyone.

Not even me.

All I can think is who? Who did I fuck that wasn't the *right* man? I mean the list isn't exhaustive, but it's not exactly count on one hand either.

I close my mouth after that and focus. As soon as the doors open, the two alphas on either side of me have to get out. With a bit of luck, I can make my escape and just keep running and running until I finally outrun them. It is my only option. I'm not staying here with these arseholes. They can get knotted. I just need the courage to say it out loud to their faces.

I sigh. Yeah, none of that is likely to happen.

If I can't escape them, I will live out my days as their slave because I hate confrontation and I'm a people pleaser. I will try one last time to get away, but I don't have enough fight left in me to attempt it again after that.

I don't know how much time passes. I stare out of the window, the headlights cutting through the dark, the rain drops glittering as they fall past the glow.

Eventually, we pull up to a large estate and drive though the enormous iron gates with a coat of arms on that I don't see for long enough to recognise.

Up the long, long private road lined with trees and around a circular driveway at the top to pull in line with three wide paved steps, which lead up to a huge black door.

I brace myself to bolt like a hunted deer across the land-scaped lawns, but there's no chance. Marshmallows grips my arm tightly and drags me out of the car with him, holding me up as I fall out, so I don't land flat on my face.

"Lock her in her room until she stops any thoughts of

running away," Seb says and marches off into the dark house, leaving me to be picked up again and carried up the sweeping stairs. Along the hallway with huge, creepy portraits, I'm placed in a bedroom, the door shut, and a key turned in the lock, then removed.

"Fuck!" I shout out and kick the door, stubbing my toe. "I'm still tied up!"

No answer.

I scream and scream at the door until my voice is hoarse, and I'm coughing and spluttering like a maniac. Exhausted, I rest my forehead against the white-painted door and cry tears of frustration rather than fear.

I bring my bound hands up to bang on the door again, but it's weak and quiet, my fists bruised from previous attempts. I turn and slump down until my arse hits the floor, hunched forward because my backpack is still somehow on my back.

My tears stop suddenly when I remember my phone in the back pocket of my jeans. I scrabble with the tie, pulling viciously at it with my teeth until I've loosened it enough to slip my hands free. Feeling in my pocket, I curse, bunching my hand into a fist.

Marshmallows must've taken it from me when I was slung over his shoulder in the park.

Now, I'm truly alone with no idea what is about to happen to me.

All I know for sure, is that my twenty-first birthday is days away, and if I'm still here when I go into my first heat, I'm doomed.

## Chapter Twelve

Harvey

Knowing exactly where Sebastian has holed up, I march into the wine cellar, kicking the doors in because my temper is raised, and I want him to know it.

"We shouldn't have locked her in her room. She will never trust us!" I bellow at Sebastian, who is, as expected, behind the locked iron gates with the most expensive bottles this Manor has to offer.

He gives me a weary look and rubs his hands over his face. "After the day we have had chasing her down, do you *really* want to let her loose so she can try again? Because that is exactly what she will do. We agreed not to use excessive force, but this day turned into a shitshow. It's *not* how I foresaw this going."

"Yeah, me either," I agree, looking down and kicking the large wooden table that somehow doesn't wobble on this ancient, stoned floor.

"I need you to go back upstairs and make sure that Xander doesn't do something...Xander-ish," he adds with a sigh.

"Can't you?" I don't want to play guard dog to Xander today. "Or Ben, even?"

"If I leave this cage, I will end up in her bed and it's not the right time. She is affecting me on a level so deep, I fear what I might do if I don't calm down first. That purr..." He inhales sharply and lets out a soft growl.

"I feel the same way," I point out softly. "And she wasn't wriggling around all over you."

"That's why you need to stay over there. Her scent all over you is driving me crazy. Crazier. Just go and sit outside her door, or something. Please, Harvey. You are the only one who will keep your hands to himself right now."

I'm not sure whether that's a compliment or not. I feel quite insulted. It's like he doesn't think I'm as affected by her as he is.

"Fine." I give the table another swift kick as I leave the wine cellar, needing to get away from him before I plant my fist in his face. It's not his fault. This day. Her. Christ, we don't even know her name yet.

"Find out her name," Seb calls to me softly. "I need to know it before I see her again."

"Makes two of us," I mumble under my breath.

But I do as I'm told. As usual. I don't create waves. I'm not the wildcard that Xander is, or the deceptive psycho that Ben is. I'm just me, trying to get along in this world without making a big deal out of shit like everyone else.

I think it comes from my mum's side. My dad's side is all fiery Scots, whereas Mum's family are laid back English folk. Stiff upper lip and all that shite.

Making my way back up to the first floor, I let out a sigh at the top of the stairs. Xander is already sniffing about.

"Go," I say in a voice that holds no emotion. It's the one

he tends to respond to the most. The barest hint of anything and it sends him swinging one way or the other.

"Nope."

"Don't make me haul your arse back to your bedroom. Seb said stay away."

"Can't." He is on all fours sniffing under the door for fuck's sake.

"Give her a bit of peace and dignity. You're like a dog with a bone." I snicker. "Make that boner."

He lifts his head up with a wicked smile. "When do we get to see her again?"

"Tomorrow. Leave her be tonight."

Xander, surprisingly, does as I ask, and moves away, loping down the hallway on all fours. I don't think I've seen the last of him yet.

Moving over to the door, I sit down, legs outstretched, facing it. It's quiet inside. I guess she must've been exhausted and fallen asleep. One can only hope anyway. I don't want her to be scared or worried. Although this isn't the best situation. I never expected her to bolt like she did. She is definitely running from somebody. Whoever it is, I intend to find out and remove that threat from her life.

"What's your name?" A soft voice filters through the door.

"Harvey, what's yours?"

"You don't know?" Her surprise is evident.

"Nope."

"Faith."

I smile. "It's a beautiful name."

"Thanks," she murmurs. "Why have you abducted me?"

"Who are you running from?"

She pauses at my question asked instead of answering hers.

"No one."

Her reply was short and evasive.

"Don't believe you."

"Can you smell lies as well?" she asks archly.

I snort. "No, that's Xander's trick. He is very in tune with his inner alpha."

"Xander?"

"Blonde, feral…"

"Ocean-breeze."

"Pardon?"

"He smells like the ocean," she says, almost wistfully.

"Oh." I blink, a bit annoyed by her tone.

Silence.

Then I hear her giggle.

"What's so funny?" I growl.

"You're dying to ask what you smell like to me, aren't you?"

"No," I say defensively, crossing my arms with a huff.

"Now who's lying?" Her sly tone catches me off guard.

I narrow my eyes at the door. What game is she playing here?

"Not lying," I grit out.

"Marshmallows," she says.

"Huh?" I wrinkle up my nose.

"That's what you smell like to me. It's heavenly." I hear a soft thump on the door and wonder if she's resting her head on it.

I scoot over and lean my back against the door now, also resting my head against it. "Strawberries with honey and cream," I murmur.

"That sounds delicious," she practically pants.

"Mmm."

"Are you getting it?" she asks after a beat.

"What?" I shake my head, slightly confused.

"I'm starving."

"Oh. Oh! Shit, of course. But no," I say, standing up with

55

a smile, and placing my hand on the door separating us. "That's what you smell like to me. To us."

Nothing.

"I'll get you some food," I murmur, embarrassed that she didn't respond.

I walk away, back towards the stairs when there's a soft weep.

"Thanks," she mutters.

Her sadness breaks my heart.

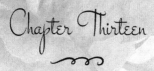

## Chapter Thirteen

Benjamin

It has taken everything I have, not to go to her in the night. I managed a few minutes sleep with Matt's shirt on my pillow, but that was about it. Now, it's nearing dawn and I feel that I've been restrained enough.

I'm relieved to see that Harvey is still outside the door, which means Xander would've been thwarted in his quest to gain entry to her bedroom.

"Hey," Harvey says when he spots me loitering near a huge tapestry of the second St. James.

"Everything okay?"

"Apart from having to kick Xander's arse once or twice, yeah." He yawns and stands up. "You here to take over?"

I nod, even though that is not strictly why I'm here. "Did you speak to her?" I ask curiously before he turns to leave.

"A little bit. Her name is Faith."

"Faith," I repeat with reverence. "It's beautiful."

"So is she."

"You've seen her?" I frown, not liking that he's had this time with her.

He shakes his head. "I went to get her some food but when I opened up the door, she snatched it from me and then slammed the door in my face."

"She shut *you* out?" I let out a soft laugh. "She has fire, this one."

"Yeah, no shit. Listen, I'm fucked. Here's the key." He hands it to me, and I weigh it in my palm.

"Go sleep," I tell him.

I watch him stumble tiredly down the hallway and then turn to the door. I wait all of two seconds before I slide the key in the lock and turn it.

Pushing the door open a crack, there's no sound on the other side. I peer inside, but see the bedroom is completely empty and the covers have been taken from the bed. Instantly, I cross to the window to see if she made an escape, but it's closed and locked from the inside. That's when it strikes me.

I turn slowly towards the small walk-in wardrobe and smile. Crossing over to it, I reach for the handle and quietly open the door.

She's there, Faith, all curled up asleep in her nest of duck down duvet with its white Egyptian cotton cover, all four pillows and the sheet. She looks so cosy and warm. I want to reach out and touch her.

She has Sebastian's tie wrapped around her head, Rambo-style, with the wide end resting against her cheek, probably so she can smell his scent in her sleep. She has fallen for him. Big time. It's not surprising. In fact, it's welcome.

Her eyes flutter open and then go wide when she sees me.

She cowers slightly, but I crouch down quickly so I don't appear as intimidating.

"Hi, Faith. I'm Benjamin," I say, pressing my hand to my chest.

"Summer rain," she murmurs.

"Hm?"

She shakes her head. "Tired."

"I know, sweet girl. Go back to sleep, you are safe here."

She murmurs something I don't catch and turns over, nestling further under the duvet. She is asleep again in seconds. On impulse, I take my white cotton t-shirt off and tuck it in near her face, stroking her light blonde hair that is strewn out over the pillow. She breathes in deeply and a small smile plays on her lips. She turns her face into it.

I feel like a king.

"I'll get you some food and drink," I whisper and stroke her forehead, feeling how warm she is. She is in her pre-heat, which means in about three days' time, she is going to be in full heat.

What that means for us, I don't know. But I do know that Sebastian needs this information now.

Standing up, I carefully and quietly shut the door to the wardrobe and creep out, closing the door behind me and locking it. I pocket the key.

Heading down the stairs, taking them two at a time, I make my way through the kitchen and ask the cook to whip up a feast for me to take back on my return. She is eager to please and sets about doing as I ask.

Taking the steps that lead down to the wine cellar, I see Sebastian leaning against the iron gate, his hands gripping the bars above his head. He looks like hell. His shirt is all untucked and rumpled, he needs a shave, and his hair is all mussed.

"Bad night?" I ask with a smirk.

"Fuck off," he growls. "Get me that key."

I bend down to retrieve it from the middle of the floor where he would've thrown it after he locked himself in. He is completely reliant on one of us opening up the cage for him.

It's quite an honour really, but also, sometimes, I can't help but play with him.

I taunt him by dangling the key just out of his reach. "Not yet."

"Ben, I swear I will rip your dick off if you don't let me out of here right now."

"Threats won't get you anywhere," I point out, unnecessarily. "We need to talk, and I need you to listen. Then I'll let you out."

He closes his eyes in defeat. That surprises me. He is exhausted. Mentally rather than physically. Something is bugging him, and I bet it has everything to do with the nesting omega upstairs.

"Her name is Faith," I begin.

His eyes widen. "Faith," he repeats, in much the same tone I did. "Suits her. Is she okay?"

"She is nesting in her wardrobe."

If his eyes go any wider, his eyeballs are going to fall out.

"Nesting. She's in pre-heat?"

I nod my confirmation and warily speak my thoughts out loud. "I think this is her first time."

Eyes narrow this time. "What makes you say that?"

I shrug. "Just a hunch."

"Shit," he mutters and rubs his hand over his face.

"Yeah."

"Fuck."

"Yep. What the fuck are we going to do?"

"I guess that's up to her. We need to find her in a lucid moment and speak to her. Tell her our intentions. It seems she feels safe here now, or at least she does in the wardrobe."

I nod slowly. "We are going to have to chain Xander up, or send him away or something," I say, as I go to him and unlock the cage. "He will not keep away from her and we can't pounce on her in full rut her first time in heat. It's not fair. I would hate myself."

"My thoughts exactly and so would I. She is ours to protect and that's final. We will not take advantage of her. I mean, we know she isn't a virgin, but still..."

Our eyes lock and as one we launch ourselves to the steps that lead back up to the kitchen in a race to see who gets to Matt first to tell him that the omega he hooked up with is in the house, and that if he touches even a single hair on her head, he is dead.

I'm kind of hoping I reach him first.

# Chapter Fourteen

Sebastian

It's only as we head up the steps to the kitchen that I realise Ben is only wearing a pair of joggers. I don't get a chance to ask him about it as we skid to a stop in the kitchen, momentarily halted in our mission to reach Matt, by Matt standing right in front us holding a tray with enough food and drink piled on top of it to feed the five thousand.

"Oh no!" Ben roars at him and snatches the tray.

The contents wobble wildly, but steady when he places it back on the massive island in the huge country farmhouse kitchen.

"So you found her then," Matt says, his eyes lighting up in a way that makes my blood boil.

"What makes you say that?" I ask nonchalantly, even though I want to lay him out flat to stop him from going to her.

He draws in a deep breath. "Strawberries and cream, right?"

The low growl that escapes my lips, cuts off suddenly as Ben and I lock gazes. I can't help the smug expression that falls over my features.

"That's all you smell?"

Matt looks between me and Ben, and nods warily.

"That just proves you have no business being with her. Her scent has subtler undertones that your beta nose just isn't equipped to deal with."

Matt glares at me but doesn't respond to my dig. I'm not usually so ornery with him. I actually like him and consider him a member of this family, but this omega situation – the *Faith* situation – has made me more possessive than I expected to be. I've often thought about how I would be with our mated omega. Caring, loving, attentive, great in the sack, but possessive and ready to kill for her without even knowing her name has taken me completely by surprise.

"If it's not clear already, you need to stay away from her," I state, just so there are no misunderstandings.

"I wanted to clear the air," he sulks. "We left things...not nice."

"Which is everything to do with you. You treated her like shit and now you want to 'clear the air' because she is right here when you thought you'd never see her again. Sorry, mate. Not happening. If she will see you when she is more comfortable here, then by all means, have a conversation with her." I'm not telling him about her pre-heat. It will get him in a tizzy. He may not be an alpha, but he will feel a pull towards her of some kind, mild as it may be.

He gives me a look that speaks volumes. I've called him out and he knows it. "Fine."

He stalks off and I let out a shallow breath. Blinking at Ben, who picks the tray up again, I ask, "Why are you half dressed?" The suspicion in my tone makes his eyes go hard. The thing with Ben is, he is the perfect gentleman. He will

63

open your door for you, allow you to go first, insist on paying for your half of the meal, smile, make great conversation, but underneath...there lurks a beast quite vicious who takes pleasure in other people's pain. Not that of his pack, but outsiders.

"What's it to you?"

"Curious. Did you give her your clothes to nest with?"

"Yes."

"Fucker," I snarl, stepping forward with my hand outstretched.

He takes a step back, hands full of tray.

"Before you kill me, know that she still has your tie and has it wrapped around her head like Rambo. Trust me. You have nothing to worry about."

My hand drops and my heart swells with something that I've never felt before, so I don't recognise it, but I know it makes me feel warm and cuddly. Two things that are not familiar to me either. "Really?" I feel the need to confirm this as fact because if he's just saying that to deflect from his own actions, it will gut me.

"Yes, really. See for yourself." He shrugs it off as if it's no concern to him.

I know differently though. If I tied her up and abducted her off the fucking street and she still nested in my home with an item of my clothing that same night, it means her instincts are ruling her, and the more she gives in to them, the better that is for all of us. While her full, *lucid* cooperation in being here would be preferred, right now knowing she feels safe here means a lot and will pave the way to the rest.

I follow Ben through the kitchen and up the stairs, pausing outside her room.

"Should we both go in?" Ben asks, weirdly unsure of himself for once.

I nod and see the relief in his eyes.

"Key's in my pocket."

I glance down at his joggers. "Seriously? Just hand me the tray."

He snickers and passes it over before digging around in his pocket for the key that will ultimately unlock our destiny.

I hear the click and watch as he pushes the door wide open. I take a step forward, suddenly nervous. I mentally roll my eyes at my ridiculous behaviour and hasten forward, dropping the tray lightly on the nightstand before I turn to the wardrobe.

Knocking lightly, I say her name. "Faith."

"Mm."

Her murmured reply is all the encouragement I need to open the door and peer inside.

The sight before me takes my breath away.

She does, indeed, have my tie wrapped around her head, which makes me smile affectionately. I drop to my knees, fixing my eyes on hers.

"Hi. I'm Sebastian."

"You're a dick," she says, but it's not full of malice. Just a statement.

I chuckle. "You caught me. King Dick here. Are you comfortable?"

Her beautiful face twists with confusion. "Are King Dicks supposed to care?"

"When it comes to you, yes. You are all I care about."

"I need answers. Why did you abduct me?"

"Are you up for a retelling?"

She nods, but then holds her hand up. "Wait. I need to pee, eat, have something to drink, probably pee again and then get comfortable. I'm feeling out of sorts."

Her admission of vulnerability fills my heart with a joy I've never known before and never sought out. I shuffle back, holding my hand out to help her up.

She glares at it for a long moment before she hesitantly presses her palm against mine.

I breathe out slowly.

Baby steps.

# Chapter Fifteen

## Faith

I let Sebastian help me to my feet, only because I feel a bit like a pile of shit, and the urge to pee is nearly breaking me. Luckily, I happen to be locked away in a prison of luxury. This room is absolutely beautiful. It is all white apart from the light brown wood around the windows. It is as big as the whole of the downstairs in Pete's shithole, and it has an en-suite bathroom with a gorgeous, old-fashioned bathtub on feet as well as a shower that is big enough to sleep in.

I snatch my hand back from Sebastian's as soon as I'm on my feet and hobble indelicately to the bathroom. Wincing slightly at the pinch in my ankle, but it seems to not be as bad as it felt yesterday. Thank God. I open the door and then give it a good solid slam to show these knobheads that I'm not theirs.

*Not yet.*

*Shut up, inner bitch.*

I grimace as the war inside me starts all over and I flick the switch near the door.

The spotlights above my head make me cringe and scrunch my eyes up.

"Too bright," I mumble and stagger to the toilet.

A few minutes later, I wash my hands and grab the brand-new toothbrush that I find in a fancy holder. Squirting the toothpaste on, I feel like a million quid once the fur is brushed clean from my teeth.

Okay, slight exaggeration.

Ten quid will about cover it.

I wash my face and dry it, only then noticing the tie wrapped around my head.

"Oh, Jesus Christ, you utter twat," I mutter, yanking it off and scrunching it into a ball in my fist.

What must he think of me?

He is probably regretting his decision to snatch me off the street and thinks he's been lumbered with a raving lunatic.

I shove it in the pocket of my jeans and shudder. I could really do with a shower and a change of clothes, having slept in these ones last night out of sheer exhaustion after building my nest. I know, even though I've never experienced it before, that I'm in my pre-heat. It's a bit exciting, but also very daunting and scary, especially seeing as I'm now a prisoner of this pack of, admittedly hot, alphas. What is going to happen to me in a few days' time? Will they pounce, leave me alone, what? I'm not sure which would be worse. I've heard it's not that nice to be without a knot to come all over when you're in your heat. But do I really want these felons to be the ones to relieve me? What will that say about me and about how I feel about what they did? Plus, more than one? Sounds like fun, but I've never done that before. What would they expect of me?

"Okay, Faith. Stop overthinking this. You will drive yourself crazy. *Crazier.*"

Deciding that these arseholes can wait while I shower, it's the fucking least they can do, I march back into the bedroom, to Sebastian and Benjamin waiting patiently in the stiff-backed chairs in the bay window. They both stand up as I enter the room, but I ignore them and with as much dignity as I can, I bend down to retrieve my backpack from the nest and then I return to the bathroom, once again slamming the door closed and sliding the bolt across to secure my privacy from these beasts.

* * *

After spending more time in the shower than was strictly necessary, and totally on purpose to make them wait, I brush out my hair and spray on some deodorant before slipping into my comfy black joggers and a white t-shirt. I pause when I remember Benjamin's t-shirt in my nest and smile. It was sweet, and he smells so delicious. It was the total opposite to how I got my hands on Sebastian's tie. Or *around* my hands that should be. Dick. King Dick about sums him up.

"Sexy King Dick. Bet you have a big dick to go with that title, don't you?"

I pucker up and apply a smear of lip gloss, my only make-up choice and then I'm ready.

Turning towards the door, I pause and bend down to pull the tie out of the pocket of my folded-up jeans that I'd placed on the small chair in the corner of the bathroom. Without thinking, I wrap it around my wrist and tuck it in tightly, so it doesn't unravel.

Happy now and deciding I've left them waiting for long enough, and also eager to hear why they chose me to abduct, I open the door and then freeze.

All four of them are assembled.

Xander, formerly known as Ocean-breeze, snaps his head towards me, his eyes narrowing and his lips parting.

"Strawberries," he pants.

He takes a step in my direction, which makes me take one back into the bathroom, prepared to lock myself in again, when Harvey Marshmallows grabs him by the collar, halting his progress, at the same time that Benjamin lays a hand on his arm almost in warning.

That makes me cautious.

Harvey said he was feral. And he was the one who sniffed me in the car.

"I won't hurt you," Xander says, his tone soft. "You don't need to be afraid of me."

Blinking, I don't say anything. I don't know what to say. *Afraid* isn't the word I'd use, but I'm definitely wary. Not just of him, but of all of them.

"Here," Harvey says, letting go of Xander and holding out my phone.

He waits for me to come to him, which takes me a hot minute. The only reason I step forward and snatch it from him, is to check if Derek got back to me.

I glance at the screen and see dozens of messages. Some from Pete and some from Derek.

I open them and read the thread, ignoring the four waiting men in front of me.

"Fucker," I mutter under my breath when I see that he wasn't ignoring me on purpose, but his phone was dead, and he was in the Home Counties at an all-day meeting. He claims he didn't know his phone had died until late on last night.

A likely story.

"Feel free to ring whomever you like to let them know you're safe," Sebastian says.

I look up at him with a sad expression.

I have no one *to* ring. Except Derek, and so far, he has proved to not be very reliable. Maybe I'll make him wait and if these four end up killing me and eating me, he can hear about it on the six o'clock news with everybody else and be wracked with guilt until the end of days.

Did I mention I like to hold a grudge rather than face confrontation? Pretty sure it's tattooed on my arse. Will *definitely* go on my headstone.

Here lies Faith.
She did what you wanted, but resented your arse forevermore.
Expect a haunting in the future.

I shove the phone in my pocket and glance at the tray of food. My mouth starts to water. It's all delicious looking sandwiches and biscuits, cake and juice. Bottled water as well.

I pick it up and kick the door to my nest further open. I place the tray on the floor and step over it to curl up in the softest, cosiest duvet I've ever known and start to eat.

What they do next is up to them.

I'm not stopping what I'm doing to please them.

Not this time.

They can totally get knotted.

## Chapter Sixteen

Faith

I wait for them to do or say something, but nothing happens for a few minutes. Just me eating my way through the gorgeous feast in front of me.

I soon start to feel a lot better, not just in myself but about this situation.

"Am I a prisoner here?" I ask bluntly after I swallow a mouthful of the most delicious, fresh cream Victoria Sponge.

"No, of course not," Sebastian says quickly. "Are you ready to hear our explanation?"

"I was ready the second I came out of the bathroom."

"Oh, ah...of course."

I try to hide my smile. Despite this being a very scary situation, having been hunted down, bound and snatched off the street by four strangers and locked in a room overnight, I don't actually feel like I'm in danger.

Maybe my judgement is impaired by the pre-heat. Maybe not.

Sebastian clears his throat and leans over to rest his elbows on his knees. Xander drops to all fours and crawls over to me slowly.

I keep my eyes on him warily.

"Can I sit near you?" he asks quietly, his eyes screaming his plea at me.

I blink and nod slowly.

His look of relief twangs over my heart as he settles against the wall to the side of the wardrobe door.

"About three months ago our pack beta, Matt, came home from a night out at a pub in the East End called the Hand and Dagger," Sebastian starts, drawing my gaze back to him.

*East London.*

*Three months ago.*

*Beta.*

*Oooooh, shit.*

I give him a guileless look and stuff more food into my face.

He snickers softly. "Indeed. As no further explanation is needed about *that*, I will move swiftly forward. When he returned home, the four of us practically fell on him. Your scent was all over him, and it affected us on a deep, profound level. To be completely transparent, Faith, we were days away from deciding on our omega. We had three excellent candidates..."

The scoff that erupts from me stops him dead in his tracks. All of their gazes focus on me. I feel like crawling under my duvet and staying there until the end of all time.

Fixing his blue-eyed stare on mine, I'm unable to look away. My breathing goes a bit heavier; my heart beats a little bit faster. He is a good-looking man. Well, that's an understatement. He is completely gorgeous. I was trying not to think about it, what with him being a criminal and all, but when he looks at me with those eyes and his scent fills my lungs, I forget the danger.

When he speaks again, his tone is dark, low and sexy. "They all paled in comparison to just your scent. We didn't even know your name, or what you looked like, but we knew we wanted you. *Needed* you. We have searched for you for three months."

"I don't live in London," I whisper, my stare still locked with his.

He laughs softly. "So we figured. Matt thought you were blowing him off."

"He's a dick." I pout which inadvertently sets the four alphas alight with the flames of desire. They edge in closer to me, their primal instincts going off the charts. I shrink back and fix my mouth into a more neutral expression, trying to ignore their scents which are suddenly overwhelming me in a mix of deliciousness that makes me go a little damp between my thighs.

"He's all right," Harvey says to break the tension.

I've figured out his role straight away. He's the buffer. The reasonable one. The mediator. He diffuses situations. Although, him slinging me over his shoulder to whisk me away wasn't exactly a soothing experience.

"Anyway," Sebastian says, drawing the attention back to the matter at hand, "We searched and searched and then yesterday, there you were, right in front of us. It threw us off guard a bit. When you ran, it hit us here." He thumps his chest.

"Who were you running from in the first place," Xander asks quietly.

My gaze cuts to him quickly and I clear my throat. "No one."

"Lies, Strawberries," he murmurs. "I can smell them, and I don't like it."

I shiver. I'm not sure if he means the scent of lies or the fact I'm lying to him to begin with. The need to apologise sits on my tongue, but I'm frozen in place. I can't even speak.

"We will circle back to that," Benjamin says. "The point is, Faith, that you landed in our lap, and we weren't letting you get away from us. We had hoped we could have a reasonable conversation with you, explain our side and all that, but you shot off before we could and we were forced to hunt you down. Then you fought like a hellcat and well...here we are."

"Hmm."

"The effect you have on us has marked every single one of us. We have all been faithful to the idea of you, Faith," Sebastian says, his expression one full of deep meaning.

*What? No, that's not possible for alphas. He's lying.*

I raise an eyebrow which shows my disbelief at his comment.

"You don't believe me," he states. "Fair enough. We will have to prove to you how much you mean to us. In the meantime, we are so glad you are here, and we hope that you'll stay."

"You're giving me the option to leave?" I squeak.

"Of course. You aren't a prisoner."

There is something about his tone that makes me not believe that for a second. They haven't searched for me for three months and found me, just to let me go. Nope. Not going to happen. Thing is, do I *want* to stay?

"Who were you running from, Strawberries, and don't lie to me this time," Xander murmurs.

I let out an exasperated huff. "My stepdad, okay. He is a mean bastard, abusive and was going to sell me to a nasty pack just for the money. I had to get away. So, yesterday, I packed my bag and I left. Then I fucking run into you and had to keep running."

"You thought he'd sent us after you?"

I stare at Xander, those light green eyes, so pretty, so full of emotion.

"Yes, that's what I thought. Why wouldn't I?"

"I'm so sorry," Sebastian says, which shocks me to my core.

Since when do alphas apologise?

Never, in my experience.

"We didn't mean to scare you further. That definitely wasn't our intention."

"Yeah," I say with a sigh. "I get that, I guess."

"He was going to *sell* you?"

My head snaps back to Xander. He is absolutely furious. His face has contorted into a menacing mask of terror, his tone dark and dangerous.

I nod slowly.

"You deserve so much more than that," Sebastian says carefully, almost as if he is trying to hold onto a deeper emotion. "We can give you everything your heart desires. You will want for nothing."

"I'm not going to agree to stay just because you live in a big fancy house filled with delicious food," I snap, insulted. "That's as bad as what *he* was going to do."

His eyes light up at my fury. He smiles slowly, seductively. "That isn't what I meant."

"Humph." *I bet, King Dick with the king dong.* "I'll think about it."

"Of course."

Two words spoken that mean nothing. I'm staying here, regardless of whether I want to or not.

"We do need to discuss what you'd like us to do in the next few days," he continues matter-of-factly.

My cheeks flame when I get that he's talking about my heat.

"You have several options. We can either take care of you,

which is, of course, our preferred option, but if that doesn't suit you this time, we can get you some accessories to take care of yourself. You can lock yourself in here and we will leave you alone until you are ready. It's entirely up to you."

"What if I decide I'm not staying?" I ask archly. He's taking a massive leap assuming I'll agree to anything.

"If you think any of us will allow you out on the street with nowhere to go during your heat, I'm insulted, but will ignore it because you don't know us. None of us would allow any harm to come to you. You are *ours*."

And there it is.

The possessive and growly alpha I was expecting a while ago.

I'll admit it makes me feel all warm and fuzzy inside.

Oh, what to do, what to do?

"I'll let you know," I murmur, even though I know I'm staying. Wild horses couldn't drag me away from this nest.

Speaking of which, I yawn.

"We'll leave you to rest," Benjamin says, standing up.

Sebastian's stare is still on mine, but I lower my eyes. "We'll check on you again in a little while."

I nod.

"Think about what I've said," he adds quietly. "We really need you here with us, Faith."

"I will," I reply just as softly.

Xander's eyes meet mine filled with sadness. "Can I stay?" he asks so no one else hears. "I'll be out here. I want to make sure you're safe."

I hesitate for the longest time, until I nod once and then curl up, my eyes closing, and sleep falls over me again.

# Chapter Seventeen

Xander

I watch her, softly snoring and smile.

I edge closer and pause.

Then I move closer still until I'm in the wardrobe with her. She snuffles in her sleep, and I freeze, hoping I didn't disturb her.

She settles again and I carefully lay down, staring into her beautiful face. I can't resist leaning over to kiss the tip of her nose.

She smiles and takes my hand, lacing our fingers together. "You're really sweet, aren't you?"

I snort. "Pah, hard as nails."

"Nah, don't believe you. Is Xander short for Alexander?" Her eyes open and I fall deeply into their aqua depths.

"Yeah, but no one calls me that. Not anymore." I try to keep the bite out of my tone, but I think some of it filtered through.

She gets it, though. "Xander, it is."

Her eyes close again and I go back to watching her.

"Stop it," she murmurs. "You're making me self-conscious."

"I don't mean to. I just can't stop looking at you now you're here."

Her eyes open again. "I hope I live up to what you expected."

"Surpassed. Not that I really thought about it. I focus more on scents and sounds."

She blinks sleepily. She probably doesn't understand where I'm coming from. "Did he mean what he said?" she asks so quietly, I barely heard her.

"About which part?" I think I know, but I want to hear her say it.

She looks down shyly and bites her lip.

It's fucking adorable.

There isn't a being in the entire world that can stop my next action.

I lean over and press my lips to hers.

Her eyes shoot up to mine, so close together as our mouths are joined. She lets out a soft breath, parting those plump red lips. I take it as an invitation and slip my tongue inside her mouth.

She moans and fists her hand into my hair.

Twisting my tongue around hers, I suddenly freeze. I don't kiss women, females, people in general. Whatever drove this need to claim her mouth with mine isn't instinctual. It was something else entirely, but I'm not sure what it was.

She hesitates and pulls back, puzzled. "Sorry," she murmurs.

"Why are *you* apologising?" I splutter.

She shakes her head, her hair tumbling into her eyes. I reach out and brush the light blonde strands out of her face.

"I'm not used to being…" I bite the inside of my cheek as words fail me.

"You aren't used to kissing women?" she asks astutely.

I nod, my turn to be shy.

She cups my face. "You're a good kisser. You should practise more."

My eyes wide, I choke on my own saliva. "I don't want to…I mean…wait, with you? Do you mean with you?"

"Yes," she giggles. "I mean with me."

I breathe out in relief. "Okay, maybe."

She gives me a secretive smile. "What Sebastian said about being faithful…why would any of you do that? You didn't owe me anything. Still don't."

"You have no idea the impact you have had on this pack, Strawberries." I inhale slowly and fall back to her pillows, stuffing one under my head. "Even during the rut, none of us took an omega to our beds. Not even Ben."

"Not even Ben," she repeats slowly, picking at the cover. "Does that mean he sleeps around a lot?"

"Used to," I point out firmly. "He has been strangely withdrawn the last few weeks. Not himself. I think abstinence has taken its toll on him." I say this out loud because I feel like I can tell her anything. I know I should mention Gertie, I'm just waiting for the opener.

"You're making me feel guilty."

"Don't, and sorry, I don't mean to. Just answering your question."

She nods. "What about you?"

"What about me?" *Tell her. Tell her now, you idiot.*

"Has it taken its toll on you too?"

I shake my head. "This is going to sound, I dunno…" I shrug.

Faith looks up at me. "What? I said before that you don't owe me anything."

"I—,"

"Xander! Faith is meant to be resting," Ben snaps as he re-enters the room before I can spill the sex doll beans.

I see Faith eye him up, probably wondering how many women he's shagged.

"It's okay," she says.

He gives her a soft look which is in sharp contrast to the scathing glare he gave me. "He can come back later."

He holds his hand out for me to take so he can help me up. I have no choice. I take it and he hauls me to my feet.

"I'll see you later," I whisper, my heart already hurting from being forced away from her. She brings me a peace that I've never known and will likely crave now until I see her again. I scowl at Ben as he escorts me out of the room and as soon as the door closes behind us, I turn on him.

"She wanted me there. You had no right to remove me like I'm some kind of nuisance."

"Please just leave her to rest for now. She is going to need all her strength when her heat comes. This is her first time. She doesn't know what it's going to be like."

"Oh," I say, and my anger deflates. I get why he's being so protective now. "You could've just told me that before."

"I've told you now," he says and stalks off, his shoulders tense, his back straight.

Narrowing my eyes, I watch him go back to his bedroom. Something is definitely up with him and whatever it is, isn't doing him any favours.

He'd better hope that it doesn't hurt Faith in any way, or he will have me to deal with. "I'm watching you," I growl and slide down the door to wait until I can see Faith again. I *will* tell her about Gertie, and I will also get her to tell me more about this arsehole who hurt her and tried to sell her. There isn't a chance in hell he will take another breath once I find him.

# Chapter Eighteen

Benjamin

I can feel Xander's eyes on me as I storm off down the hallway. Opening my bedroom door, I enter and close it behind me with a lot less vigour than I wanted to. But I didn't want to disturb Faith. She needs her rest. I rub my hands over my face and then slip into the bathroom to glare at my appearance.

I'm a mess.

I came off the rut suppressants a few days ago. I was warned to not take them for longer than three months at a time. It stopped the recent rut, so that was enough for now. Coming off them cold turkey was not advised, but I cut the cord and now I feel like hell. At least I don't ever have to go back on them. We've found Faith and everything will fall into place now. My eyes are bloodshot, and my head is banging. Turning to the shower, I strip off and step inside, blasting the frigid water onto my feverish skin, cooling it down instantly. It eases my head, but my bones start to ache with the icy cold water.

With a sigh, I turn the temperature up moderately and stand there, letting the lukewarm water cascade down over my head and body. Closing my eyes, I lean my hands on the cool tile in front of me.

I feel the stirring deep inside me before it goes to my cock.

Faith.

She is here.

She is ours.

She is so precious, so beautiful, I just want to hold her close and kiss her before I tie her up and smack her arse until she squeals.

I groan as my dick goes stiff. I haven't had a sexual release in months and it's killing me. Her pheromones are all around, zinging off my senses and I need to do *something* to relieve the tension.

With a grimace, I grip my cock in my fist and tug gently. The ripple of the hardening tissue against my palm feels so good. Still leaning with one hand on the tile, I jerk off, slowly, enticingly, closing my eyes and imagining it is Faith's small hand wrapped around me.

"Faith," I murmur. "Oh, yes, Faith."

I can feel the pleasure building up quickly now. Picturing her blue eyes, filled with a raw lust as she opens up her mouth to lick my dick and twist her tongue around it, I pump harder. Faster. My breathing speeds up, my heart hammers in my chest.

"I'm coming...oh fuck, Faith, I'm coming," I whisper.

At the precise second that my cum shoots out of my cock, the door to the bathroom is flung open and Sebastian marches in.

"Ben!" he yells. "For fuck's sake, where are you?"

I muffle my groan by biting my lip, and when I'm done with my climax, I snap, "Having a fucking shower, you prick. Fuck off."

"We need you downstairs," he snaps back, ignoring me. "We have a visitor."

Fully alert now, I slide the door across with a frown. "Who?"

"Some arsehole who climbed over the gate. Now, please."

"Yeah," I mutter and turn the water off.

"Are you wanking in there?"

"Get fucked," I retort, not copping to the fact that I've been caught with my dick in my hand. No way. I would never live it down.

"Whatever. Hurry the fuck up." Sebastian has already gone by the time I step out of the shower, so I grab a towel and dry off with haste. I choose my clothes carefully but quickly. Black combat pants and a tight black shirt. White will show blood stains, and be a pain for the maid to get out. I get why Sebastian is so anxious for me to join him. I'm the enforcer of this pack. Anyone who comes within a fifty-foot radius, trying to cause trouble gets their arses kicked by me. I enjoy this role. It thrills my darkened soul on a level that is hard to explain. The mood I'm in right now, whoever has dared to cross over into our territory uninvited is going to seriously regret being born. Especially with Faith in the house. My protective side has just inflated a hundredfold, and I will murder anyone who tries to set foot anywhere near her.

Shoving my boots on, I pick up my pace and take the stairs quickly, striding across the entrance hall where Sebastian and Xander are assembled, the former keeping the latter on a tight leash with great difficulty as Harvey barricades the doorway with his enormous Celtic body.

"I know she's in there! Faith! Faith!" the intruder yells, trying to duck around Harvey.

"About time," Harvey says to me, annoyed. "You know I prefer not to smash faces in unless I have to."

"Step back, Scottie, Daddy's got this," I inform him with

an arrogant smirk, which makes him laugh despite the severity of this situation.

The second Harvey removes his bulk from the doorway, the intruder tries to rush forward, but he hits a wall of solid alpha in the form of me. I place my hand on his chest and shove him backwards, making him stumble and fall on his arse.

I glare down at him. He's got light blonde hair and blue eyes, the same shade as Faith's. I narrow my eyes and cross my arms over my chest as he scrambles to his feet.

"I want to see Faith," he says, waving his phone at me. "I know she's here; I tracked her phone."

"Not a chance," I state.

"You can't keep me from her."

"Actually, I can. You are on private property and the last idiot to trespass isn't here to talk about it."

My brain races to figure out who this fucker is. He can't be her stepdad, they look too much alike and he isn't old enough, so I'm going with her brother. But the question is, did the stepdad send him to retrieve his slave? That's what I'm going to enjoy beating the crap out of him for.

"Faith!" he yells again. "Faith!"

"Shut the fuck up," Xander growls. "You aren't getting anywhere near her. She is *our* omega. You aren't getting your hands on her."

"She is my *sister*, for fuck's sake!" her brother growls.

Definitely an alpha, but a packless one it seems, seeing as he is here solo.

"Bullshit," Xander snarls.

"Shut it," Sebastian snarls at him.

I grab the guy by his shirt front and growl in his face. "Who are you?"

"Derek," he says. "Faith's brother. I know she's here, so you let me see her now before I start kicking some arses."

Sebastian snorts, but lets Xander go.

I haul Derek into the entrance hall at the same time as Faith stumbles drowsily down the stairs.

"Faith!" he shouts out.

"Derek?" she asks with a frown. "What the fuck are you doing here?"

"Trying to find you," he says desperately. "I'm here now, you don't need to stay with these pricks. Come back to my place where I can keep you safe."

"She's safe here," I inform him.

His eyes pin mine furiously. "No, she isn't. You think I trust a pack of alphas around her at this time? Get knotted. Give me my sister back or I'll call the Inter-pack Parliament and report you for abduction."

"Derek," Faith says, "It's okay. I'm okay."

"My father is the head of the Inter-pack Parliament," Sebastian says smugly. "Not sure you'd get very far."

I watch as his face falls, but he rallies and focuses on Faith. "Faith, tell them you want to come with me." He holds his hand out for her.

All stares go to Faith at the bottom of the stairs, her hand on the banister for support.

"Faith," I say calmly. "Tell him you want to stay."

She looks from him to me and licks her lips.

In the next second, Derek flies out of my grip as Xander launches at the intruding alpha, flattening him against the expensive plush carpet. His fist connects sharply with Derek's nose before he grips his shirt, lifting him up only to smash his head back against the floor, knocking him unconscious.

"Jesus," I say with exasperation. "Someone put a leash on him, will you?"

# Chapter Nineteen

Faith

My senses snap together when I see my brother laid out on the floor with Xander smashing his head in. I lurch forward at the same time that Benjamin grabs Xander's shirt at the back and hauls him off Derek, growling like a wild alpha.

"Xander," I say quietly. "It's okay, he's my brother."

He turns to face me, his eyes feral and unfocused. Every cell in my omega body winces and wants me to run, but I force myself to inch further forward.

"How do you know your stepdad didn't send him?" he snarls angrily, but I don't think the rage is directed at me.

I shake my head. "He wouldn't do Pete's bidding. He hates him as much as I do. I was running to him yesterday, but he was...unavailable. He obviously tracked me down."

"Can't risk it," he clips out and turns back to Derek, ready to beat on him some more, even though Benjamin still has his fist bunched in the back of his t-shirt.

"Xander," I say and take another step forward.

"Faith," Harvey's quiet, steady voice cuts over what I was going to say in warning.

I glance at him and shake my head before I edge in right next to Xander. I know in my bones that he wouldn't hurt me. Not even when he is like this.

I reach out and place my hand over his heart.

Benjamin's hand comes down softly over my wrist to pull me away, but I shake him off.

"I know here," I say to Xander, tapping him lightly on the chest. "He isn't here to cause me harm."

Xander stares at my hand. I force myself not to pull it away. When I first touched him, I felt his racing heart. In the last few seconds, he has calmed down. I doubt it is my words, so he is reacting to my touch. I figured him for being wired slightly differently upstairs. He wanted to be near me, whereas the other three kept their distance. I don't know how it works yet, not even in the slightest, but it's clear that my touch affects him.

He reaches out, his hand hovering over mine. Benjamin's hand hovers over his. It's a waiting game to see what he will do. He must be a bit unpredictable if the other alphas wait to take their cues from him.

Xander's hand drops onto mine and he grips my fingers, tightly, but not crunching them.

"Are you sure?" he asks, raising his lovely green eyes to meet mine.

I nod. "I'm sure."

He takes a step back and Benjamin lets him go. I take him to the side, lacing our fingers together that are still resting over his gently beating heart.

Benjamin hauls Derek up and over his shoulder, stalking away into a downstairs room with Sebastian and Harvey following.

I look up at Xander. "Do we follow?"

"You should go back to rest," he replies, turning towards me and curling my hair behind my ear.

I shake my head. "I think I need to speak to Derek. Find out what the fuck is going on."

"He'll be out for a while."

I giggle, surprising him. "Fancy yourself as Mike Tyson?" I ask.

He snorts. "I know how hard I hit. Trust me. He won't be coming around anytime soon. Sorry."

I shrug. "I guess he could've tried a bit harder to explain what he was doing here."

"He trespassed. That's not okay." A frown clouds his features.

"I know. I'll tell him."

"Are you staying, Faith?" he asks me after a pause.

"I think so," I reply hesitantly. "Apart from the way you brought me here, I haven't felt in danger or scared since. You've treated me well..."

He interrupts me. "We care about you."

"I get the feeling that you do, but this is still not what I had in mind when I met a pack I wanted to be with." I say it carefully because I'm not sure how he will react to my words. I don't mean them as an insult or to be mean in any way, it's just a fact. My head is spinning and really, I kind of want to see the beta to make sure that they're telling me the truth about that. Not that I'm going to ask to see him. Pretty sure that wouldn't go down very well, but catching sight of him, maybe even speaking to him would be a good indicator that things are on the up and up.

"I understand that more than you know," Xander's voice interrupts my musings.

I want to ask why, but it doesn't seem like the time.

"Do you want to go back to your nest, and I'll come and get you when he's awake?"

I debate that point for a moment. What if they use my absence to get rid of my brother in a permanent sense?

"He'll be safe from us, I promise," he adds with a soft smile. "We would never do anything to hurt you, Faith."

Taking him at his word, because I actually do believe that they won't hurt me. Not to blow my own trumpet or anything but I'm a relatively pretty, unmated omega about to go into her heat. What's not to like? Even if their objective is just to use me, which I don't think it is after all the trouble they went to because let's face it, unmated omegas are ten a penny, hurting me would go against what they are trying to achieve.

"I can bring your duvet and pillows down if you would rather stay with him," Xander concedes when he sees me dithering over this quandary.

"Can you bring him up to my room?"

His green eyes flash with danger and his heart starts to beat faster again.

"Uhm, okay, it's okay, I'll stay down here with him," I stammer, trying to backtrack and fucking fast.

Clearly having a strange alpha in my room, even if he is my brother, does not sit well with him.

He nods stiffly and leads me into what appears to be a massive, fancy drawing room type affair. I look up at the frescoed ceiling and the pretty covings with wide eyes. There is a huge chandelier, bigger even than the one we were standing under out in the hallway. Gilt edging all around the walls and doors and thick, gold fabric curtains hang at the enormous bay windows. Three of them, I count, that look out onto the perfectly manicured lawns to the front of the house. Mansion. Whatever it is.

My mouth drops open in awe as I look around. I feel Sebastian's gaze on me, so I meet it and he smiles at me. He is pleased that I find his home so lovely. Bless him. It's important to him for some reason.

I spy Derek on a straight back chair with Harvey binding his wrists behind him with a curtain tieback.

"I don't think that's necessary..."

"Intruders are all dealt with the same until we determine if they are a threat or not," Sebastian states, his blue eyes darkening slightly.

I would be a fool to argue with him, and I ain't no fool.

Usually. I have my moments, but this isn't one of them. I lower my eyes and accept he is the prime alpha in charge of this situation.

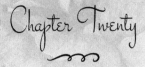

## Chapter Twenty

Harvey

After about ten minutes, I see Faith's eyes start to close again. She is curled up on the comfiest couch in here, which isn't saying much. This room is very much an old country manor room. I prefer the informal sitting room further down the hall.

"I'll take her back upstairs," I murmur, taking a step forward.

Sebastian gives me a nod of confirmation. I think he would rather she wasn't here when Derek wakes up. He wants a clear run at him without her influencing the way he deals with it.

I scoop her up gently and cradle her against me, inhaling deeply, her scent filling my nose and falling over me, almost putting me in a thrall. She is one of the most amazing people I have come across. She has taken all of this in her stride so far. I'm guessing though she is processing, and it will all come out at some point in the near future and our arses will get kicked. I'm quite looking forward to it.

I smile to myself and carry her up the stairs, enjoying it when she snuggles in even closer to me, her face pressed against my chest. Her instinct is definitely telling her she belongs with us. I just hope her head catches up soon.

Entering her bedroom, I make my way over to the wardrobe and lower her gently to the nest. The urge to curl up with her is overwhelming, but I straighten up after tucking her in. Hesitating, I bite the inside of my cheek. Sebastian's blue tie is on her pillow, and I think that's Benjamin's white t-shirt next to it.

I glance at the door and then back to her. "Fuck it."

Stripping off my green and black plaid shirt, leaving me in my green t-shirt, I drape it over her like a blanket. Just as I'm about to close the door, I see her grip it and turn over, bringing it up to her nose with a soft, sleepy smile.

My heart nearly bursts with joy.

Closing the door enough to make her feel safe, but not all the way closed so she can get some air, I cross over to the sash window and open it a crack. The cold winter air seeps in but she will be nice and cosy where she is.

Reluctantly leaving her, I make my way back to the drawing room just in time to see Sebastian punch Derek in the face.

"Why are you really here?" he growls.

"I told you already..."

Sebastian bunches his hand up and smashes the alpha in the nose, making it bleed profusely.

"Fuck's sake," Derek groans, his head lolling forward.

"Once more," Sebastian says quietly.

The drop in his tone chills me.

I step forward and place my hand on Seb's shoulder. "How about we try this a different way?"

When his eyes meet mine, I see that the thrall of Faith has dropped over him as well. He will do absolutely anything to protect her, including beating her brother to near death because he doesn't like the look of him.

After a hefty pause, he nods grimly and steps back.

I pull up the matching chair to the one Derek is tied up in and sit in front of him. "Ben, ask Lindsey to bring him some ice, please."

Ben nods and crosses over to the pressbell on the wall and pushes it, alerting the maid that she is required in the drawing room.

Minutes later, after Ben's instructions, she comes back with some ice and a tea towel on a tray. I take it from her and wrap some ice up before I stand up and untie Derek. Then I sit back down and hold out the makeshift ice pack.

"Try to run and Ben will stop you before you've gone two feet," I inform him casually. There's no threat in my tone. It's merely a statement.

He gives me a vicious glare from eyes that are just like Faith's. I'd noticed it before, but until we know his intentions, brother or not, he is a threat to Faith's safety.

"Why are you here?"

Derek snatches up the ice pack and places it on the back of his head where he must have a huge bump from when Xander smashed his head on the floor.

"To pick up my sister," he replies curtly.

"She is safe here."

"Says you."

"She is about to become our mate."

"Is that what *she* wants? Because this is news to me."

"Tell me about yesterday."

My tone is soothing and non-accusing, and this is why I'm the mediator for this pack. The other three deal in fists and violence, but sometimes it's not needed.

He sighs. "It's none of your business."

"Actually, it is. Faith was running *from* your stepdad, and she said before that she was running *to* you. Why weren't you there for her?"

"Look, I will tell Faith my side of the story, but it's nothing to do with you. It's family stuff."

I sit back and cross my legs at the knee. "I'm not letting you anywhere near Faith until I know what you're going to say to her. She is in a delicate state right now and I don't want anyone upsetting her."

"You have no right to keep me from her." Fury emanates from his eyes as he places the ice pack against his nose now.

"I don't want to, but I will."

"Fuck's sake," he snarls. "You are so fucking arrogant. I knew I'd come up against it, the second I saw your crest on the front gate."

"Yet you still climbed over it and trespassed onto our territory."

"To save my sister! How many times do we have to go over this?"

"Until I'm satisfied with your answers. Of which, you have given me none, so until you do, we will sit here."

He sees I mean it and while he debates with himself over what to tell me, if anything, I see when he finally decides it's easier to co-operate than to butt heads with me. Especially with the three frustrated alphas at my back, practically slobbering with the need to kick his head in.

"Where do you want me to start?" he says with a heavy sigh.

"Start with the stepdad. What's his deal?"

"He's a fucking dickhead arsehole," Derek snarls, the rage in his eyes making them go almost black.

"Then why leave your sister with him?"

95

The guilt that fills his eyes is good to see. At least it shows he cares about her.

"What I'm about to say, cannot leave this room," he says eventually.

"We don't gossip."

His gaze flicks to Sebastian, but then lands back on me. "I want his word that he won't go to his father with this." He points to Seb.

"Have you committed a crime?" Sebastian asks archly.

"No."

"Then I have no reason to mention you to my father."

I hold my hands out in a there-you-go gesture, before crossing my arms.

"It goes back to our father," Derek says. "Faith was so young when he died, not even sixteen. She was absolutely devastated, but too naïve to see that things didn't add up."

"What do you mean?" I prompt when he stops speaking, his expression filled with sadness.

"They say he died of a heart attack, but that's not possible. He was as fit as they come, ate right, didn't drink or smoke or do drugs. One day he was there and the next he was gone. I know that's how death works, but there's more. They took him away and we never saw him again. They wouldn't even let our mum see him. We buried him without seeing him again. That never sat right with me. I started to investigate, here and there at first. Then our mother got involved with Pete." He spits out the name.

"Your stepdad?"

Xander growls in response to the name. I do hope that Benjamin has him restrained somehow. We are finally getting somewhere, although we are quite a way from where we need to be.

"Yeah. Fucking prick. He moved into my dad's house, wore his clothes, drove his car, spent all of his money until there was nothing left, and we had to move to a shitty house in a shitty area, tearing Faith from her family and friends."

"You used to be well off?" It doesn't matter, I'm just asking questions to keep him talking. It seems to matter to him, or he wouldn't have mentioned it.

He nods. "My dad used to be in Parliament. He was outspoken and not everyone agreed with him…" Derek's glare shoots to Sebastian again.

"What was his name?" I ask.

"Oliver Halstead."

"Oh," Sebastian says, I think before he could stop himself. "Halstead?"

Derek nods.

"I remember him. My dad used to get so mad with him," Sebastian says with a laugh, which is quite out of character for him. "But I think he quite enjoyed the debate. I remember when he died. Dad was upset. Are you saying you think he was murdered?"

We all look back at Derek.

"Originally, yes. After we moved, and Pete started to become even more of a dick, I looked deeper and deeper into Dad's death. Pete found out one day and threatened to sell Faith to the first pack who offered him cash for her. She was nineteen. I stopped looking, knowing I had to protect Faith, but then a job came up in London and it was the perfect excuse to get out of the house and start investigating again. I hate that I had to leave Faith but if I'd told her any of this, she wouldn't be able to keep it to herself, and if it all came to nothing, I would be stabbing her in the heart again. I wanted to believe she was better off where she was, then me dragging her into this."

"You say originally? You don't think that now?" I can't help how madly curious I am about this. So are the others, judging from the deflated aggression.

Derek shakes his head, wincing at the pain and then placing the ice pack on the back of his head again. "No, now I think he is still alive."

"What?" Sebastian asks. "How?"

"This is what I'm trying to find out."

"If you're right, then I do need to speak to my father about this," Sebastian says. "He can help. We have resources..."

"No!" Derek snaps. "If it gets back to Pete, there is no telling what he will do to my mother."

"We can help with him," Xander says, his voice low, dark and dangerous. "Just point me in the right direction."

Derek's gaze fills with interest, but is quickly squashed. He doesn't rely on anyone to fight his battles, it seems.

"My turn to ask some questions," he says boldly. "How do you know Faith?"

I sit forward and uncross my arms, leaning my elbows on my knees. "Our beta met her three months ago."

"In London?"

I nod carefully.

"She was visiting me. She lives about a hundred miles from here."

"Oh, for the love of God!" Sebastian snaps suddenly. "A hundred miles? We'd have been searching for her for over a fucking year, longer."

"Hmm?" Derek murmurs. "And you just decided that you wanted her?"

"Kind of," I say.

"Does she want to be here? Does she know who you are?"

"Does it make a difference who we are?" I ask, instead of answering.

"You're the most superior pack in England. Yeah, it makes a fucking difference. That's a lot of responsibility you're thrusting onto her. She isn't even twenty-one yet. She is days away. She will be going into her heat. I don't want her here when that happens. You all have reputations and you're all about ten years older than her."

"Only five in my case," I feel the need to mention. "However, our intentions are to mate with her." I point this out before Sebastian, to his annoyance. "If she'll have us."

"Mate? You seriously want to mate with her?"

"That's the plan," I say with a soft smile. "If you're worried about how she will be treated here, you don't need to be. She will be cared for, respected and given everything her heart desires. We have waited a long time for her, you do not need to worry about her safety."

"I need to speak to her," he says firmly. "I want to hear it from her lips if she wants to stay."

"Of course," Sebastian says. "Now that we know you aren't here to hurt her, you are free to see her when she wakes up. But think about what I said. If you are sure there is foul play involved in your father's death or disappearance, then the Parliament can help. It's what we're there for, and anything to help Faith. We want her to be happy."

He nods grimly. "I'll think about it. There are still a lot of unanswered questions."

"Then let's find some answers," I say.

I stand up and give Sebastian a smug smile. He rolls his eyes at me, but he can't deny that my approach worked. One day he will learn that violence doesn't have to be the first port of call.

I just hope that when Derek speaks to Faith, she tells him she wants to stay. It will hurt my heart and that of the other alphas if she decides she doesn't want us now that her brother is here to save her. Something tells me violence will definitely ensue if that's the case, even from me.

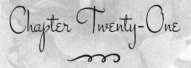

## Chapter Twenty-One

Faith

I wake up with a lazy stretch and wonder how on earth I got back into my nest. I must've fallen asleep downstairs and one of the alphas must've carried me up here. I can't get over how much I'm sleeping lately. It's crazy and a bit annoying. I want to be up and learning stuff about this pack, not sleeping my arse off in the fucking cupboard the entire time.

On that note, I stand up and stretch again as I step out of the wardrobe. The room is dark, the moon glowing full through the window. I gasp in surprise and run over to it, looking up at the vision above me. Stars for miles and miles in the cloudless sky. I shiver from the cold breeze that filters under the slightly opened window and I shut it, flicking the lock. The heating is going full blast which makes it nice and warm in here. I wonder how they can afford to have the central heating on in this huge house. If I was back at home, I'd be shivering under my thin duvet.

"But you aren't at home, Faith. You are here." I smile at

my words, my heart feeling warm and full of a joy I haven't known since my dad died.

That doesn't mean that everything is bells and whistles, but I know that despite a rocky start, this pack actually does want me to be their mate. The pull is too strong to deny. I can feel it. I know they can as well. I rub my fingers over the inside of my wrist where Sebastian bit me in the park. Frowning, I rub harder. I don't like that he marked me as a possession. However, if he had tried to give me a mating bite, I'd be less than impressed about that. He hasn't earned that yet. None of them have.

With a sigh over my vastly conflicting feelings, I make my way over to the door and open it, peering out into the dimly lit hallway. I wonder if Derek is still here, and if he is, where is he? Hopefully alive and not buried under a bush in the garden somewhere. Xander was not happy with him being here. I hasten out into the hallway and down the stairs, past the creepy portraits that at this time of night, in the semi-dark and eerie quiet. They freak me out a bit. I feel like their eyes are following me.

I make it to the bottom of the stairs without a Scooby Doo incident and run smack bang into a solid wall of male.

"Sorry!" I pant and look up as he grips my arms. "Oh. It's you."

My tone makes the beta I hooked up with raise his eyebrow and give me a smirk. "Oh, it's you too."

"Pah, like you didn't already know I was here."

"Back at you. You stalking me?"

"Fuck you," I spit out and then jab him in the chest. "You are the one that set these alphas on my tail."

He shrugs. "I can't help that you smell like heaven to them. Try masking your scent with some severe BO or something."

My cheeks heat up with indignation, but the comical

expression on his face is too much. I snort loudly and in a very unladylike manner. Mortified, I slap my hand over my nose and mouth while he chuckles.

"Listen," he says after a few seconds. "I'm really sorry for being a dick that night. I really fancied you, and I wanted to see you again. I really thought you were blowing me off."

"I could've tried harder to explain," I say, immediately taking the blame.

"Maybe we both could've done better," he says.

"I'm kind of glad to see you actually. You're the whole reason I'm here. It's nice to see that you're...you know..." I chew my lip nervously, knowing I sound like a bumbling idiot.

He scrutinises my face for a moment, but then nods. "I get what you mean. But you have nothing to worry about. These alphas can be huge douches, but seriously, deep down they are a good pack. They know what respect is and don't expect everything to just land in their laps. Although in your case, that might have been preferable. They were getting majorly cranky." He snorts with laughter.

"Thanks," I say, looking down and tucking my hair behind my ear. "That helps. A lot actually. Unless you're just saying that..."

"Not my style," he interrupts me.

"What's your name?" I ask suddenly, realising I never got it that night.

"Matt."

"I'm Faith."

"Yeah, I know."

I nod and give him a tentative smile. "Friends?"

"Definitely."

"Have you seen my brother around?"

"Yeah, he's in the kitchen."

I wait, but nothing happens. "Which is where?"

"Oh! Duh, yeah." He turns and points to a door a way down the really imposing hallway.

"Thanks," I murmur and duck around him, heading to the door he pointed at.

As I approach, I hear a burst of laughter and then several voices all talking at once, a can opening and a rustle of a crisp packet. Curious, I push open the door and see the four alphas hanging out around a humongous kitchen island with my brother, laughing at something he said.

I smile in surprise, glad that he isn't under a bush and lean against the doorway. "This looks fun," I say when they all turn towards me.

I'm shocked when the four alphas all race forward, eager to reach me first to draw me further into the kitchen.

"You need to eat," Harvey says. "I'll make you a sandwich."

"I'm okay," I say, shaking my head, not wanting him to go to any trouble for me.

"No, you need to eat now. Fill yourself up before...you know..." he says with a sidelong glance at my brother.

"My heat?" I say and watch his cheeks go a cute shade of pink.

"Yeah, that," he splutters, avoiding Derek's stare.

"Faith," my brother says, "We need to talk about that."

"I'm staying," I say before he can add anything else, taking in the astounded, but happy gazes of the alphas around me.

"You are?" Sebastian says, almost cautiously.

I hear Xander's slow inhalation and give him a smile.

Then, I nod and pick up an orange from the fruit bowl in the middle of the island. "As much as I appreciate your attempt to let me know I'm free to leave, I know as well as you do that I'm not going anywhere. But that's okay. I don't want to. I'm not sure what's going to happen in a few days, there's still a lot to learn about each other, but..." I shrug and start to peel the orange. "I like what I see so far. There is one thing that is bugging me though."

"What's that?" Sebastian asks, his eyes swimming with a desire that is flattering to see aimed at me.

I hold up my wrist. "This bite mark. I don't like it. I'm not a possession."

"No, you aren't. I was wrong to do that to you. It was in the heat of the moment, and I wasn't thinking clearly. I will replace it with a proper bite when you tell me that's what you want."

"I appreciate that. Thank you. I will let you know," I say and turn on my heel, throwing the orange up in the air and catching it as I leave them to their boys' night. I have plans with a massive hot bubble bath and not much is going to deter me from this. Smiling, I make my way back upstairs, happy with my decision to stay. Now all I need to figure out is what the hell I'm going to do when my heat hits in a couple of days.

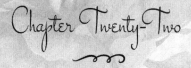

## Chapter Twenty-Two

Faith

Stretching, I stick my arms above my head and then shiver. I poke my head out of the wardrobe and remember that I opened the window last night after my bath. I was feeling a bit feverish and wanted some cool air in the room. I crawl a few feet and then get to my feet as there is a knock at the door.

"Uhm, yeah?" I call out awkwardly hovering in the middle of the huge, white bedroom.

The door opens and the four alphas troop inside. "Are you up?" Sebastian asks, his eyes on the cupboard, but then he sees me standing shivering near the bed. "Oh, it's freezing in here."

His gaze shoots to the open window and me standing here like an awkward lemon, a suspicious expression descending on his handsome features.

"Everything okay?" he growls.

I nod, momentarily speechless. "I was too hot last night, so I opened the window. I fell asleep before I could close it again."

The suspicion immediately turns to concern, and he crosses over to me, taking my elbow and leading me to the bed. "You're like ice," he murmurs, and flicks his fingers to the window.

Harvey crosses over to close it and lock it. I instantly feel warmer.

"Better?" Sebastian asks.

I nod, dumbstruck by the care they are giving me.

"Good, we wanted to discuss something with you if you are up for it?"

"Sure, but where's Derek?"

"He went back to his place early this morning. He said he'd call you later."

"Oh," I say, a bit disappointed. I'd hoped he would stick around so I could ask him where he was a couple of days ago when I needed him. "Okay, what did you want to discuss?" I cross my arms over my chest because I'm currently dressed only in my thin white cotton pjs with no bra and my jugs are swinging in the wind.

Not that any of them are gawking at me. They are all staring into my face. Too sweet and very unnatural, so they definitely noticed the girls were unencumbered.

While they make themselves comfortable, I dart towards my nest and pull my duvet up over me, feeling much safer and more secure. Not that any of them were making me uncomfortable. It's just me and my lemony weirdness.

I watch as they all adjust their seats to face me in the cupboard, trying not to laugh.

"Sorry," I murmur. "Cold."

"Wait a minute," Xander says and disappears.

He returns a few moments later with a balled-up pair of socks. He unfolds them and holds them out, one in each hand with a wicked smile. "Show me your feet."

I giggle like a fiend and stick my tootsies out from underneath the covers. He drops to his knees and picks up the right one.

"Jesus, they're like ice," he comments when he rolls the sock onto my foot and then picks up the other one.

"Hope they're clean," Sebastian remarks.

"Lindsey will be pissed if she overhears you," Xander retorts. "Of course they're clean. I wouldn't taint Faith with gross, sweaty socks."

Giggling, I lower my eyes. "Thank you."

He rubs his knuckles over the sole of my foot. My toes curl in as it tickles. I hope he decides to stay next to me, which he does, in the same spot he was in last time we were all assembled in here.

Only last time I had food. Where's the food?

Almost as if on cue, there is a soft knock and a woman enters, Lindsey, I presume, pushing a trolley filled with breakfast foods and a delicious smelling pot of coffee. Harvey gets up to fill me a plate up with bacon bagels, croissants, toast and a variety of other yummy things while Benjamin pours me a mug of coffee.

I accept them readily and dive in while they sit their fine arses back down.

"As you have agreed to stay, we wanted to ask if you'd like to spend some time with us individually over the next couple of days, to get to know us better," Sebastian says, diving right in.

"Oh. Yes, I'd like that. That's really sweet of you." I smile warmly, glad that they aren't just leaving me to my own devices and are taking some responsibility for getting to know me as well.

"Good," he says. "How do you want us?"

I look at each of them all eager for first dibs, but there is only one way in which this will be fair. "Alphabetically," I say with a smirk.

"Yes, I win!" Xander says.

"How do you figure?" Benjamin snarls. "Unless she's going backwards."

"I'm 'A'," he says, jabbing his finger into his chest, way harder than I'd like. He probably gave himself a bruise.

"You go by 'X', so fuck off," Benjamin snaps, standing up. "Now everyone get out. This is *my* time."

"Uhm," I say, catching Xander's eyes. I didn't mean for this to turn into an argument. I thought it was clear.

"You agree?" he asks.

I put my coffee down and crawl over to him, cupping his face. "Last but not least," I murmur against his lips, before I press my mouth to his, shocking him and the rest of the alphas at my bold move.

Xander pulls his head back, his eyes full of heated desire. "Unless you want us all to jump on you right now, maybe less of that," he mutters.

"Boo," I pout and sit back, picking up my coffee again. "Benjamin. You are first, what would you like to do?"

The expression of raw lust on his face tells me exactly what he would like to do, so I stop looking at him and stare at my coffee instead.

"I'll come and find you when you're done," Harvey says stiffly, and escapes the room where the pheromones are bouncing around all over.

I'm getting closer to my heat. Maybe this isn't such a good idea after all.

"Same," Sebastian croaks and leaves as well, swinging by Xander to yank him to his feet and haul him out of the room, only to stick his head back inside and fix Benjamin with a glare of epic proportions.

"You touch a single hair on her head, and I will rip your pubes out one by one."

Benjamin gives him a death stare for all of a second before

he concedes to the prime alpha and holds his hands up. "Hands to myself."

Sebastian narrows his eyes and then leaves us alone.

Benjamin's gaze softens when he looks back at me.

"Can I shower first?" I choke out, needing to get out from under his scrutiny.

"Of course."

"Alone," I stammer.

He chuckles gently. "Yes, alone." He holds his hand out for me and I take it, trusting him. There's something about him that makes me know he will behave.

Smiling, I let go of his hand when I'm on my feet, wishing I could bring it to my mouth to lick and taste his skin. Licking my lips instead, I rush to the bathroom, locking the door behind me.

* * *

Standing in the middle of the bathroom a few minutes later, I realise my faux pas. I only have my pjs or a towel to cover up in.

I didn't bring any other clothes in with me.

"Dammit," I mutter and consider changing back into my jammies, but I threw them over the basin after I brushed my teeth and got in the shower, and they have wet patches. "Fuck."

Glancing at the door, I chew the inside of my cheek. I can't stand in here indefinitely. The guys have taken time out of their day to get to know me and so I can get to know them. That's hardly going to happen with me dithering in the bathroom like a fucking idiot.

Making a decision, I wrap the towel tightly around myself,

and open the door. Stepping out of the steamy bathroom, I see Benjamin standing at the window, staring out over the grounds.

"It's a nice day. Do you want to go for a walk in the grounds?" he asks, turning to face me.

I blink and stand my ground when his features change to reflect his feelings about me dressed only in a towel in his presence.

"Jesus," he mutters, rubbing his hand over his face. "You are beautiful, kitty. So, so beautiful." His tone is almost reverent as his gaze takes in every inch of my body.

"K-kitty?" I stammer.

He smiles, slowly and sexily. "Do you like it?"

I nod and hastily walk to the wardrobe intending to get inside, close the door and get dressed in the dark.

However, I don't make it.

Almost as if he is made from speed, he is in front of me before I make it to the safety of my nest. He slaps his palm against the door and shuts it, blocking me from my safe haven.

"Uhm," I murmur, glancing around warily.

But there is no escape.

He moves to the back of me, his hands going up to my bare shoulders. He strokes my skin, inhaling deeply. "So soft."

He places a kiss at the base of my neck, brushing away the wisps of hair escaping from the messy bun I'd bunched my hair into to shower.

I shiver under his touch.

"Can I touch you, kitty?"

"Yes," I murmur not wanting him to stop. His hands feel so good against my sensitive skin.

"Fuck," he groans. "Tell me to get away from you."

"No," I say, my voice stronger. I stare at my reflection in the full-length mirror of the wardrobe door, my breath coming in short, shallow pants.

He presses his body closer to me, his hand snaking around to grip my throat gently. "Be a good girl and tell me to get away from you, kitty."

"I can't do that." My heart is beating rapidly, making me go lightheaded.

"You're going to be naughty?"

I nod.

He increases the pressure on my throat. "Bad girls get punished."

"What are you going to do?"

His hand drops from my throat to the top of the towel, and he flicks it open, letting it drop to the floor at my feet. His breath hitches.

I lift my gaze to latch onto his. His hazel eyes are grey and beautiful when he looks back at me. His expression is one of torment. I want to let him off the hook and tell him to step back, but when I open my mouth to say the words, nothing comes out.

"You have completely unravelled me, Faith," he groans softly. "I am a creature of restraint. I'm not ruled by my dick or my base instinct to rut everything that moves. But you bring that out in me."

His hands trail lightly down over my breasts as he presses his body closer to mine, pushing me up against the cold surface of the mirror.

I whimper softly.

He closes his eyes, inhaling deeply, his hands cupping my breasts. "You are everything, Faith. Everything I never even knew I wanted, but now crave. Now that my hands are on your skin, I have to keep touching you or I will perish."

One hand drops between my legs. He cups my pussy, squeezing gently. "Tell me to step back, Faith because that is the only thing that will stop me now."

"I don't want you to stop," I say and follow that up with a soft purr when his fingers slip inside me.

"Fucking hell," he groans. "Faith."

His other hand fumbles behind me, releasing his cock from his sexy black combat pants.

"You're everything," he says again, that posh accent drifting over me, turning me on even more.

I slick on his fingers, drenching them with my sudden need to have him. "P-please."

He removes his fingers from my pussy and lifts one hand up above my head to place my palm against the mirror. His gaze fixed on mine in the mirror and unwavering, he pulls back on my hips, so my arse is sticking out. He guides his cock to my entrance and slowly slides into me before he takes my other hand and plasters it to the mirror.

"Ah," I cry out as his massive cock invades my pussy, coating him with slick.

"Fuck, yes. You feel so good."

I have no words. His cock buried deep inside me feels so right, I want to weep with joy. It proves everything to me that I was trying to deny or shove aside. I belong to him. He belongs to me. I am destined to be his mate and I want nothing more than to be tied to him and the other alphas. He brings his hips back, only to thrust deeper inside me again, our gazes transfixed to each other in our reflections.

"Soak my cock, kitty," he whispers.

I tremble against him, my slick covering his cock. Already I can feel my climax building. It's going to hit me like a freight train. He pounds into me, harder, deeper, faster. I open my legs wider, stick my arse up higher to give him even more access. He lets go of my hands and grabs my hips, slamming up against me, exhaling heavily, making the wisps of my hair tickle my neck.

"Benjamin," I cry out as the orgasm slams into me. I

release a long, low purr. He growls in response, gripping my hips harder. He places his mouth to my neck and opens up. I tilt my head, so ready to accept his mating bite, but with a snarl of irritation he pulls back and bites my shoulder instead.

My pussy clenches around his cock, tightening its hold on him possessively, never wanting to let him go.

"That's it, kitty, hold onto me. Never let me go."

"Ah!" I cry out again, shuddering wildly, my nipples so hard, they are aching.

My skin is red hot, I can see my flushed face in the mirror. Benjamin is panting as he pounds into me, thrusting fast and furious.

He lets out a loud grunt when he shoots his load into me, his fingers digging into my hips and bruising me.

"Faith. I've waited so long for you. Faith. You're here. You're mine," he whispers into my hair and then he withdraws from me, leaving me wanting more. I knew not to expect a knot from him. I'm not in my heat yet. He isn't in his rut. But it makes the decision for me that in a couple of days, I will take them all into my nest and let them relieve me. I will come all over their knots until I can't come anymore, and I can't fucking wait.

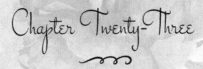

# Chapter Twenty-Three

Faith

My breathing slows down. I press my hot forehead to the cool mirror. Benjamin runs his hand down my back, and I flex my shoulders, feeling the deep need inside me for him to keep touching me.

"Sorry," he whispers before he gives me a soft kiss behind my ear. "I shouldn't have done that. You are precious. You deserve more."

"More than a fucking good shag with a hot guy?" I ask before my runaway mouth can stop itself.

He chuckles. "It was a fucking good shag. You have no idea how much I needed it with you. But I should have restrained myself, and now I need to go and tell Seb." His sigh speaks volumes. He is going to get his arse kicked. Severely.

"Let me clean up and I'll come with you."

He turns me around, a look of surprise on his face. "As much as I appreciate the protection you will undeniably bring me, I'm a big boy. I can handle it."

The girly giggle erupts, and I press my lips together to try to stop it, but it's too late.

He gives me an arched eyebrow. "Glad that my impending arse-kicking is amusing to you."

"It's not that," I choke out before I laugh for real. "It's—it's, well, no one has ever said I could protect them. The big bad alpha being protected by the little omega. It's funny and not at all true, but I want to face the music with you. It's only fair."

He laughs gently. "You still have no idea the effect you have on this pack, do you?"

I lower my eyes, embarrassed by his intense gaze.

To my surprise, he doesn't push it. He just bends down to retrieve my towel and he wraps it around me, covering me up.

"Let me clean you up, Faith."

I shake my head, mortified. "No, no, you don't have to."

"I *want* to," he says firmly and scoops me up in his arms so I can't escape him.

He takes me to the bathroom and places me on my feet while he turns the shower on. "Your skin is on fire," he murmurs. "You're getting close. Cooler?"

I nod, really loving this side to him. Caring and attentiveness didn't seem to be his style. Regardless of no words, I'm learning about him anyway.

He takes my hand and helps me step into the shower. I stand there as he picks up the washcloth and soap, lathering up with way more than I'm used to using back at home. I tilt my head back, so my hair doesn't get wet and part my legs, watching him with interest. He kneels down on the outside of the shower and starts to wash my feet before moving upwards. My blood runs slightly cooler when I realise, he's done this before. It brings me back to what Xander said about him.

"I suppose we should actually learn stuff about each other," I murmur.

"What do you want to know?"

"How did you become a member of the most prestigious pack in England?"

He looks up at me, those gorgeous eyes smiling. "Seb's dad and mine went to Harrow together. I practically grew up in this house, even though I only lived a few houses away."

"Oh," I say, that makes sense. They're so posh, although Sebastian has more of an edge to his accent where Benjamin's is refined. "Can I ask something really personal?"

He nods. "Of course. Open book for you."

I love the added touch of 'for you'. "Did you grow up in a pack or solo?"

"Solo. All of the St. James alphas chose to be solo mated couples. It is only recently that packs with one omega became the norm."

"I know," I say lightly. "My mum and dad were a solo mated couple."

"Sorry," he says. "I didn't mean to sound patronising."

"You didn't. So, what do you do for a living?"

"I'm retired," he replies with a wicked smirk.

I blink. "Oh. How old are you?"

He snorts. "Thirty-two. It's not as entitled as it sounds. I invested wisely."

"Now I'm intrigued. What did you *used* to do?"

He runs the washcloth up the outside of my thigh, making me tingle. "Investment banking."

"Ah, okay. That makes sense."

He nods. "It's still a full-time job though to make sure the investments stay profitable."

It's all over my head so I just nod. I freeze when the washcloth slips between my legs, and he cleans up my slick mixed with his cum. He is holding his breath, his eyes dark with lust.

"You're good at this," I murmur and then wince as his eyes shoot up to mine in question.

"Ask what's on your mind," he says quietly.

"It's nothing."

"Faith. I have no secrets from you," he says seriously.

Again the 'from you' goes a long way.

"It's just something that Xander said that's playing on my mind."

He stops what he's doing for a moment, but then proceeds to run the washcloth over my stomach. "What did he say?"

"Don't blame him. I asked him if Sebastian was being honest when he said that you'd all been faithful to the idea of me. I found it a bit unbelievable."

"And he told you what about me?" His tone is steady, but his eyes tell me he is furious.

"He said that none of you had taken an omega to your bed during your rut. Not even you."

"Not even me." He tuts in annoyance, shaking his head. "No, I didn't. I haven't taken a woman to my bed since the second I smelt your scent all over Matt. But clearly, you have further questions."

"He made it sound like you were a bit of a player." *Why am I saying these things?*

"I was. I enjoyed sex, especially sex with omegas. I maintained a sense of full control over the situation and that is what thrilled me more." He finishes cleaning me and stands up, replacing the washcloth and fixing his glare onto me.

"Sorry," I murmur instantly. "It's not my business."

"It is definitely your business. If you want to know something about me, I want you to ask. Yes, I like to be dominant during sex, but I also have a kink for praise. It really arouses me to dirty talk to you and then praise you during sexual acts, especially really filthy ones."

My eyes go wide with shock. I've never been with anyone like that before. It occurs to me that my sex life is very boring. A quick shag here or there with men who are nowhere near as *manly* as Benjamin. They seem like boys with no clue what they're doing in comparison. I can't help the tingle that goes across my clit.

He crosses his arms. "I won't do anything with you that you don't explicitly ask me for."

"Thank you," I murmur like a fool. I have no idea what else to say.

He smiles and drops his defensive stance. He leans in and turns the shower off before grabbing a fresh towel and wrapping it around me. I baulk at the decadence. He picks up the previously used towel and drapes it over the radiator and then picks me up again, cradling me in his arms to carry me back to the bedroom.

"I can walk," I say, slightly breathless again at his nearness.

"Let me take care of you, Faith. I enjoy it. It isn't a chore for me."

I just nod because what do you say to that?

I turn from him and hurriedly get dressed, replacing Xander's socks on my feet because they are so soft and warm, and still dry as they didn't hit the wet sink with my pjs.

I curl up in my nest and hold my hand out for him. He joins me, spooning around me and we talk for ages. He asks about my family and my dad. He avoids any mention of Pete, which is sweet. It would totally ruin our time together. I find out more about his family and laugh at anecdotes from the posh family that sound like a lot of fun despite their stiff upper lip.

"I can't wait for you to meet them," he murmurs in my ear, which thrills me.

I don't get to answer because there is a swift knock on the door before Harvey strolls in. "My turn," he says with that cute smile.

Benjamin smiles secretively at me and whispers in my ear

after he kisses me chastely. "Don't tell them. I'll come clean with Seb but leave them out of it."

I nod and let him go, feeling a bit desolate by his absence.

But then I glance at Harvey, and it disappears. "Are you up for moving?" he asks. "I want to show you my favourite room in the house."

Eagerly, I climb out of my nest with an enthusiastic, "Yes!"

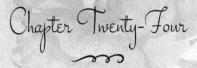

## Chapter Twenty-Four

Faith

Harvey holds his hand out for me, and I take it. In my socked feet, he towers over me. He must be at least a foot and half taller than me. I have to admit that I'm madly curious what drives this gentle giant. He definitely is not like the other alphas. He is calmer, more rational. I'm guessing he is the mediator of the pack.

"Matt says that you two made up?" he asks casually as we make our way down the stairs.

"We did," I reply cautiously.

"We've sent him away for the next few days. Just because of your heat. It's got nothing to do with you and him hooking up."

"Okay, thank you."

He gives me a curious look. "You're thanking me for us keeping you safe and secure?"

I shrug, still not used to this level of care. From practical strangers no less. "Guess I'm used to living on the less safe side of things."

A low growl rumbles out of his throat, but he says nothing. He leads me down the long hallway, deeper into the Manor and then pushes open a door halfway down.

"Oh wow!" I exclaim when I take in the room, or more to the point, the enormous TV on the wall. It must be a hundred inches at least. There's every kind of games console you could think of, a pool table and dart board, plus a bar in the corner opposite the door. "I see why this is your favourite room."

He grins. "Do you want something to drink?"

I shake my head, so he leads me over to the huge couch and sits down. I sit and curl my legs up, facing him. I rest my arm on the back of the couch and lean my head on my hand. The best place to start is the same with Benjamin.

"So, how did you become a member of the St. James pack?"

"My grandfather on my mum's side was a member way back when," he replies.

"So that means your dad's side is Scottish?"

"Yep. They are an old family of landed gentry."

My eyes widen. "Oh, fancy."

He chuckles. "Used to be. Doesn't mean as much these days."

I nod knowingly, even though I don't have a clue. I'm so naïve next to these older, way more sophisticated alphas.

"And what do you do for a living?" Okay, so my repertoire is limited, but it worked with Benjamin, so I'm sticking with it.

"I don't work," he says cagily.

I raise an eyebrow at his tone. He is defensive. "Trust fund brat?" I ask, making a joke out of it and it works. He laughs loudly. It's infectious.

"You could say that," he chuckles.

"Well, you'd never know."

"I'll take that as a compliment, petal."

"It is."

"Can I ask you what you do?"

My face falls. "Nothing. I wasn't allowed to work."

His eyes narrow. "Oh?"

"My stepdad wanted me at home to play maid."

"Ah," he says, "I see. He sounds like a real wanker."

I snort. "That's putting it mildly. He beats my mum, hit me once or twice, but realised if he hurt me, I couldn't do the chores, so he left me alone after that. Physically, anyway."

"Oh, Faith," he says with a sigh. "I'm sorry."

I shrug, trying not to cry in front of him.

He takes my hand and draws me closer. I take the opportunity to crawl onto his lap. He cups my face. "You are so special. I hope you know that we all worship you and you will never be treated with disrespect in this house."

"You are all very sweet," I murmur.

"Not really, we just know a treasure when we have one."

I blush furiously. "I don't get why you all think I'm so amazing."

"Because you are."

"You don't even know me."

"We know what we feel in our hearts when you're near. That's enough to know that we want you in our lives forever."

"Fuck off," I croak, my throat thick with emotion.

He laughs and leans forward to kiss me. When his lips touch mine, I shiver in delight. I take the initiative and slip my tongue into his mouth. He wraps his around mine, deepening the kiss, slowly, erotically, thrusting his tongue in and out of my mouth almost as if he is trying to show me what he wants to do to other parts of me with other parts of him. I want to, but I've already gotten Benjamin into trouble by being a wanton omega on the verge of her heat. I don't want to divide this pack by opening my legs for another alpha before the alpha prime has even had a crack at me. It's a sign of huge disrespect and I have a horrible feeling that Sebastian is going to be seriously pissed off with me when he gets through with kicking Benjamin's arse.

So, I settle for a fantastic kiss that fills my heart with joy and desire for the alpha underneath me.

He breaks the kiss after a few minutes with a shy smile. "We'd better stop, or I won't be able to help myself."

"Same," I murmur to his delight.

He clears his throat and then regards me closely. "I want to apologise to you, Faith."

"What for?"

"For being a complete bellend the other night. I don't usually go around throwing women over my shoulder to stuff into the back of a car and drive away with them."

I giggle like a fiend. I've laughed more this last day than I think I have in the last five years. "Bellend," I gasp in absolute hysterics. "You're fucking adorable."

He waits patiently, trying his hardest not to laugh as well until I calm down. "Be serious for a minute, will you," he chides me gently.

"Sorry!" I clap my hand over my mouth. "Sorry, really, sorry. And thank you. I accept your apology."

"Good," he says, relieved. "It's been playing on my mind a lot how we got you here."

I sober up and smile. "But I'm here now and I'm staying."

"Half of me wonders why?" His eyes search mine.

I place my hand over his heart. "Because I feel this."

Harvey smiles softly and clutches my fingers, bringing them to his mouth to kiss. "Can I ask you something?"

"Of course."

"The pack your stepdad was going to sell you too, do you know who they are?"

Not having expected that, I freeze momentarily. "Uhm, no. I just overheard my mum saying they weren't very nice. Had a bad reputation around town."

"Are they going to come looking for you?"

The seriousness of his question throws me completely off guard. I hadn't even thought about it.

"I don't know. I don't think they'd paid for me yet." Those words coming from my lips angers me. I feel hot spots appear on my cheeks.

Harvey strokes my face with the back of his hand. "I don't want to upset you, but this is stuff we need to know. You know we want to mate with you, if there is another pack out there who wants to do the same, then we need to be aware of who they are."

"It's okay. I'm not upset, just angry. And you're right. I didn't even think about it." I let out a heavy sigh.

"We will protect you, Faith. Please don't worry about them. They will not get their hands on you, but I need you to do something for me, okay?"

"What's that?" I ask suspiciously.

"Stay on the grounds for a while. Even after your heat, don't leave the safety of the estate, okay?"

I nod slowly, thinking there must be something else to that. Am I at risk for being the potential mated omega to the St. James pack, or is it something else? "Okay," I say brightly, trying not to show my worry or my questioning concern.

"Good girl," he murmurs.

I can't help the beam of pride I give him.

"So how old are you? Same as Benjamin?"

"No, I'm twenty-six."

"Oh," I say with surprise. "You seem older than that."

He snorts. "Thanks, I guess."

"I don't mean that in a bad way, you've got this way about you..." I trail off and shrug not knowing how to describe it.

He gives me a smile and leans forward to kiss me again. "I can't seem to stop doing this, petal," he murmurs.

I respond immediately, enjoying his kisses immensely. "Me too."

"Are you hungry?" he asks after a few heated moments.

"Yes. Starving."

He chuckles. "Let's go fill you up." He takes my hand again and off we go to the kitchen where he makes me a dinner of pasta, sauce and garlic bread, which annoys the cook, but thrills me because it means I don't have to cook the whole time. I don't mind it, but doing it night after night like I did at home is a pain in the arse I could do without. Also, a *cook*? He tells me they also have a maid, an entire team to tend the gardens, someone who comes around to clean the tapestries and paintings, three drivers who also clean and take care of the garage full of cars, and a fucking chimney sweep. What happened here? Did we time travel back to the Victorian era? All in all, my time with Harvey is fun, enjoyable and I decide he is definitely the one that will be a best friend as well as a lover.

# Chapter Twenty-Five

Sebastian

I look up from my desk as Ben enters my office. He looks like he has something to say, but what I have to say takes precedence.

"Good, I was just about to come and find you."

"What's up?" he asks warily.

"Derek just rang, he is on his way back home, to their mum and stepdad. He did as we asked and contacted them to ask if they'd heard from Faith to throw the trail off him. They fell for it and now he's going home all concerned that she's missing. While he's there, he will find out who this pack is that tried to buy Faith and we can deal with them in an appropriate manner."

He lets out a growl that borders on just this side of too aggressive. Something is definitely bugging him beyond this. "By that, I hope you mean kick their arses."

"Obviously. In exchange I will send all the info he has on

Oliver's disappearance to my dad for him to investigate," I say and then sit back. "Got something you want to say?"

He nods slowly and stands in front of my desk, an almost defiant look on his face.

Narrowing my eyes, I remain quiet, even though I just want him to spit it out.

"Something happened earlier," he starts. "With me and Faith. We had sex."

His words sink in, and I see red.

I stand up abruptly, my chair kicking back a few feet. "You did what?"

He puts his hands up. "I know how it sounds, but let me explain."

I don't even think about my next move. I place my hand in the middle of the desk and use it to assist my leap over to land in front of Ben. I smack my hand to his chest, flattening him to the floor.

He lets out a grunt of annoyance, but stays down.

I crouch next to him, my hand fisting in his shirt. "You took advantage of her."

"No, that wasn't it. Let me explain. I need you to listen, Seb."

His almost desperate tone catches me off guard. I expected arrogance, smugness, even. My hesitation gives him time to get out of my grip and to his feet.

I stand up, not ready for him to be let off yet. I grip his shirt again and slam him up against the walnut panelled walls. "I'm listening," I snarl, although whatever he has to say will only delay his painful death.

"I didn't mean for it to happen. I didn't set out to seduce her. You have to understand that the way it happened took me by surprise, her as well. This wasn't devised to disrespect you or hurt you. I know I've done both, as well as disappointed you. She went to take a shower and when she came out of the bathroom, she was dressed only in a towel. In hindsight, we both realise that she forgot to take a change of clothes into the bathroom with her. If it had been *anyone* else, Seb, I would have turned around and walked away. But it was *her*. I tried. I really tried to stop myself. I asked her twice to tell me to stop. She didn't. She didn't want me to. I'm not blaming her. Not at all, this is solely on me. I should've had more restraint. But it's been so long since I gave in to my alpha instincts. I've been the epitome of well-behaved. But Faith, in a towel, so close to her heat scrambled my better judgement. I went to her, and I took her. With her absolute consent. I'm sorry. I really am, Seb. You know that I would never disrespect you as my friend, or my alpha prime in this way intentionally. I know it doesn't help."

I don't know what to say. I'm so fucking furious with him, I could kill him. "I told you to keep your hands off her," I roar in his face.

"I know," he replies softly. "I know." His moan of sorrow does cut through me, just a tiny little bit. But I tighten my grip on him and shove him up against the wall harder.

"Did you bite her? Did you claim her?" If he has, so help me God, he will die right now.

"No. I wanted to, Fuck, Seb, I almost did. But I stopped myself in time. I bit her shoulder instead."

"Christ's sake, Ben! Which part of ripping out all your pubes one by one did you think was an idle threat?"

"None of it," he says, eyes lowered. "You are right to punish me. If you want to spend the next few months with some tweezers, I'll accept it. If you want to hurry it up and give me a wax, I won't complain. I deserve it and more for what I did to you, to her and to this pack."

"Fuck's sake," I growl and let him go. "You're an absolute knob."

He looks back up. "I know."

"I'm not going to rip your pubes out. It'll be over too quickly, even with the tweezers. What I will make you do is wait. If Faith gives us the go ahead to be with her during her heat, you will wait. You will be last, the absolute last one she takes. You will watch all of us knot her, our cocks covered with her slick and you will sit and wait and not even touch her. Once she is satisfied, on the very last day of her heat, then you can take her. Got it?"

He lowers his eyes again, but I saw the fury flash in them. He is beyond livid, but I don't give a shit. He shouldn't have done what he did, and he knows it.

"Fair enough," he mutters.

I step back from his personal space. He strides to the door and pauses.

Looking back at me, his eyes full of sorrow and anger, he says, "Don't take this out on her. This was my fault. She doesn't deserve to be raked over the coals about it. Please, don't blame her for this. If you have to double my punishment, then go ahead, I'll take it."

I ignore him.

He sighs and leaves me alone. The rage bubbles up even more now that he's gone. I turn with a growl and swipe the entire contents off my desk and onto the floor. It all goes crashing down. One of the glass paperweights smashes as it flies so far across the room, it hits the fireplace.

I have no words, only anger and betrayal. Two emotions that need to be gone by the time I see Faith in the morning. I know she has spent time with Harvey and has gone up to her nest now. She will sleep until morning, and then it's my turn to spend time with her. I don't want it tainted with these feelings. I will let her know how angry I am, but calmly and without the emotion clouding my judgement.

I march over to the side table and pour out a glass of Scotch, right to the brim. It's probably a quadruple, but I don't care. I need it to numb the pain that is currently trying to worm its way into my heart.

I sit on the small sofa to the side of the roaring open fire, ignoring the broken glass and the desk mess. I glare into the flames and sip my Scotch until I feel my eyes burning with exhaustion and I close them, just for a few minutes.

* * *

My eyes snap open to see an Angel hovering over me.

"Faith," I croak, my voice hoarse with lack of sleep and too much Scotch.

"Morning," she says with a beautiful smile. "I'd ask if you're ready to spend some time together, but it looks like you could do with a bit longer."

I rub my head and sit up.

Her eyes go to my hair. Her smile widens as she leans over to smooth it down. It's the cutest thing ever, and I smile at her. "Give me ten minutes to shower and change and I'll be with you. You'll probably go into your heat tomorrow, so you need to see me and Xander today."

She nods and steps back. "I'll be waiting."

I give her a grim nod and get to my feet. Neither of us has acknowledged the mess, so I continue to ignore it and walk out, heading upstairs to shower and get my head on straight.

Ten minutes later, I walk back into my office dressed in black jeans and a casual black shirt. Faith is dressed in the same jeans we abducted her in, although now washed and pressed and a white shirt which accentuates her glorious tits. I make a fist to stop myself from shouting at her about what she did with Ben, and instead watch her as she bends down to pick up the last remaining thing from the floor and place it on the desk.

She sees me staring and looks down. "I didn't go noseying," she says, "I just tidied up. Lindsey came to sweep up the glass. I hope that's okay?"

"You didn't need to do that. I would've tidied it later," I say carefully.

She shrugs. "I'm used to cleaning up the mess," she says, cautiously. "I want to apologise and get this out in the open and out of the way. I'm really sorry for what happened with Benjamin. It wasn't intentional, but just something that happened unexpectedly."

"So I hear," I growl under my breath.

"I know I've disappointed you and hurt you, and the level of disrespect makes me feel disgusted with myself. I will accept whatever punishment you want to give me. I'm truly sorry, Sebastian. I hope you can forgive me in time."

I stare at her completely dumbfounded. Her hands are clasped in front of her, her eyes lowered in a contrite pose that is completely genuine. The fact that she came in here, owned up to her mistake before I'd even said anything and then asked for my forgiveness, has staggered me and completely turned the tables around. I feel like an absolute dick for being angry with her in the first place.

"You have nothing to apologise for," I say slowly. "Ben is the one responsible for letting you down. He is your protector, and he didn't do that."

"Please don't place all the blame on him. It was both of us," she says, shaking her head. "I don't want to come between you two. I would hate myself if you stayed angry with him over this."

"I gave him a direct order," I state, trying to justify why I'm still so angry. But it turns out that I'm not even angry with her. Not at all. "You were vulnerable, and he took advantage of you." I wait to see her response.

"No," she says vehemently. "That isn't what happened. He didn't take advantage of me. He asked me to tell him to stop and I didn't. This is more on me than on him. I should've been stronger. I'm sorry, I should've..."

"Faith, stop. I'm not angry with you. Ben is still in the doghouse, but you have nothing to apologise for." To make it clear to her that I'm telling the truth, I go to her and cup her face. I can't resist running my thumb over her full red lips.

"Please don't be angry with him," she whispers, her cornflower eyes looking up at me, pleading with me.

Jesus. How can I stay mad with anyone when she asks me and looks up at me like that? She has shown balls that I've never seen on a woman before by admitting point blank what she did instead of trying to blame Ben or twist it somehow into not her fault. I guess that shows the type of women I've been dealing with in the past.

Those not worth it.

Faith is worth it and so much more. She is perfection.

"Do you regret what you did?" I ask as a test to see what she'll say.

"No," she says instantly. "I'm sorry about what we did because it hurt you and disrespected you, but I don't regret it. If anything, I'm glad it happened. It made me realise a few things."

She passed that with flying colours. I gave her an out and she didn't take it. She stuck to her guns, and I think I've just fallen in love with her. She has more strength than she knows.

"What things?" I ask lightly.

Her eyes fill with a wicked sense of desire that sends a bolt of lust straight to my cock. "I know I want you all in my nest when my heat hits tomorrow."

I raise an eyebrow and give her a curious look. "Oh?"

She nods, biting her lower lip and looking down again, an adorable blush tinging her cheeks. "My raw instinct is telling me that we all belong together. I don't have enough experience to know any better than to just listen to it. I *want* to, no, I *need* to trust what I feel. Is that okay?"

She's asking me if it's okay to rut her during her heat? *Fuuuuuuck's sake.*

I groan, the restraint of not touching her killing me.

"More than okay," I murmur. "I won't claim you though, Faith. Not this time. You haven't been with us long enough to make that decision with a clear head. Know that none of us will attempt to do something you aren't ready for yet. We will treasure you and keep you safe."

She smiles up at me. It's slow, sexy and she has no idea the effect it has on me. "Deal."

I return her smile, and deep down I know she is my mate. I can feel that I'm on the verge of a rut and so soon after the last one, that can mean only one thing.

She is ours.

Fully and completely, and I can't wait until she is ready to be claimed.

# Chapter Twenty-Six

Faith

My insides are quivering. I was so scared to face Sebastian alone with my apology, but he accepted it with grace, and I thank God. If he'd gotten angry and wanted to throw me out, I'd have been gutted on a level that shocks me. I want to stay here so badly with these alphas, it's frightening.

He takes my hand and leads me over to the sofa near the fireplace. Lindsey, the maid, had restarted the fire while Sebastian was in the shower, and I was tidying up. She seems nice, but the idea of having a maid when I used to *be* a maid of sorts is quite daunting. I don't think I can get used to someone cleaning up after me. Perhaps, I'll have a word with her to leave my stuff and I'll deal with it.

"So, what do you want to do today?" I ask when he doesn't say anything.

"This," he says and wraps his arms around me, drawing me close to him.

I inhale his gorgeous woodsy-rain scent and smile. "I guess

I don't have to ask *you* how you became a member of this pack," I say with a laugh.

He chuckles. "Long line of it being passed down from father to son."

"So you'll need a son to pass it along to," I say before I realise what I'm saying. "Err..." I blush like a fiend, my cheeks on fire.

He gazes at me, those blue eyes dancing with amusement. "That's the idea."

"How come you decided to mate a single omega as a pack?" I ask to deflect from the idea that I'm the one who is supposed to give him a son. What if I don't? What if I only give him daughters? Or no babies at all?

"Well, that's easy," he says, settling back with me in his arms. "We are a very close pack. If we had all gone off to mate separately, we wouldn't be as close anymore. None of us really wanted that, plus Xander is...high maintenance. He needs us."

"That's really sweet, that you care about him so much."

"He's my brother. I wouldn't abandon him for anything in this world. But it's not just about him. It's something we want to do as a pack. I assume you're okay with that?"

*Oh, more than. It's all I ever wanted to have more than one to love and have them love me back.*

"Mm-hm. Have you ever shared a woman before?" I ask, wanting to get that out there before I chicken out.

The look he gives me is tinged with surprise, admiration as well as something akin to shyness. "No," he states with such finality, I know that subject is shut down dead.

"Oh."

An awkward silence descends. Well, it probably isn't awkward for him. It's just me being that lemon again. "And what do you do for a living?"

*Dammit, Faith.*

I am so fucking boring. I hope they don't meet up to discuss what I asked them. I'll be so humiliated.

"I work with my father at the Inter-pack Parliament. I'm a facilitator, of sorts."

"What do you facilitate?"

"Stuff."

I blink and turn my face away from his. Christ. He must think I'm a complete numpty that he can't even explain his job to me.

"Sorry, that was rude," he says after a beat. "It's complicated."

"You mean you sort out inter-pack problems using force?" I ask to his surprise.

He lets out a small laugh. "Something like that."

"You don't have to hide yourself from me, Sebastian," I point out huffily. "The idea of this time is to get to know you."

"I am not trying to hide myself, just that part. I don't want you to think less of me." He is avoiding my gaze by staring into the fire.

"I wouldn't do that. I don't judge."

He faces me again with a soft smile. "I know. I'm cagey about it. Some people don't like it."

"I'm not some people."

He leans over to kiss my nose. "No, you aren't, and you deserve better than me including you with them."

"Can I ask you about the other omegas you were considering before?" I'm wildly curious.

"Of course. What do you want to know?" He is curious himself where I'm going with this.

I don't really know, if I'm being honest. "Were they pissed off when you didn't choose them?"

He smiles. "I have no idea. We put all of our effort into

trying to find you. Are you worried they will turn up here and demand why you and not them?"

"No," I snap, defensive because I've been caught out without even knowing what I was worried about in the first place. How did *he* know?

"Well, if they do, you don't have to worry. You are our mate. You have been since that night Matt came home from being with you. You may not know it yet, but we do."

I sit back then and relax in his arms, enjoying being held by him.

"There's something you should know," he says after a few minutes of soothing fire-staring.

"Okay..."

"We asked your brother to contact your stepdad saying that he hadn't heard from you and was worried. He is back with your mum and him now. While he's there, we tasked him with finding out who the pack is that tried to buy you."

"Oh," I say and sit up again, concern filling me from my toes upwards.

"He'll be fine," Sebastian says quietly. "Your stepdad won't hurt him. Derek is capable of taking care of himself."

I nod slowly. I hope he's right. "What will you do once you find out?"

"Pay them a visit to inform them that you will not be joining them."

His cold tone chills me to the bone.

Suddenly, a wave of emotion sweeps over me, and I let out a strangled sob. I stand up and start to pace in front of the fire. "My mum!" I shriek. "You have to get her away from him. You can do that. Arrest him or something." I spin back to him, the plea brimming with my tears.

He gives me a cautious glance before he sighs. "He hasn't committed any crimes that we can prove," he says steadily.

"I'm sorry, Faith, officially we can't just burst into his house and arrest him."

"Why?" I shriek at banshee level. "You are all powerful, you can do whatever you want! Why won't you do this?"

He stands up and regards me cautiously. My change in temperament has caught him by surprise. I know the sudden shift is hormones. I've been mostly okay since my pre-heat started with a weepy moment here and there in private, but this is going full force now with Sebastian as the enemy who won't help me.

I hiss at him when he approaches me slowly, his hands held out as if he's trying to capture a scared rabbit.

"Faith," he says calmly. "Come to me."

"No! You don't understand. He hurts her every day. She is a shell of who she used to be! Please, Sebastian, help her! Help me."

The wave of anger crashes over me and dissipates as quickly as it rose and when he reaches me, I let him take me in his arms. Now all I feel is utter sadness.

My sobbing becomes uncontrollable, and my knees buckle with the agony my heart is feeling that I've been trying so hard to keep at bay, to be strong for her and for me. He sinks to the hearth with me, stroking my hair and kissing the top of my head.

"Faith," he says quietly. "I said officially. If you are prepared for the consequences of what you ask, we will take care of him for you. Anything for you, Faith. Anything for you."

I hear his words and it calms me.

My weeping quietens down and I don't really need to know anything else about him.

He will step up when I need him.

What else is there to know?

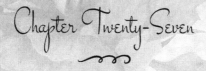

## Chapter Twenty-Seven

Faith

After I'd calmed down – which took longer I'd have liked, I told Sebastian that I wanted to find Xander and get back to my nest by early afternoon. He was quite happy with that arrangement, so now I'm walking hand-in-hand with Xander across the grounds of this huge country estate, on this chilly, yet sunny winter morning. The sky is azure and completely cloudless with the low sun shining brightly.

"Are you sure you're okay to be outside?" he asks me. "I prefer it, but if you're cold, we can go back inside."

I shake my head with a smile. "I've been cooped up for a few days. It's nice to be able to roam free but still be safe."

"Always safe here," he murmurs, drawing me closer to him.

I lean my head on his upper arm, and smile to myself. He isn't as tall as Harvey, but he is still pretty tall. I quite like being so short next to them. Makes me feel precious or whatever.

"This is my favourite place," he says a moment later, leading me into a space between two perfectly manicured hedges. "It's a little sun trap."

"Oh, lovely." I look back up at the Manor in awe. It is so imposing and beautiful with its red brick walls and ivy crawling over some parts of it. It's way bigger than what I've seen of it so far. I look forward to exploring it one day.

Xander sets up a blanket for us and lightly drops the basket he was carrying before he helps me sit down. I cross my legs and peek in the basket as he settles himself on the other side of the blanket, leaning back on his elbow and stretching his legs out.

He stares off into the distance and after a minute, I wonder if he's forgotten I'm even here. "Are you hungry?" he asks, into the silence.

"Always," I say with a laugh.

"You can dive in, you don't have to wait for me," he says with a smile.

I take him at his word and open the basket, pulling out a punnet of strawberries and popping one into my mouth. I chew thoughtfully for a moment and then ask the question that now makes me cringe. "So how did you become a member of the St. James pack?"

"Well, my story isn't as illustrious as the others. I'm the first of my line."

"Oh," I say surprised. "That's awesome. How come?"

"I went to school with Seb and Ben…"

"At Harrow?" I interrupt him with this knowledge that I've gleaned, and he beams at me.

"Yep. Old boys club and all that. But I was a rank outsider. Wealthy and from a good family, but I was always different. Not wired the same as the others. I was shy and awkward and a complete klutz. I hated sports and P.E., I can't sing for a dime and acting? Yeah, not happening. I was too shy to debate, I'd stammer and make a fool of myself, so basically, I was the idiot in the corner with no mates. Until Seb and Ben came along and took me under their wing. I have no idea why, but they found me and protected me from all the bullies."

"I hate bullies," I spit out, thinking of Pete.

"Me too," he murmurs. "After my accident, I was even more of an outcast and Seb's dad, Anthony, took me into his home, here..." He points over his shoulder, "...and told me that I was always welcome and that he would be happy for me to join the pack once Seb took over. So, I did."

"That's sweet. Accident?"

His eyes cloud over and the goosebumps that ripple over my skin under my hoodie and old coat, have nothing to do with the cold air.

"Yeah, my family life was a bit shitty after my dad left my mum."

"Left?" I choke out. "He *left* his mate?"

Xander nods slowly. "My mum didn't want to be alone, so she took up with the first alpha who would look after her and he was a mean fucker. He didn't want me around. He beat me regularly. One day he went too far, and I ended up in hospital in a coma for six weeks."

"Jesus, Xander," I murmur and edge closer to him. I stroke his face. "I'm sorry. You don't have to talk about it."

He shrugs. "By the time I came back to the land of the living, Anthony had arrested him and thrown him in jail and my mum blamed me."

"*What?*" I spit out, startling him. I rise onto my knees, my hands clenched into tight fists. The rage that is boiling up inside me is making my head spin. "That bitch! How dare she! How could she...I'll kill her!"

He takes my fists in his hands. "It's okay, Faith. I'm over it. She's a weak bitch and I want nothing to do with her." He also gets to his knees and cups my face. "You are so sweet. Thank you for caring."

I let out a low growl which he smiles seductively at.

"Don't do that, you're going to make me do something Sebastian will make me regret. Anyway, I waited ten years for that fucker to come out of prison and when he did, I killed him." He says it so bluntly, his eyes on mine, I wonder if he's testing me somehow.

"Good," I snarl. "I hope you made it hurt."

He sits back down and pulls me onto his lap. "I am willing to avenge you as well, just tell me where to find him."

I cup his face, enjoying his bloodthirstiness. Enjoying it within myself. I've never felt so protective and fierce over anyone before. I've never had to, but now I really would kill to protect this sweet, misunderstood alpha. "You are so beautiful," I murmur.

He rears back slightly. "That's my line."

"No, seriously, Xander. You, your mind. People don't understand you, they think you're broken but you're not. You are completely whole; you just need to be around the people who care about you. Nobody else matters."

"Oh, Faith," he murmurs. "You are the best thing that has ever come into my life. I'm sorry for what I did during the rut."

I blink and then leap off him. "What?" I snap, even though I have *no* right to be annoyed. I didn't even know they existed then. But those hormones have reared their head again and with all the emotional conversations I'm having today, I'm about to spin out of control like a complete berk.

He pulls me back down and kisses my lips. "I didn't take a woman to my bed. Sebastian was absolutely truthful about that. But I feel I need to come clean about something."

"Okay," I say cautiously.

"I'm not that strong," he says, avoiding my eyes. "Not like

Ben and Seb. They deal with stuff, and it doesn't affect them. I'm more...feral. I need to feed the alpha inside me in ways that they can control."

"I understand, Xander. You don't need to explain anything to me." The surge has died down again and I'm back to calm me.

"I do. You deserve to know. I had a sex doll made to look like you. Or at least, how Matt described you. I tried to get it right." He scrunches his face up. "During the rut I fucked the doll."

I press my lips together, trying not to laugh. He is so embarrassed; he can't even look at me. "That's actually quite sweet," I reassure him that I'm not mad. Why would I be? It's better than the alternative, which even though I have no right to be jealous about, I am, and I don't even care. The mere whiff of them being with another woman, another *omega* makes me want to gouge eyes out.

He cracks an eye open. "Sweet?"

I nod. "Please don't think I'm upset about it. I'm not. Thank you for telling me, but that wasn't necessary." To reinforce my words, I lean over and kiss him, swishing my tongue into his mouth, and giving him a kiss to remember.

He groans and squeezes my arse, dragging me against him so that my pussy is pressed against his hardening cock.

"Faith," he murmurs. "You are perfect. Even if you had been a complete bitch, we would still have needed you, but the fact that you're sweet and caring and kind, makes this so much more than just a mating."

"I agree," I whisper back, unable to beat that with any words I know and can string together. I rotate my hips, grinding down on his cock, wishing we were naked so I could ride him like a cowgirl, but that can't happen. I have already pushed that limit with Benjamin, I can't do the same with

Xander. He presses his hips up, smashing our bits together, turning me on so much, slick fills my knickers.

"Fuck, Xander," I rasp, grinding down harder.

"Jesus, Faith. I'm going to come..." He groans and unzips his pants, pulling his cock out a second before he erupts all over his hand. "Fuck, that was better than full sex with Gertie."

I snort, unable to help myself. "Gertie?" I splutter and cough, but luckily, he takes it in his stride.

"Dirty Gertie," he informs me with a big beam, wiping his hand on the blanket, which makes me giggle even more.

I howl with laughter, and he joins in, making this a really special moment. "Can I meet her?"

He chokes back a noise of surprise. "You want to?"

I nod. "If you still have her."

He stashes his dick and helps me stand up. I've got a pool in my knickers, but I ignore it as he scoops up the blanket and shoves it in the basket. We didn't get to eat, but this is way more fun and intimate. He picks up the basket and takes my hand, leading me back to the house.

"Was she expensive?" I ask.

"Cost me about a grand," he replies.

"Wow, that's a lot of money."

He just shrugs it off, which reminds me how very different we are. But none of it matters. When he leads me into his bedroom a few minutes later, he drops the basket and pulls out a huge bag from under the bed.

He unzips it and pulls out the life-size blonde sex doll with tits pretty much the same size as mine and big blue eyes. Her mouth is shaped in an 'O' for reasons that don't need explaining.

I reach out and stroke the lifelike 'skin'. "Jesus," I mutter. "And here I thought you meant a blow-up thing, like out of that episode of *Only Fools and Horses*."

He lets out a loud guffaw. "Oh, my God! The scene where it inflates behind the bar! No," he splutters. "I'm not that desperate."

"What does it feel like?" I murmur.

"Close enough to the real thing that it got me through the rut."

"Well, she's pretty."

"She can be disposed of now you're here." He zips her back up.

"Wait," I say on impulse. "It seems a shame to get rid of her. We could, you know, maybe, you know..." *Spit it out, Faith seeing as you got this far.* "Have some fun with her, maybe?"

"Really?" he asks, scrunching up his nose. "You'd be up for that?"

I shrug. "Why not? I feel a bit sorry for her," I say, mirth threatening to bubble up again.

"You know what? Me too. She was there for me when I needed her. I'll keep her. If you decide she can come out and visit, then we know where she is." He stuffs her back under the bed and it suddenly hits me, I'm in his room. I need to leave now before I do something I will definitely regret.

"I'd better get back to my nest," I murmur.

"I'll see you to your room," he agrees.

We walk down the hallway in silence and when I push open the door to my room, I let out a cry of surprise at the sight in front of me.

Tears well up and fall down my cheeks as Sebastian turns to me and asks, "Do you like it?"

# Chapter Twenty-Eight

Faith

My emotions overwhelm me and I ugly cry while kicking off my shoes. I alternate with a squeal of delight and clapping my hands before I cry again, snot and tears pouring out of my face. I crawl over to the huge nest that Sebastian and the other alphas have built, teepee style in the middle of the room. Heavy white and gold brocade curtains that somehow, they've attached to the ceiling, spread out to make a tent.

I crawl up to Harvey, who is on his knees, piling up blankets and pillows in the teepee while Sebastian hovers uncertainly.

"I FUCKING LOVE IT!" I bellow at him before I shove Harvey out of the way and dive into the nest filled to the brim with comfort. "Marshmallows, Summer rain, Ocean breeze and Woodsy rain," I croak out, rolling around in the blankets like a joyful kitten. I sit up suddenly and stick my head out of the teepee, fixing Xander with a glare. "Did you know about this?"

He laughs. "Yes, another reason why we went outside."

"Fucking bastard," I grouse, but give him a smirk, so he knows I'm joking. Then I disappear from their sight and roll around again, grabbing a woodsy rain smelling blanket and rolling myself up in it like a sausage roll. "You guys," I sob, the tears coming again. "You didn't have to do this."

Sebastian's head appears in the teepee opening. "Actually, we did. We won't all fit in the wardrobe."

I giggle like a maniac, hysteria descending as the nerves hit me, then it turns back into sobs again. "Thank you. Thank you so much."

"You're welcome," he says. "I'm glad you fucking love it."

"I do. I really do." I breathe in his scent off the blanket deeply. "These are all your blankets and pillows."

"And yours as well from the cupboard."

"I adore you," I murmur into the blanket.

"As I adore you. We will leave you to rest now, baby girl. We'll bring you something to eat later on tonight."

"Thank you."

I wait for all the men to leave before I unravel from the soft pale blue blanket and strip off naked. I flop back to the nest, a sense of wellbeing and care overwhelming me. The fluffy blankets and soft rugs underneath are absolute heaven. With a smile on my face, my eyes close. Surrounded by a level of safety and comfort I have never known before, and knowing that despite our rocky start, I think I might just be falling for these alphas. Even though I'm totally out of my depth and feel so naïve and innocent next to them, they haven't done anything to make me feel uncomfortable. Only the opposite. My stomach is once again tied in knots as I think about the next few days. My anxiety level spikes, and I whimper, burying my face into Sebastian's blanket. I'm on a roller coaster of emotions right now. I just hope that I don't make a fool of myself tomorrow around these older, way more experienced alphas. That would be the worst.

* * *

I hear the bedroom door open, but I ignore it. What comes next is harder to ignore though.

"Happy Birthday, Faith!"

This greeting is bellowed into my nest, forcing me to open my eyes.

"Whu?" I mumble, still mostly asleep and feeling hot and bothered. I kick off the blankets and force my gritty eyes to open.

All four faces of the St. James alphas swim into view, along with a birthday cake in the shape of a strawberry.

"Happy twenty first," Sebastian adds, more quietly this time.

"Fuck." I shove my hand into my hair. "I'd totally forgotten with everything else going on." How fucking daft can you be? The whole reason I've gone into my first heat is *because* of my twenty-first birthday.

He chuckles and crawls into the nest. "Am I okay to be in here?"

"Of course," I reply, confused as to why he is asking.

He leans over and gives me a soft kiss on the top of my head. "Do you want some cake? You didn't eat last night."

"Oh, sorry. I didn't even hear you come back."

He shrugs. "It's okay. We figured you'd be sleeping, but wanted to make sure you had something if you woke up starving."

"Always starving."

"That's what we figured," Xander says, also crawling into the nest and curling up near me but not touching me.

I glance over to the teepee opening and beckon the other two men inside. "Don't stand out there," I chide them. "Party's in here."

Benjamin snickers and crawls in, followed by Harvey. It's full of gorgeous, masculine, delicious smelling alphas. It's cosy and beautiful.

And that's when it hits me.

The absolute, desperate need to have sex with all of them, as many times as I can to satisfy the dull ache deep inside me that is twisting my stomach into a further knot.

I meet Sebastian's blue-eyed stare with a sultry one of my own and his smiling face descends into something darker, sexier and irresistible.

I shove the blanket back and as naked as the day I was born, I pounce on the prime alpha, with a slick coated pussy, ready to devour every inch of him and then move on to the next after I've come all over his knot.

I slam him back to the soft floor of the nest, my hands pressing down on his chest. He grabs my wrists and asks, "One last time, baby girl. Do you want us all in here to relieve your heat?"

"Yes," I pant. "A thousand times, yes."

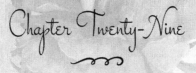

# Chapter Twenty-Nine

Sebastian

With Faith wiggling about all over my cock, I knew I had to ask her before my mind goes fuzzy with the mix of her heat and our rut. It has kicked in and now all I want is to bury my cock so far into her, she will scream my name. I want to hear it. I *need* to hear it.

Her fingers are already working to get my cock free of the joggers I'm wearing and with her pussy totally bare and out there for anyone to fall into, I will be the first.

Okay, second.

Well, *third* if you count Matt, for fuck's sake.

I let out a low growl as I remember that Ben has already had a taste, but it's quickly squashed when she writhes around, pressing her tits up against me and her mouth latches onto mine.

"Fuck, Faith," I groan.

She is grinding down on my cock. Her slick is wet and hot, and I catch the scent of her. Inhaling deeply, surrounding myself with the delicious strawberries, honey and cream aroma, I close my eyes and kiss her, flipping her over so that she is underneath me. I take her hands and restrain them out to the sides, my tongue wrestling with hers as I taste her for the very first time.

She is heaven.

There is no other word for it.

My whole life has been leading up to this moment and now that it is here, I can't hold back any longer. I want to breed with her. I need to. There is a driving force that is overwhelming me. As much as I want to give her the attention she deserves, I just can't. The rut is in full swing and if I don't get a knot soon, my cock is going to burst. I tell myself that there will be time enough for afterplay later. Foreplay is off the table. I pull back from our kiss and stare into her bright blue eyes. My cock is so stiff I don't even have to grip it to guide it into her. It's already there, ready and waiting to slip inside her slick filled pussy and pound her until she comes so ferociously, she screams loud enough for the neighbours to hear. Which, considering they are a good mile or so away, *that's* how hard I want to fuck her.

She opens her legs, ready for me. She doesn't even stop to ask for me to lick her clit or finger her. She raises her hips up and wraps her legs around me. I sink into her pussy with a low groan.

"Fuck, yes. Fuck, Faith..."

I savour every inch of my above average-sized cock sliding into her.

I've had a fair bit of sex in my years, but nothing has ever compared to this. Her pussy grips my cock tightly, just as her soul wraps itself around mine, tying us together in ways that were beyond my comprehension until this very moment.

I draw back until I'm about to fall out of her and then I slam back inside her. She cries out, arching her back. I pound into her a few more times before I roll us over to give the other guys access to her. She steadies herself with her hands on my chest and I grip her fingers tightly. She smiles serenely, completely lost to her heat now and works her hips over me. She rides my cock slowly at first before she rises up and slams down on top of me. Harvey and Xander are latched onto her nipples like starving men needing to feed their desire for her. She cries out and flings her head back. I grab her hips to keep her from toppling over, watching her face, enjoying the arousal and sheen of sweat on her forehead. Xander growls low and bites down on her, making her yelp, but it doesn't slow her down. She rotates her hips and then shudders on top of me, coming spectacularly quickly, thrilling me to my very core.

"That's it, baby girl," I groan, feeling her pussy clench around my cock. Her slick is dripping out of her pussy and onto my balls, going cool and sticky in a luscious feeling of sheer eroticism.

"Sebastian!" she cries out.

"Say it again," I demand, needing to hear it from her lips.

"Sebastian, fuck me harder. I need your knot, please, please."

"Jesus," I practically whimper and tighten my hold on her hips so I can lift her up slightly and thrust upwards, high and deep, fast and relentless. Ramming my cock so deep into her, I'm surprised there is anywhere left for me to go. The juices are flowing freely, making a delicious slurping sound over her moans of desire and Xander's panting. Harvey has taken his cock in his hand and is tugging wildly, while he kisses her, devouring her. I glance at Ben. He is pale, motionless and sweating.

He meets my gaze and I see the pain my punishment is causing him.

And I let it go.

I indicate with my head for him to get in here. He needs no encouragement. With a grateful smile at me, he focuses solely on Faith as he dives into the fray, his fingers going to her clit as I smash against her pussy, driving my cock deeper and deeper.

When the orgasm hits me, it makes me go dizzy.

"Oh fuck," Faith cries out when she feels my knot expand and lock inside her as my cock shoots out so much cum, I wonder where it all came from. On and on the climax goes, sending me into a state of sheer hedonism. Nothing else matters except Faith and her climaxing all over my knot, which she does in spectacular style, slick pooling out of her pussy, soaking me, drenching the blanket underneath us, as we rock together, locked in place until my knot goes down.

"Faith," I croak, my voice hoarse with lust. "Are you okay?"

"Fuck, yes," she pants, wrapping her arms around me. "Oh. Fuck. Yes."

# Chapter Thirty

Faith

I bury my face in Sebastian's chest, a bit embarrassed that I pounced on him like a nympho. Not that he is complaining, but still. Cool hands run down my back, knuckles digging into my spine to ease the tension. I groan with contentment, still locked onto Sebastian's knot.

"This feels so good," I murmur, practically slobbering all over him, wanting to orgasm again, but it's just out of my reach for now.

"You have no idea," Sebastian murmurs, his hands tangling in my hair.

I peek up at him. His awe-filled expression catches me off guard. It's like he's never done this before, but I know that can't be true.

I don't say anything, I just hide my face again, but turn my head to the side so my ear is pressed against his chest, over his heart.

"Baby girl, look at me."

I turn my head, so my chin is resting on his chest.

"Ask what's on your mind."

I shake my head.

"Faith," he says. "I can see something bugging you. Was it not what you expected? Did I hurt you? *Am* I hurting you?"

"Oh, Jesus, Sebastian," I snap at him. "Don't be a pillock. It is better than I expected, and no, you aren't hurting me. I'm just...your face is..." I huff as Benjamin snickers.

I glance at him, wondering why he took so long to join in, before I slide my gaze back to Sebastian's.

"I think she means you look a bit stunned, maybe like you've never experienced it before," Benjamin says quietly.

"Fuck off," I mutter and hide my face again.

"Faith," Sebastian says, tugging gently on my hair to lift my head up. "I haven't ever experienced anything like that before. The knot, yes, of course, but with you it surpassed anything that I've felt before. It was real, true, the whole purpose of being what I am was to do this with *you*. No one else. Don't ever feel embarrassed to ask a question that's on your mind. I will answer it honestly and without judgement."

"Okay, now you need to fuck off as well. Why are you so nice? Aren't alphas supposed to be dicks?"

"Oh, I'm a dick," he says at the same time as Benjamin says, "He's a fucking knob."

They exchange a good-natured grimace, and then Sebastian continues, "But with you, I only want what's best for you."

I nod slowly, trying to take that in. I remember my mum and dad together. Sort of. I wasn't really paying that much attention, truth be told, but they were loving and caring towards one another. Pete's way has scarred me for life. I don't think I will ever get over thinking alphas treat everyone like shit. Well, maybe I will. Maybe these four can convince me.

"I suppose I have yet to see King Dick in action," I murmur and then feel my cheeks heat up even more.

"What?" he asks with a laugh. "What are you thinking?"

"Is my face that fucking expressive," I snap.

"Oh, yes," Xander pipes up, crawling back into the teepee from wherever it was he went. Looking over, I see he retrieved the cake.

I'm not even that bothered when my stomach growls slightly.

"Tell me," Sebastian says, playfully tugging on my hair again.

I can feel his knot going down now and within a few seconds, I think I can leap free.

I'm right. I make a dive to the left and bury myself under the blankets, ignoring the damp one that is covered in slick.

"I was right in thinking King Dick had a king dong," I mutter from under the protection of the blankets.

"What?" he splutters as the other three men laugh their arses off. "Well, gentlemen, you heard it here first."

"Christ." My curse is muffled by the blankets, which are peeled away to reveal a piece of cake, hovering in front of my face.

Xander has the small plate balanced on his fingers, like a posh waiter. A wicked sense of fun descends over me, and I sit up, swiping my fingers through the perfect frosting and wiping it all over his bare, well-defined chest.

He looks down and blinks. Then he does the same to me, circling my nipples with frosting. He drops the cake and dives on me, sucking it off, one hand fisting into my hair, making it sticky with cake and the other diving between my legs, his fingers thrusting deep inside me.

There is nothing on this planet that could stop me now. He has riled me up and the heat induced lust for him has just increased tenfold.

Shoving my tongue deeper into his mouth, I wrap my legs around him, encouraging him to ram me with his cock as hard as he can.

He doesn't disappoint.

I squeal as his rampant thrusts jolt me over the blankets. He drives deeper, longer, harder, with a feral growl which I respond to with a loud purr. It sets off the other alphas and suddenly, it's a mesh of mouths, limbs, fingers, cocks. Every part of them is touching every part of me somehow. It's incredible. I feel like I'm flying on a red-hot rainbow of decadence and my prize at the end is a hard knot to come all over.

"Please! Yes!" I scream as fingers are thrust inside me alongside Xander's cock, tongues licking me, lips kissing me, hands splayed out on my feverish skin.

It's a frenzy of debauchery and as soon as Xander's knot expands inside me, I orgasm in an intense way that convulses my body, straining my stomach muscles as Xander's dick latches inside my body with a refusal to quit.

"Fuck," he roars, shooting his load into me.

My head is swimming and somehow, I got turned around so that I'm reverse cowgirl on him. The pressure of his knot is just beyond anything I ever could've imagined. I gasp and come again, slicking so much, it pours out and Benjamin drops his mouth to my pussy to lick it all up with a low growl that sends a ripple over my skin. My nipples are aching, they are so peaked. Harvey bites down on one, making me moan and purr at the same time.

"Jesus, Faith," Benjamin murmurs, his mouth full of slick. "Fucking hell. You are the sexiest creature I've ever come across. You taste..." He sighs with happiness and then laps at my slick again, flicking my clit with his tongue so that I can't help but treat Xander to another orgasm, my pussy clutching him too tightly, I rasp with the sheer pleasure firing through me.

"Oh, God!" I cry out, the pleasure reaching the point of it becoming unbearable. "Help!"

"Fuck, Faith," Xander pants. "Oh, fuck that feels so fucking good. Don't stop, don't stop. Tighter, tighter. Squeeze me until I burst."

"Aah!" I scream as my pussy has suddenly developed a mind of its own and has decided it's not letting go of Xander's cock for love nor money.

"What is going on?" Harvey asks, his eyes meeting my wide, horrified stare. "Faith, are you okay?"

"Oh, fuck, yes," I whimper, tears pouring down my face as it just becomes too much.

The pleasure overload makes me go dizzy and my eyes close as I slump against Sebastian, who has shoved Benjamin out of the way to get to me in concern.

"Xander?" Sebastian's voice cuts through my foggy haze.

"Squee-squeezing so tight. Can't breathe," he pants from what sounds like a great distance away, but that can't be because I'm stuck fast on his dick.

"Help!" I rasp, unable to stop the orgasm that floods over me like a tidal wave of every type of porn known to man. I squirt all over Sebastian, causing him to groan loudly and drop his mouth to my clit, sucking me with gusto.

My whole body trembles violently as Xander and I knot each other, although how the fuck I'm doing it, I don't know. I've never heard of it before, and I doubt I will ever do it again. My head lolls to the side, my eyes closed in exhaustion. My heat frenzy recedes slightly, and I sob, tears seeping out of my eyes.

"Faith," Xander pants. "You are so fucking special. Don't ever let me go."

"Uhng," I moan and collapse face forward on the blankets. Then everything goes quiet.

## Chapter Thirty-One

Xander

I fall down behind her, keeping her close as she is still stuck on my knot. I don't want to hurt her, so I curl around her, my dick still deep inside her. She has let me go now that she is unconscious. This feels really weird, but I have no choice but to stay inside her. I've never been into somnophilia before but the sudden urge that strikes me to keep shagging her is a little overwhelming.

I blink and then get yelled at by Sebastian after the shock has worn off, I'm guessing.

"What the fuck was that?" he bellows.

"You'd have to ask her," I reply, tightening my hold on her.

"Jesus," he snaps and runs his hand through his hair. "She's passed out."

"She's fine. Her heartbeat is steady."

"Fuck's sake." He lets out a low growl, but it doesn't bother me. There is nothing I can do about what happened, nor where I'm currently situated. If anything, it makes me smug. Really, really, Jeremey Clarkson type smug.

That must reflect on my smug face because Seb bunches up his fist and shakes it in my direction.

"Have any of you experienced this before?" he asks quietly.

A unanimous 'no' resounds around the teepee.

"Hmm, interesting." He gives me a thoughtful look. "Why you?"

I shrug. "Why not me?"

He acknowledges that with a raised eyebrow.

Faith groans softly and all attention goes back to her.

"Faith, petal, are you okay?" Harvey is the first to reach her and lays down so he can look her in the eye.

I feel my knot deflating and groan inwardly. I'm going to have to let her go. I don't want to. She feels it and wiggles away from me, rolling over onto her back.

"Fuck," she says breathlessly. "Fuck." She sits up suddenly. "That was intense."

"So it appeared," Sebastian says, taking her hand. "How do you feel?"

"Fine, great, glad to be free," she says with a laugh and an apologetic look at me.

I don't take it personally. I know she was scared. I loved every second of it, but it must've been frightening for her.

"How about we run you a nice, hot bath?" I murmur.

Her grateful expression warms me. "Please. I do feel a bit achy. Food as well," she says and giggles when I pick up the cake that somehow survived the romp in one piece, minus some frosting. I pick it up and hold it to her lips. She grins and takes a bite.

"Oh fuck," she mumbles. "That's divine."

"Happy Birthday, Strawbs," I murmur, watching her mouth as she eats.

"Fanks," she says, her hand to her full mouth.

Harvey disappears, probably to run her bath and Ben sneaks in behind her, sitting with his legs on either side of her and kissing the nape of her neck. "You are so precious, kitty," he murmurs.

She giggles and leans back, tilting her face to his for a kiss. As he claims her mouth, she holds her hand out for me, making a gimme gesture.

Seb snickers and hands her the cake, right in the middle of her palm. She pulls back from Ben, and I let out a loud guffaw as she smashes the cake into his face with a gleeful whoop before she dives away from him and scrabbles to get out of the nest before he can retaliate.

"Oh no!" he exclaims, wiping cake from his eyes. "Get back here."

"Catch me quick," she pants and ducks out of the nest, with Ben hot on her heels.

I stick my head out and see the door to her room slam closed.

"Here, kitty-kitty," Ben calls out, and now this has turned into a chase.

The alpha instinct, not that deep inside me sticks its ears up at the thought of a hunt. Sebastian shoves me out of the way, his own primal instinct at the forefront in the face of a chase.

Ben yanks the door open and marches down the corridor calling, "Kitty? Where are you?"

We hear her giggle and aim for the stairs.

It's a good thing we sent everyone, even the maids away so Faith could have her heat in relative privacy. Right now, as I lean down over the railings, I see her running down the hallway to the front door, her hands over her tits to stop them bouncing around. She looks back over her shoulder with a wicked expression, inviting us to follow her. Her heat will have been satisfied for a short while, but it will flare up again very soon.

In the meantime, I join in the hunt for our omega, who is leading us on a merry dance, to the absolute thrill of each and every one of us.

Harvey joins us, all completely naked on the chase outside. It's fucking freezing, but Faith won't be feeling it so much with her heat running rampant right now. It's a good thing that we live on a very private estate, because the sight of a naked omega being chased by four naked alphas would be a sight indeed to anyone observing.

"Strawbs, we can smell you!" I call out.

"Come and get me then," she shouts back, and we all turn towards her voice.

I growl and lope forward, as she spins and runs away, laughing wildly. She is free and happy and full of joy.

When I see her stumble, I pick up my pace. She overestimated how great she felt after the knotting and now she is overexerted. She slows down, and turns to me, her breathing heavy.

"Do you concede?" I ask, slowing down and stalking towards her.

She nods, her cheeks flushed. "Think…" She gasps. "Think, I got giddy."

I reach her and scoop her up. "You need to take it easy. But you definitely got us all riled up."

I turn with her in my arms and Sebastian takes her from me. I don't begrudge it, even though having her soft, warm body nestled up against me felt like heaven.

"Naughty, baby girl," Sebastian murmurs. "Making us chase you."

"It was fun though," she purrs, responding to his deep tone full of meaning.

"Bath time now, then eat and sleep if you can before we

need to sate your heat again," he says, still in the same soothing tone. "Even goddesses need to listen to their bodies."

She beams and snuggles into him.

He has a way with words that I don't have and never will, but I know this isn't a competition. The way she is with each of us, I know in my heart that she is falling for us. It may take her some time to accept a mating bite. She is young and we *did* abduct her. Even though she seems to have adapted, she still needs time to trust us completely. But she will, and when she does, she will be ours forever.

# Chapter Thirty-Two

Faith

Happy to sink into the hot bubble bath that Harvey ran for me, I smile tiredly. Even as my eyes start to close, I feel the urge to fuck like a bunny. Sitting up, I reach for the closest alpha to me and drag him into the bath.

Harvey lands with a splash, drenching the floor and making me laugh uncontrollably before I climb on top of him, snaking my hand in between us so I can grip his cock tightly. He groans as I wiggle on his lap before I take his eye wateringly huge dick and sit on it. Shoving it deep inside me, I slide down over it. I clasp my hands at the back of his neck and start to ride him. The water sloshes out all over the bathroom floor, but none of the other alphas bats an eye.

Closing my eyes, I struggle to keep up with the enormity of his girth and length. I tire quickly and he sees it. When he tightens his hold on me and stands up, my eyes fly open. He climbs steadily out of the bath with me still on his dick, and steps into the huge shower instead. He gently presses me up

164

against the cold tile and turns the water on. It gushes down over us like a beautiful warm waterfall. Then he grips my hips and takes over, thrusting deep and slow. The other two alphas were in a frenzy of their rut and my heat, making it a rampant orgy. This is completely different.

As much as my heat is screaming at me to take over again and shag him until the cows come home, I don't. I want to feel what he is giving me, which is pure and complete *love*. It's amazing and I want this to last as long as possible.

"Yes," I moan, closing my eyes again when his long, even strokes continue to stoke the fire burning deep inside me.

My toes curl as the orgasm starts there and slowly works its way up my entire body until it hits my clit, and then ripples out in waves up to my heart and then my head. My limbs go floppy, but it's okay. Harvey is there to hold me up, thrusting deep and almost withdrawing, thrusting deep and almost withdrawing.

I want to weep with the pleasure, and it lulls my heat, cradling it gently while he pays attention to me.

"Oh, petal," he murmurs, pressing his mouth to mine. "You're so hot, so wet."

His words increase the slick that is already coating my pussy and pulsing out with the orgasm that won't quit.

"You're so huge," I gasp when he starts to speed up, needing his own release. The rut has taken him over now, his grey eyes are darker, his stare intense as I stare back at him in rapture.

"Fuck," he grunts when his knot inflates inside me.

My breath hitches and my eyes go wide when I feel him shoot his load into me. I wrap my legs around him tighter, tilting my pelvis so that his huge cock presses down on my g-spot.

I tremble again, a tired whimper escaping my lips as we

lock together. I close my eyes as shower water drips into them and lean forward so my head is resting on his shoulder.

"After Benjamin, I need to sleep," I mumble.

"Oh, kitty, don't be silly. Sleep first," Benjamin says quietly.

"You sure?"

"Of course."

I nod sleepily, feeling terrible. You'd think having passed out on Xander's cock earlier, I'd be more rested, but nope. This heat and all the fucking is taking it out of me. I've never shagged so much in one go, ever. I need to build up my stamina if this is going to be a quarterly thing. Maybe hit the gym or go running. There again, just because my heat is quarterly, doesn't mean that's the only time the shagfest will happen. I stifle my groan of exhaustion just thinking about it.

I yawn loudly and snuggle further into Harvey's chest.

"Come, petal. Let's get you back in your nest."

I nod, keeping my eyes closed.

The shower is turned off, a towel is wrapped around me and the parts of me that can be reached are patted dry. Somehow, Harvey manages to get back in the nest with me still stuck on his cock.

Moments later, I feel him release me and I think I'm asleep before my head hits the pillow.

* * *

When I wake up, my heat has ramped up another notch. My skin is hot, and my vision is slightly fuzzy. Luckily, Benjamin is right next to me. I grab him, pulling him on top of me. He chuckles quietly and kisses me first before he drives his cock deep inside me. There is nothing to this fuck but a way for me to get through my heat and for him to have a knot.

I feel glad we had a good time the other day. Yesterday? The day before? I've lost track of time now.

He pumps away, knowing I'm half asleep.

"Sorry," I murmur. "Next time."

"Don't worry about it, Faith. Just let me take care of you."

I nod and eyes still closed, I focus on the matter at hand. He speeds up, slamming into me and I cry out softly as the climax roars through my weakened body, but I'm not able to enjoy. I'm too exhausted.

I wait for Benjamin's knot, but nothing happens. He comes inside me with a curse and then withdraws, hauling himself to his feet.

"Wait," I cry out weakly, left wanting.

He storms out of the nest, the other guys giving him curious looks, but Sebastian leaps into action first, tugging on his semi-hard cock before he falls on top of me, bracing himself on his elbows, and shoves it inside me.

"Find out what the fuck," he grits out as he pounds into me, knowing if I don't get the knot, I'm going to suffer.

Harvey follows Benjamin out of the nest.

"I don't understand," I sob. "Did I do something? Was it me?"

"No, baby girl," Sebastian croons, kissing away my sudden tears. "It *definitely* was not you." His low growl is pissed off and when he knots me, it's less than fantastic. I sob harder as it sinks in.

It's a pity knot.

# Chapter Thirty-Three

Benjamin

"Just. Don't. Even." I lean heavily on the counter in my bathroom, after slinging a towel around my hips.

Harvey, who also had the decency to cover up before he came in here, crosses his arm and glares at me. "What the fuck?"

"None of your business."

"Actually, it is. Whatever is going on with you has affected Faith."

"Get me Sebastian," I hiss. There's nothing for it. I'm going to have to come clean – again. He is going to fucking kill me this time.

"He's a bit preoccupied," Harvey snaps.

"Of course he is," I growl.

"So, you might as well tell me while I'm here."

I shake my head, eyes closed, jaw tight. "No. I'm only going to say this once. Come and find me when he's ready."

I shove past him back into my bedroom, and head for the

wardrobe. I pull out a pair of joggers and drag them on, chucking the towel onto my bed to deal with later.

Storming out of the room, leaving Harvey slightly bewildered about what is going on, I march down the stairs and into the kitchen. Searching through several cupboards, it takes me a minute to find the bottle of aged Scotch. When I do, I snatch it up and pour out a glass way larger than an average measure.

Dutch courage.

I'm going to need it. I was hoping this could slide under the radar, but clearly not.

"Faith," I mutter. "Jesus." What must she think of me?

"Right," Sebastian's voice echoes around the silent kitchen as he kicks the door open. "What the fuck was that?"

I sigh. "It's a long story."

"I've got time," he grits out.

"The night that Matt came home, and we decided that Faith was going to be our omega and we would search for her until we found her, I had a feeling it was going to take a while. We had absolutely nothing to go on. No one at the pub even remembered her. How were we going to find her?"

"Thanks for the recap, but get to the part where you've fucked up," Seb growls, interrupting my flow.

I pause, disrupted from what I was saying. "As the days went on and we went around in circles, I knew I had to do something. The rut was coming and there was no way I was dealing with it in the way I usually did. So, I asked one of the omegas that I used to hook up with to get me in touch with her heat suppressant dealer. He gave me the number for a guy who sold me rut suppressants. I know it was..."

"You fucking what?" Sebastian snarls, striding over to me and wrapping his hand around my neck. "You know that shit is illegal."

"Yes, I'm aware," I growl back, slapping his hand away. I've had about enough of being chastised by Seb. Prime alpha or not, he is still the brother that I never had and vice-versa.

"Ben…" The warning in his tone is unmistakable.

"Listen, I know I fucked up," I snap. "But you *know*, you all know, how I am during a rut. I wouldn't have been able to help myself and then I'd have been pissed off and hated what I did. I did what I thought was best for me and for Faith. I'm sure she can appreciate *that* more than the bitter disappointment from today."

"You'd better bloody hope so," Xander says, quiet and almost a bit pensive. "She was in tears, thinking it was her, that she'd done something wrong."

That stabs me in the heart so badly, I let out a moan of pain. "Fuck."

"When did you come off them?" Sebastian barks, all business now.

"About a week ago. I knew I couldn't stay on them or risk permanent damage, so I came off them. When we found Faith, I thought, I *hoped* enough time had passed for them to clear my system, but obviously not."

"Obviously."

His scathing tone riles me, but I don't have a leg to stand on.

"You had better hope to *fuck* this is not permanent, Ben, or so help me, I will throw you out of this pack." His rage rolls off him in waves and I cringe inside. I knew he'd be pissed, but the disappointment I can sense hurts more. His threat would be a punishment worse than death. To be thrown out of a pack would render me useless in our world. I'd be shunned despite my good, old family name.

"I'm sorry. I was trying to do what was right for Faith."

He pauses storming out of the kitchen and draws in a breath. "You need to apologise to her the instant she wakes up. I don't care if she sleeps for the next twelve hours. You will wait by her side and before her eyes are even fully open, you will tell her what a fucking dick you are and none of this is her fault."

"I will," I say, hating this so much I could curl up in a corner and cry. Seeing as I have never cried in my life, that I can remember anyway, this feeling is horrible and not something that I want to repeat.

"Here," Harvey says, thrusting a big bottle of water at me. "Drink up, hold it for as long as you can then piss it out. It'll flush your system."

"Thanks," I mutter, taking it, eyes lowered in shame.

I was trying to do the right thing, but it backfired and now I'm the pile of crap prick anyway.

"I don't regret it," I say as Harvey and Xander turn to leave. "It's better than the alternative, and you both know it."

"Yeah," Xander says, still so quietly, it's freaking me out. "We know."

That's about as much sympathy and redemption I'm going to get.

But I'll take it. This will be forgotten by my pack by tomorrow. Faith, however, is another story.

I rip the lid from the bottle and glug down a few mouthfuls, hoping and praying that this helps get rid of the suppressants. I don't know if it will or not, but I'd dance naked in the rain on the Stratford line Underground if I thought it would help right now.

Slowly, I leave the kitchen and take the stairs, my mood sombre and thoughtful about what words I will use to explain this to Faith.

As it turns out, as soon as I push the door to her bedroom open, a vase comes flying at my head, hitting me, thudding to the floor unbroken and rolling away as Faith shrieks at me in a tone I think only dogs can hear, "You fucking knob!"

171

# Chapter Thirty-Four

Faith

"Ow!" Benjamin cries, rubbing his head where the vase hit him.

My instinct is to laugh like a hyena but that would defeat the purpose of showing him how pissed off and hurt I am.

"You have made me feel worthless!" I yell.

"I know, and I'm sorry," he says, holding up his hands.

He's clutching a bottle of water like a lifeline, and the fear on his face is pretty funny. I can't help it.

I giggle.

He scowls at me.

It doesn't help stop me in the slightest.

He breathes in and straightens up, cautious, but less fearful, until I start bawling my eyes out and crawl back into my nest, flicking the curtain over the entrance to inform him without words that he is *persona non grata*.

"Faith," he calls out.

"You are not welcome in here," I say with a sniff, just in

case he didn't get the memo.

"I know. I wanted to say how sorry I am, and to explain."

"Rut suppressants," I hiss, knowing this is the only thing that could possibly be the cause, because I know it isn't me. I thought it was in the heat, pardon the pun, of the moment, but then logic struck for a moment before I went all ragey. I saw this with one of Derek's friends back when I was too young to really understand what was going on. I found out years later he was gay and didn't want to rut until he figured out how to be a gay alpha. Which he did. Apparently, he is very happy now. But Benjamin doesn't have that excuse. The only thing I can come up with is that he didn't want to rut with *me*.

It fires up my engines again when he gingerly lifts the curtain up to peer inside. "You can totally get knotted, you prick."

"Please let me explain."

The desperation in his voice makes me pause. He takes advantage of it and continues quickly. "Yes, it was rut suppressants, but it's not what you're thinking."

"How do you know what I'm thinking?"

"You have a very expressive face, remember."

"Dammit," I mutter.

"It was to stop the rut prior to this one. The one that came while we were searching for you. I didn't want to act on the rut, and be unfaithful to you, so I suppressed it. It's not your fault, it's mine. I'm a pillock and yes, I should get knotted. But, please, Faith, don't think it was your fault. You did absolutely nothing wrong."

I blink and take that in. I didn't think of that.

"Why didn't you tell me the other day when we were talking about that kind of stuff?" I ask, expecting a truthful answer.

"I wanted to. I should have, but I hoped it wouldn't come

to this. I thought a week was long enough for it to be out of my system."

"You really did this so you wouldn't fuck an omega during your last rut?" I know I shouldn't, but I feel a bit smug that he would do that for me when he didn't even know me.

"Yes. God's honest truth. I was trying to do the right thing for me and for you as well. I'm sorry that I made you feel even for a second that I didn't knot because of you. Never in a million years would I ever want to hurt you, Faith. It's the whole reason I did this to begin with. Fuck."

He drops his face into his hands.

I bite my lip and then sigh. I crawl over to him and take him in my arms. I can't help it. He seems so lost, so alone.

"You really didn't think you could get through the rut without it?"

"I know I couldn't."

"Could you not have borrowed Gertie?" I try to keep the laugh out of my tone, but I think some of it seeps through.

He peeks up at me through his hands. "You know about Gertie?"

I nod. "Xander doesn't keep stuff from me."

"Ouch," he mumbles. "In hindsight, maybe a Gertie wouldn't have been such a bad idea."

"Well, you know what they say, everyone has twenty-twenty vision in hindsight."

"Do you forgive me, Faith?"

"What for?" I ask, genuinely curious as I don't think he really has much to ask forgiveness for.

"For making you feel that it was you."

I swallow and contemplate his words. "Well, I only thought it for a minute."

"It's a minute too long."

I shrug. "It is what it is."

"Jesus, Faith. Has anyone ever told you, you are fucking

hard work to apologise to?" he grouses, almost sulking.

I giggle. "I've heard it once or twice. What can I say, I hate confrontation and I'm a people pleaser."

"The exact opposite of me."

"And that's why we will work so well together." I smile and lean forward to kiss him.

He tangles his fingers in my hair and deepens the kiss for a few seconds before pulling back. "I can't wait to knot you."

"When do you think that will be?" I ask, biting my lip.

He heaves a sigh. "I wish I knew. Harvey said to drink up." He indicates the bottle of water.

"How does he know?" I scrunch up my nose.

He blinks, once, twice and then says slowly. "You know what? I have no fucking idea."

"Hm. Seems the alphas of the St. James pack have many secrets."

"Not anymore. Not from you. I swear I have no other skeletons hidden."

I nod slowly, knowing that I'm keeping something from them, but now isn't the time to mention it. Besides, all this rational talk is making me weary, and the heat is dropping over me again.

"Guess you'd better get me an alpha who can knot me," I say.

"Fuck," he says, shaking his head. "I'm so sorry, Faith."

I cup his face. "I will forgive you if you go and find me a fucking alpha WHO CAN KNOT ME!" I end up yelling right in his face.

He rears back in shock and then leaps into action. "On it! On it!" he exclaims and scrabbles out of the nest to hopefully find me a knot I can sit on and fucking fast before my stomach lining detaches itself with the cramps that are ripping through me, and I die alone, vomiting up my own insides.

"Yeah, not being dramatic at all, Faith. Not. At. All."

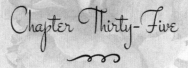

# Chapter Thirty-Five

Faith

Gasping, I wake up to a beautiful sensation between my legs. I crack an eye and look down to see Xander fervently licking my pussy, drinking my slick as if it's slaking his undying thirst. The look of bliss on his face makes my heart thump a little faster.

"Morning," I croak.

He doesn't stop what he's doing, just waggles his fingers at me in a half wave before he grips my thighs again.

"How many days left?" I ask, sleepily.

"How do you feel today?" Sebastian asks.

I contemplate my feelings. "Less fuck me now, more let me sleep."

"Probably your last day then."

"Good," I groan. These last few days have all mashed into one and I'm exhausted. All I've done is fuck, eat and sleep. Sounds like a good time on paper, but yeah, could do with a break. I yawn and wiggle closer to Xander's face as he increases his efforts and I come spontaneously, flooding his mouth with more slick. He groans and slurps it up, sticking his tongue deep inside me as his fingers work against my clit.

"Need you," he mumbles, dragging his tongue upward, over my stomach, in between my breasts, before he traces it over my neck to my jugular.

He pauses, breathing in deeply.

My omega side is crying out for him to bite me, claim me, mate me, but the other side is hesitant. Not because I don't want them, I do, but there are still some things that need ironing out before we make it official.

He slides into my pussy nice and slow, and I reach for Sebastian. He kneels next to me, knowing what I want. I prop myself up on my elbows and take his cock in my mouth, sucking him with the same rhythm that Xander is fucking me.

He groans, holding his base so that he doesn't drop out of my mouth. I moan softly, the vibration of the hum driving him wild.

"Fuck, Faith," he pants, shoving his other hand into my hair and tugging tightly. I stop moving, giving him the green light to fuck my mouth as hard as he wants.

"Oh, yes," Xander rasps as he pounds away inside me, speeding up now and ready for release.

I drench his cock with my slick, feeling another orgasm about to rocket through me and then to my surprise, Sebastian pulls out of my mouth and comes all over my face with a loud, feral grunt that makes my skin tingle.

It pushes Xander over the edge and he knots, big and beautiful, and fires his cum deep inside me.

"Dirty girl," Harvey murmurs, jerking off over me when I fall back to the pillows, still covered in cum.

Xander braces himself on his hands, out of the way of the big Scot, watching him closely as he pumps away at his cock and then splashes my face and tits with warm sticky cum. I run my hand over it, mixing his and Sebastian's together before I bring my hand to my mouth to lick clean of the heavenly cocktail.

"Jesus," Ben whispers. "You are being such a good, filthy little kitty, aren't you?"

I gasp at his words, the tone especially. It's dark, low, soothing almost, as he praises me for being dirty.

This is what he talked about with me, what gets him off.

It gets me off too. I want to do more filthy stuff. I try to think of something I can do to please him, and I shiver when it comes to me.

I sit up, pushing Xander back and awkwardly straddle him. I shove him so he's lying flat on his back, his inflated cock still buried deep inside me.

"Benjamin," I purr.

He growls and is at my back in an instant.

"Use my slick to lube up my arse. Take me while Xander's dick is still inside my pussy."

"Oh, fuck, kitty. Now, you've done it."

He scoops up as much of my slick as he can from around Xander's cock, then he pushes me over. With my arse available for him to prepare, I tense up. I've never done this before. I did anal once a couple of years ago. It was okay, but nothing I craved and needed to do again. But this feels right, and it's only fair. I have the holes, they have the cocks to shove into them. Why not have them use me at the same time? Plus, I know Ben will either withdraw before he knots, or he still won't knot. I know he won't rip me apart in his rut-induced frenzy.

He slides the tip of his finger into my rear entrance. I draw in a sharp breath, tensing up slightly.

"Relax, baby girl," Sebastian murmurs in my ear.

I do as he says. I'm overcome with the need to do precisely as he instructs. It makes sense. He is the prime alpha and despite what my head says, my omega soul knows he is my mate.

I focus on Xander's eyes. He smiles at me, it's cute with a wicked edge. He is going to enjoy this as much as I'm pretty sure I am.

After a few minutes of inserting and stretching, Benjamin murmurs, "Are you ready, kitty?"

"Yes." My voice is hoarse with desire.

He presses his tip to the puckered hole.

"If you want me to stop, just say, okay?"

I nod, unable to form words as he slowly sinks his large cock into my rear passage.

Exhaling, I clasp my hands around Xander's neck, closing my eyes and feeling an overwhelming sensation that definitely did not occur the last time. "Oh, fuck, yes," I murmur.

"Good, filthy kitty?"

"Mmm."

"You are so hot, so dirty. Such a precious little kitty."

"Ah!"

His words are really doing it for me. The combo of the two is fucking fire. No, scratch that, it's the flames of hell.

He settles inside my arse, pausing to let me get used to the invasion, but then he pulls back. Slamming into me, I cry out, that toe curling orgasm already building again.

"Yes, Ben!" I cry out, shortening his name and not caring if he hates it or not. I have no air in my lungs for *Benjamin*.

He pounds away, Sebastian's fingers going to my clit, teasing me slowly.

I tremble in their arms, feeling Xander's knot going down, but he doesn't withdraw.

"Sit back, Ben," he says quietly.

Ben does as he says, bringing me with him impaled on his cock, so I'm reverse cowgirl. That's when Xander slips out of me, and Harvey takes his place.

"Oh, Jesus Christ!" I scream as his huge dick penetrates my soaking wet pussy at the same time that Ben fucks my arse.

I'm being held up in between the two of them as they pound away, and I lose it completely. Slick gushes out of me like a waterfall and I come so intensely, I think I'm going to break Harvey's cock.

"That's it, little whore. Let the big bad alphas use your body to please themselves. Let them fuck you until you weep for mercy. Enjoy every second of it and I will reward you like a good little slut needs to be. Do you want that?"

"Yes!"

"What do you want?"

"Reward me for being a slut!" I scream at the top of my lungs.

"Ooh, kitty," he groans, hammering into me with all of his might. "What kind of slut are you?"

"Good," I pant. "Good."

"Yes, you are perfect," he murmurs and then withdraws quickly, splashing his cum onto my arse cheeks. His feral moan of relief is a dead giveaway.

"Knot?" I ask breathlessly as Harvey continues to ram into me with that slow, steady rhythm that gives me an orgasm to die for.

"Fuck, yes," Ben pants with a laugh. "You are so in for it in a few minutes, kitty."

I smile and shove Harvey back as Ben releases me, although I'm not sure what a knotted cock does without a pussy to latch onto. I don't get a chance to investigate because I writhe around, rotating my hips, treating Harvey to a show that I will probably never be able to repeat.

# Chapter Thirty-Six

Harvey

Watching Faith's tits bounce up and down as she writhes around on my cock, is mesmerising. She is just beyond sexy. The four of us have never shared a woman before, so this was something new for all of us to begin with, but actually taking her two at a time...

I groan as my cock jerks inside her, eager for a release.

But I'm not knotting yet for all the tea in China. I want to keep watching her tits jiggle, her rosebud nipples hard and expecting to be bitten.

I give in to them and sit up, cupping her breast into a mound of creamy deliciousness before I nip her on the ripe bud.

"Ah!" she cries out, soaking my cock further.

I didn't think it was possible for her to get any wetter, but she is surpassing my expectations, and then some. I've only ever been with one omega in heat, and it was nothing like this. My ruts have always been with omegas outside of their heat.

The complications of getting involved, however brief, with an omega in heat is just something that I had never wanted. I get why Ben did what he did. I've done it myself. Although it was a long time ago and it never affected anyone except me. Sebastian or any of them, don't need to know about it. I'm supposed to be the rational one. I'll lose that if they know, so I'd rather they didn't. I did show my hand to Ben, but I think he was too far gone in his own pile of shite to notice, because he hasn't said anything.

"Faith," I groan, looking up from her nipple and meeting her light blue eyes.

"You're a big boy," she purrs, working herself hard on my cock.

"Fuck, petal. Don't talk dirty to me. I want this to last."

She giggles. "Like a bit of filth, do you?"

"When it comes from your rosy lips, you could talk smack to me, and it would turn me on."

She laughs loudly. "You're a fucking twat, you are," she says.

"Oh, baby. Call me a wanker, see how it gets me off."

She snorts and leans down to whisper in my ear. "Wanker."

I grab her hips and flip her over, so she is underneath me now. I plaster her hands either side of her head. "Say it again."

"Fucking cunting wanker."

"Oh, ow, upping the game. I'll show you cunting." I pull my cock out of her and slap her pussy with it lightly.

She nearly creams herself, wiggling about on the slick covered blankets. So I do it again.

"Harder," she pants, lifting her hips up to give me easier access.

I slap her again and then rotate the tip over her slippery clit.

I drive back into her, pounding her hard and fast until

she screams my name, clawing at my back, marking me with her sharp nails. Her pussy clenches around my cock and I give up. My knot bulges out, expanding inside her tightly, making her cry out with the pressure of the muscle locking us in place.

Grunting softly, I feel my cum fill her up and I can't help but wonder what would happen if she got pregnant now.

I would be over the moon. It's all I ever wanted was a loving mate and a family. But we've never even talked about what *she* wants. We haven't talked about anything to do with her becoming our mate, except to inform her that was our plan. There wasn't really time for a brutal, honest conversation without her heat affecting her and us.

I rest my forehead against hers, loving that she wraps her legs around me to hold me close.

I want to tell her that I love her, but it's too soon.

Isn't it?

I know I feel it. She is kind, funny, sweet, bold and caring. She will fight for those she loves, and I want to be one so badly, it makes my body ache.

As my breathing slows, my knot starts to go down. We are at the end of our rut, and this will be the last time we fuck her like this until next quarter. I want to keep her close just a little bit longer, breathing in her strawberries and honey cream scent, feeling her slick coating my cock, feeling her heart beat next to mine.

"I love you," I blurt out and the nest goes completely silent.

All I can hear is my own breathing.

If she says, 'thank you', I will be humiliated beyond belief.

She rolls us over and lays her head on my chest. "I think I love you too," she says eventually.

"I'll take it, and work on making you know it."

My heart sings with joy when she smiles up at me, and

then she is ripped from my grasp by a very horny Ben, who practically devours her face, he kisses her so deeply.

I prop myself up on an elbow to watch them, enjoying seeing the omega that I love, receiving the love she deserves from good alphas who will do anything for her to make her happy and keep her safe.

## Chapter Thirty-Seven

Benjamin

Claiming Faith's mouth with mine in a kiss so deep, so erotic after what I just did with her, sends me into a state of raw lust. I want to pin her down and rut with her until she screams for mercy, however, there is something I need to do first.

Reluctantly, I pull away, taking her hand, leading her quickly out of the nest and into the bathroom. I step into the shower and turn the water on, coolish again so she can join me.

I reach for the soap and washcloth, but her hand on mine stops me.

"Let me," she says quietly, almost shyly.

"Faith," I murmur, closing my eyes and revelling in the gorgeous sweetness of the woman I know I also love. Damn Harvey for jumping in there, but I should've known. He feels deeply and openly, and it was a dead cert he'd crash hard for this omega with a heart of pure gold with a dash of spice and sass.

It breaks my heart to think she was dulled by her family life, unable to shine as brightly as she was meant to.

I keep my eyes closed as she runs the soapy cloth over my chest tentatively. She dips lower, over my stomach and then takes my hard cock in her small, soft hand, cleaning my shaft and balls. I open my eyes and watch her do this. I jerk in her hand. She tries to hide her smile, but I see it anyway. Dropping to her knees to wash the rest of my body, I let out a whimper of restraint. I've done this so many times before to other women, but no one has ever done this to me. I didn't think I wanted them to. It's a sign of complete vulnerability. My insides wither at the thought of anyone else doing this, but with Faith, it makes me feel like a god. Like I'm on top of the world, *her* world and nothing else matters.

She finishes and I help her up, taking the soap and cloth from her.

"I want you just as dirty as when you stepped in here," I murmur, dropping them back on the soap dish.

Her breath hitches.

Her adoring blue eyes gaze up at me. If I hadn't already fallen like a boulder off a cliff top, I'd be in a landslide right now.

"You are so beautiful."

She smiles. "You are fucking hot."

I snort. "I love that you just say what's on your mind. It's an admirable trait and honestly, not one you come across very often."

She shakes her head. "I've never been this open with anyone else before. Not even my brother. I've always been the good little omega. Ready to please with a smile and no words."

"You don't have to be that way anymore," I say quietly, slipping my hand into her wet hair.

"I know. I feel so comfortable with all of you."

"I'm glad, because you deserve to shine, kitty."

She tilts her head back and I kiss her, pressing my mouth to hers. My cock stirs against her stomach when she steps closer to me.

Drawing back, I wipe the shower water from her face. "When your heat is over, I want to do things to you that I need your consent for."

Her lips part and she lets out a soft breath. "What kind of things?"

"Dirty things," I reply with a wicked smile.

"Mm, and will you tell me how wonderful I am when I'm doing these dirty things?"

"You like that, kitty?"

"It's amazing."

"You are wonderful with or without the dirty things, but yes. I will praise you until just my words send an orgasm crashing down over you. I want to see your clit throbbing as I tell you how proud I am of you for being a filthy slut."

"Fuck," she rasps. "If you're ready, I need you to take me now."

Without words, I pick her up, my hands on her arse. She wraps her legs around me and I press her against the cool tiles. My cock is aching with the need to knot inside her. She reaches for me and guides me inside her slippery wet pussy.

I groan as I feel her slick coating my cock. Nothing has ever come close to this. The feelings she invokes in me are unfamiliar, but completely wanted. I crave her touch, her kisses, her pussy clenching around my cock tightly enough to make me emit a groan of driven arousal that heightens when she responds to it with a soft purr. It makes the alpha inside me want to protect her and kill for her. I *will* kill for her if I ever get my hands on the arsehole stepdad. It makes me want to *die* for her if it means keeping her safe and protected.

"I love you, Faith," I murmur. "Don't say anything until you can tell me the same in no uncertain terms."

"It's not fair," she pouts. "You all had a bit of a head start on me."

My eyes are riveted to that rosy, red lip stuck out in a cute sulk. I lean forward and bite it gently, tugging until she gasps.

I reach up and pinch her nipples, wedging her between my body and the shower wall. "Come for me, kitty. Show me what this pussy can do."

She moans and closes her eyes. I twist her nipples, slightly harder than I know she will be comfortable with. Her squeal at the bite of pain, thrills me and I twist just a tiny bit harder and then I let her go. Her breath is coming in short, sharp pants. She is close to coming undone. Placing my thumb on her clit, I rotate it slowly and she shivers in my arms, then I feel her pussy grip my cock possessively. I ram into her as deep as I'll fit.

"Fuck, Faith," I grunt and spurt my cum inside her as the knot bulges at the base of my dick, locking us together in an intimate embrace that I never want to end.

## Chapter Thirty-Eight

Faith

Two days after my heat finally ended, after five long days of shagging the four alphas more times than I can count, I glare at the packet on the countertop in my bathroom.

"Shit."

I inhale deeply and then exhale slowly. "Shit. Shit. And more shit."

One.

There is one birth control pill left in this packet.

I knew I was running out before I left home, but figured I'd be at Derek's and within striking distance of a family planning clinic or local doctor, so I didn't concern myself too much with it. Running away was paramount. This was not.

Now, though?

"Fuck."

I chew my lip. Granted, the alphas will leave me alone for a bit after my heat. They are so sweet and caring and attentive to my every need, they will assume, rightly so, that I need some time off. But that doesn't get me very far. Eventually, they will want to insert their baby-making sticks into my, well, baby maker and I'm just not ready for the baby to be produced yet. I want kids. Desperately. But I'm not daft enough to dive into motherhood headfirst at twenty-one after my very first heat and with four alphas who are not my mates. Yet. It *will* happen. I want it to. But in time. Now isn't that time.

I'm going to have to tell Sebastian that I need more birth control and force a conversation that I wanted to put off for a little while longer.

I know he needs a son. *Wants* a son. He will make such an amazing father. They all will. But it's most important to him. I don't know where his head is at with regard to a timeline on that. We've never talked about any of this shit.

"Bollocks. Guess I'm going to have to come clean. Unless…" I purse my lips and then dart back into the bedroom and over to the window. I peer out over the grounds, but I can't see the gates from here. I can locate the nearest family planning clinic, head straight there and be back by lunchtime. No one has to know. I don't have to tell anyone anything. These grounds are big enough that if anyone comes looking for me while I am out, I can say I was all the way over there in that corner, which is about a mile away, for fuck's sake.

"Okay, this is a plan."

I huff out a breath and snatch up my phone. I do a location search for a clinic near me and find one a few miles away. I'll need to get on a bus, I think, but I still have some cash from the money I stole from Pete, so all good. I switch the phone off again, still worried that if Derek managed to track me down, Pete could as well. All I have to do is head right out of the gates to the main road and head towards a large village called Woodthorpe. Easy peasey.

Maybe.

Guess I'll find out.

I grab my backpack and stuff my phone inside and make sure the cash is safe. It's less than I'd like, especially as I could do with some new clothes, but hopefully Derek will swing by soon with the stuff I left at his place three and a half months ago.

I zip up my old coat and sling the backpack onto my shoulders and then peek out of the bedroom door. Seeing the coast is clear, I hastily, but quietly make my way down the stairs and to the front door without encountering anyone except the creepy as fuck portraits of the St. James's of yore. Even the most recent one of Sebastian's dad is all stony-faced and daunting.

Slowly turning the old-fashioned, gold-plated handle on the big black front door, I pray for no squeaks. Last time I snuck out of somewhere, the squeaks got me in shit. But this is well oiled and squeak-free.

Looking back over my shoulder one last time, I slip outside, silently closing the door behind me. I quickly head down the three paved steps and down the driveway, heading straight for the trees that line the mini private road that leads up to the house. The freezing cold air takes my breath away and I shiver. This coat is no match for the English winter weather. I'm so glad I didn't have to rough it, even for a night in the park. As terrifying as it was to be hunted by the alphas, it's worked out so far.

I just need to do this one thing, and I'll buy myself some time. Then I can be the good little omega again and stay behind the castle walls. I start jogging, mostly because this road is never-ending, but also to keep warm. Finally, I see the huge black, wrought iron gates come into view. The coat of arms takes up a large portion of the gate. I can't see what's on it from behind, but make a note to have a look on my way back in. Standing in front of the gates, I reach out to open it, but it doesn't budge.

I try again, shaking it slightly.

"Shit, locked."

I look to the side and groan. Electric. Of course they fucking are, posh twats.

Looking up, I debate with myself once more. Derek climbed over them. Maybe I can too. I'm on this mission now, and to not see it through would piss me off and put me back at square one with only one birth control pill.

Bracing myself, I lift my foot up and grip the iron bars, hauling my body up. I climb up again, but three quarters of the way up, I come a cropper. There are huge iron spikes on the top of the gates.

"Derek did this. So can I."

My pep talk does its job and I reach the top of the gates. Wondering how the fuck I'm supposed to get my leg over the spikes, I figure I'm going to have to go *in between* them. This is going to be fun. I shake my backpack off and let it drop to the ground on the other side, hoping I didn't smash my phone in the process. Then I squeeze my right leg through the spikes, squeaking when one of them pokes me in the arse cheek. I wobble and grip the freezing iron tighter. I get my foot secure and then with the acrobatic prowess, I didn't know I had until I was stuck on top of some bloody iron spikes, I swing my left leg over the top of the gate. My foot slips and I cry out softly as a spike comes dangerously close to my eye.

"Eek," I squeal as I drop down, sliding down the iron gate less than gracefully to land, free, on the other side. I do not know how I'm going to do that in reverse.

My hands trembling, I scoop up my backpack and place it on my back. Then I look right and left. I'm sure the directions said right, but it's hard to tell. The small road in front of me gives no indication. There is a huge field on the other side and trees and tarmac right and left.

"Right it is, then," I mutter and set off, blowing on my red hands to warm them up before I shove them in my coat pockets. Hunching my shoulders against the icy wind, I stick my head down and walk up the road for roughly five minutes before I come to a junction. Here I see a sign and to my relief it is signposted Woodthorpe to the left.

"Fan-bloody-tastic," I comment under my breath and head over the road to the pavement, picking up my pace and hoping to see a bus stop soon so I can thaw out, not to mention hurry this show along.

A tingle goes down my spine and I shiver. Looking back over my shoulder when I get the feeling someone is watching me, I don't see anyone on this deserted road. Telling myself, there's no one there, I face forward again and start to jog, hoping I see signs of civilisation bloody soon.

## Chapter Thirty-Nine

Sebastian

"Faith?" I knock gently on her bedroom door.

No answer.

"Faith?" I knock harder.

Still nothing.

Anxiety claws at my insides as I worry that something might have happened to her, I open the door slightly and call out again.

When she still doesn't answer, I enter the room and announce my presence. "Faith? I'm coming in."

I scan the room to see it's empty. The wardrobe is open and only filled with her meagre clothes, which is something I wanted to talk to her about now. Crossing over to the bathroom, I notice that it is also empty.

Just as I'm about to turn and leave to resume my search for her, I spot something on the counter that makes me stop.

Two strides into the bathroom, I snatch up the packet of birth control pills. There's one left in the packet. "Dammit,

Faith," I growl and scrunch it up in my fist. I shove it in my back pocket, several emotions washing over me. I'm not sure which one to listen to the most. I'm disappointed and hurt that she didn't say anything, but at the same time, I know there was hardly time to say much of anything, let alone something this personal to her. I'd hoped she would get pregnant during her heat so that she would allow us to give her the mating bite, but obviously I will be bitterly disappointed if I expect that result now. I need to find her immediately and start a conversation about where her head is at. Clearly, we are not on the same page.

I spin and stalk out of her room.

"Faith!" I shout out. "Faith!"

Xander sticks his head out of his room. "What's up?"

"Have you seen her?" I'm not going to tell the others about this yet. I want to speak to her alone first.

Xander shakes his head, concern on his face. He sniffs the air and frowns. Then he goes on the hunt. If she is in the house, he will find her.

"Harvey! Ben!"

I only have to call for them once and they are next to me.

"Either of you seen Faith?" I ask as I head down the stairs.

"No, should we be worried?" Ben asks slowly.

I grit my teeth and refrain from replying.

"Not here," Xander says, joining us a moment later. "Her scent isn't strong enough anywhere."

"Check the security cameras," I bark out. "I want her found. Now."

He nods and pushes open a door near the front door that looks like a coat cupboard but is in fact a high-tech security office. Xander is a whizz with tech and sits down at the array of screens and keyboards on the desk. Harvey and Ben squeeze in behind me, blocking out most of the light in the dark room, only the screens and various flashing LEDS give off a glow. I watch as he taps the keyboard quickly, pulling up all fifteen of the outside security cams, flicking through them one by one.

"Can't find her," he mutters.

"Keep searching."

The three of us lean over Xander, peering over his shoulder at the screens in front of us.

"Go back," I instruct after another sweep bears no fruit. "Go back an hour and scan forward."

He does as I ask.

My breathing is short, sharp and painful. If she has run, it's going to tear my heart out. I feel sick with the anxiousness running rampant through my body.

The thoughts are irrational. She left the few clothes she has, plus the pill.

*She hasn't run. She hasn't. She wouldn't.*

But it wouldn't be the first time she's run. I shouldn't taint her present with her past, but it is still very close, and my obsessive side has gone loopy with bad thoughts.

*Trust her, Seb. Don't do this.*

"Here," Xander says after a few minutes. "Forty minutes ago, she left the house."

We watch her scamper down the paved steps and then lose her.

Xander picks her up heading towards the tree-lined private road.

"What the fuck?" I snarl.

She *is* fucking running.

However irrational it might seem, she's running.

"The gates," he says quietly.

"What the fuck is she doing?" Ben asks incredulously as we watch her *climb* over them.

"Fuck," Harvey breathes out when one of the spikes jabs her in the arse.

"She really wants to leave, doesn't she?" I mutter.

"Jesus!" Ben exclaims as one of the spikes nearly takes her eye out. "No! Just no! She wouldn't run. This has to be doctored somehow."

Xander shakes his head and stands up, pushing past us. "One way to find out," he growls. We follow him out of the small room and watch him pick up a set of keys from the key rack on the wall next to the front door.

"Wait, we don't know where she went," Harvey says, trying his rational approach.

"Not this time," I growl. "Shut it and get in the car or stay here and talk to yourself."

"Fucker," he snarls back, the aggression getting to both of us.

He shoves past me and storms to the Range Rover, getting in and slamming the door. Xander is already gunning the engine. I climb into the passenger side while Ben takes the back next to the grumpy Scot. Rather him than me. Harvey is the mildest man I've ever known, but when his back gets up, you'd better fucking run, and I poked that bear good.

"Which way?" I ask as Xander screeches round the circular driveway and down the private road.

"She went right," he grits out, his hands white knuckling the steering wheel.

I open the gates with the remote control from the glove compartment when we approach. Xander takes the corner on two wheels, making us wish we'd remembered to put our seatbelts on.

Doing about seventy miles per hour down the thirty zone, he slams on the brakes when we reach the junction at the top.

As soon as I see the sign for Woodthorpe, a light bulb goes off that I refused to acknowledge before.

"Head towards the town. I know where she's going."

She isn't running. She left to get more birth control. It's not as painful, but it still stabs me in the heart and the gut and the balls. She doesn't want kids. That's *all* I want. I don't even care if I never have a son. I just want children to love and build a family with her. I wish we'd talked about this before, so we knew where she stood. What if she never wants kids?

I can't even go there.

Right now, I just need to focus on finding her.

As Xander makes his way through the busy, early morning rush hour traffic towards the town centre, my phone vibrates for a text message.

I yank it out, wondering if it's Faith somehow, even though she doesn't have my number. It's not. It's Derek.

"Fuck!" I bellow as I read the words in front of me. "We need to find her, *now*! Move this fucking car one way or another, Xand. She is in danger."

Four words that he understands and responds to.

He swerves onto the other side of the road and shoots off at breakneck speed, pretty much ignoring the speed limit, the fact he is on the wrong side of the road, the horns blaring and the cars hurtling towards us.

"Jesus," Ben remarks. "Please don't let us die before we find her."

I grip the grab handle as Xander uses his advanced driving skills to manoeuvre us into the busy town, eyes peeled desperately for Faith before she is grabbed off the street and lost to us forever.

## Chapter Forty

Faith

So far, so good.

I managed to make it to the bus stop several minutes before the small bus trundled down the road. Upon inquiring, I discovered that it goes directly to Woodthorpe, straight down this road. The fare was a couple of quid, and I had the exact change, so I feel like I'm winning at life right now as I sit on this bus, jostling about, ready to jump off when we get into the town.

I press the button when I see the high street and a few seconds later, I'm jumping off just as the shops are opening up for the day. I look around and head for the chemist. If anyone knows where the clinic is, they will. It occurs to me belatedly, and I feel like an absolute idiot, that by blocking Pete's number, that will probably block him from being able to track me as well. I roll my eyes to myself, wondering how I never thought of this before. I guess there was so much going on, it just escaped my not very tech-minded notice. Whipping it out,

I do precisely that, feeling a sense of relief that is quite liberating, and then look up the walking directions to the clinic. It opens at nine o'clock so hopefully I'll be in and out and on my way back home before I'm missed.

A few minutes later, I reach the clinic and their friendly receptionist has me booked in. I sit and wait my turn, which isn't very long at all, and then I'm sorted out and out of the door a mere half an hour later.

I'm shocked a second later, when a giant, Harvey-sized man grabs my arm and growls at me, forcing me into submission before I've even batted an eye.

I whimper and lower my eyes, my shoulder hunching and my back stooping.

"That's it, little whore. Submit. You've given us quite the runaround, but lucky for us, your brother was quite talkative once we beat him enough times."

"Derek!" I gasp. "What did you do to him?" I feel an anger descend that is foreign to me and makes me struggle in his grasp to get free so I can claw his eyes out.

He holds up Derek's phone with a savage grin and waves it at me. "Easy peasey, lemon squeezy."

"Fuck!" I hiss. I *knew* turning my phone on was a bad idea. If Pete has hurt Derek, I will kill him with my bare hands and damn the consequences.

"You were owed to us, princess, now get a move on. I don't want to pick you up and cause a scene, but I will if I have to," the bear-man snarls.

Wait. *Owed?*

Oh, shit. This isn't Pete, this is the pack that wanted to buy me.

Fuck.

Fuck.

Harvey warned me to stay inside the estate, but I didn't listen and now I'm fucked up the creek without a paddle.

"Let go of me!" I yell, making the scene he didn't want to cause.

"Shut up," he grits out.

I don't shut up. In fact, I go louder. "Help! Help!" I screech like a banshee, because there is *no way* in hell, I'm going without a fight.

Causing a bit of a stir, most people look away and walk past.

Nice.

*Great community spirit there, dicksplashes.*

I struggle and as much as he growls and tries to force me into submission, the stronger I seem to get to defy him. He drags my arm up and sniffs my wrist, the one that Sebastian bit and it sends him into a feral rage. He twists my arm back, snapping it audibly.

I scream as the white-hot pain shoots up my arm and then everything seems to happen in a haze of agony induced fog and slow motion.

Xander leaps on the bear-man, teeth gnashing and bites his neck, tearing a chunk out of it, right there in the middle of the street.

I drop to my knees, cradling my broken arm, watching in horror as the public is now definitely getting involved in this commotion.

"Faith," Harvey says, helping me up. "Come with me."

"Harvey," I croak and look up into his grey eyes. "I—I..."

"It doesn't matter. We need to get you to safety, come."

I nod, feeling nauseous from the action. He helps me to my feet and then picks me up, careful of my injured arm. The police are arriving, plus an ambulance. The small street is running amok, the confusion and violence a rarity in this small country town.

Glancing across at Xander, he is being forcibly held at bay

by Ben, while Sebastian looms over the downed bear-man and smashes his fist into his face.

"Fuck," I mutter. "What the fuck is going on?"

I'm disorientated for a moment, and I can't remember why I'm out here or what the alphas are doing here rearranging faces.

"Get her out of here," Sebastian grits out, barely heard over Xander's snarls of restrained rage.

"Take him," Ben states in a voice so cold and so commanding, I shiver with dread.

Sebastian, panting furiously, straightens up and takes control of Xander while Ben leans down and hauls the beat-up guy to his feet. He drags him along, not waiting for the alpha to find his feet.

That's when things go from bad to worse.

Coming back to my senses, I groan as Harvey stuffs me into the back of a Range Rover and after climbing in himself in the driver's seat, he drives off with me kicking and screaming because the other three alphas were just swarmed by the pack the bear-man belongs to.

"Harvey!" I scream, "They need help."

He snorts. "No, they don't, petal. Now shut the fuck up like a good little omega and sit tight. You have a universe of explaining to do and you can stew while we wait for the other guys to meet us back at home."

"My arm," I pout.

"Doc's already on his way," he says kindly, but then goes back to hunching his shoulders and slamming his foot on the accelerator, not happy with me in the slightest.

I keep my trap shut, knowing that I'm in so much trouble, if my arse doesn't get spanked at the end of it, I'll consider myself lucky.

## Chapter Forty-One

Faith

Back in my room, I sit still like a good girl while the fancy doctor takes care of my arm. After giving me some painkillers, he straps a makeshift cast on my left arm. I feel myself going a bit drowsy.

I can only hope that I don't pass out before the other alphas get home, but I have a feeling that is going to be a while. With the other pack and the police showing up, Christ knows what trouble they all got into. Harvey is nowhere to be found, so when the doctor finishes up, with instructions to head to the hospital soon, I lie back on my bed and close my heavy eyes.

Within seconds, I drift off.

* * *

Sometime much later, it is now dark outside, I hear a knock on the door. It rouses me and I sit up groggily, blinking my aching eyes.

"Yeah," I croak out, bringing my hand up to my hair, but then realising it's the broken arm. I wince and drop it again.

"Are you up?" Sebastian asks, sticking his head around.

"Guess so," I grumble.

He chuckles, which sort of puts me at ease. But is he lulling me into a false sense of security? My best guess would be yes.

"How is your arm?"

"Sore. How is your fist? And your face?" I reply, taking in two black eyes and a split lip.

"The other guy looks worse."

"I'm sorry, Sebastian," I get out before anything else can get in the way, lowering my eyes contritely.

He heaves a sigh. "There was no need for you to go out there. Especially when we told you to stay in here."

"There was a need. I needed something."

"Birth control," he says quietly. "I know we never had the conversation about this, but we need to have it now."

"How did you know?" I ask, looking back up.

He pulls the old packet out of his pocket. "I wasn't snooping, you left it on the counter."

Well, I can't argue with that. I look away and bite my lip. "I've just turned twenty-one," I start. "I'm not mated. I don't want to get pregnant, yet. Is that a problem?"

"If you mean 'yet', then no, we don't have a problem. If you don't want kids, then there are some more things we need to talk about."

His almost desperate tone forces me to look back at him. "I do mean 'yet'," I say softly. "Getting pregnant now, unmated and so young would be a mistake, I feel."

"You are right," he says, taking my good hand. "But I want a family, Faith. So do the other men. Is that what you want?" His cautious tone makes me sad that I disappointed him.

"Yes, it is. Just not right now after my first heat. Can you understand that?"

He nods slowly.

"Okay, if you are sure about that and not just saying it to get out of trouble, because we haven't even started on that yet?"

"I mean it." I sigh. "Let me have it. What punishment do you have in mind? I deserve it for being too shy to ask for help and for getting you all into trouble and hurt."

"Faith," he says steadily. "This isn't about any of that. *You* were hurt and if we hadn't arrived when we did, probably carted off to live with that pack of thugs. The only thing that I care about is your safety and you didn't consider the effect it would have on us if you got taken away or worse. For some reason, you still don't trust us, although I suppose I do get it on some level. But haven't we earned it by now? Haven't we shown you we care?"

Tears fill my eyes and I feel like the worst omega on the planet. This is the most awful thing he could do to me. "I'm sorry," I whisper. "I didn't mean, I didn't..."

"You didn't even think about us, did you?"

I shake my head.

"Do you trust us, Faith?"

I swallow and lick my lips. "Yes," I croak out. "I think so."

"You think so."

His bitter disappointment cuts across my heart.

"Please, don't take it personally," I blurt out, desperate to fix this mess.

"How can I not?" he blurts back.

"It's nothing to do with any of you. You have been kind and caring, okay apart from hunting and abducting me, but after that. It's me. I trusted my dad and he broke that trust. He died and left me, and I've suffered because of it."

"Oh, baby girl," he murmurs, drawing me to him. "I know

you have, and we will take care of that arsewipe. But if you can't trust us, then we *do* have a problem."

I snuffle into his shirt and nod. "I'm sorry. I know I have no right to ask you this, but that guy said he hurt Derek, and he had his phone... please, can you try to find him, make sure he's okay?"

"He's fine," Sebastian says quickly. "Derek is downstairs. His phone was stolen yesterday."

"Oh, thank God." I let out a relieved breath. "How much trouble are you all in?"

"None. Don't worry about us. Get some rest, Faith, and then you need to apologise to the other alphas and your brother for scaring the pubes off us. If you're comfortable enough for now, we'll leave off taking you to the hospital tonight and go tomorrow."

"I don't want to go. I'm fine."

"Doc says you need an x-ray."

"Doesn't Dr. Fancy-pants have a portable one?"

Sebastian snickers. "I suppose I could throw him an extra few grand to find one, but only because it suits *me* to keep you here safe and sound," he adds sternly.

"Noted," I mumble. "I'll come and find you when I've slept a bit more. My head is fuzzy."

He nods absently and gets up. With a kiss to the top of my head, he crosses over to the door and leaves, shutting it behind him. I hear the key turn in the lock, and I sigh.

"Yep, you deserve that, Faith. Totally and utterly deserve it."

I turn on my side and curl up, and despite the agony of the wait to speak to the other alphas, I still fall asleep again within minutes, aided by Dr. Fancy-pants' meds.

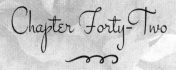

# Chapter Forty-Two

Benjamin

Pacing up and down, in front of the fire in Seb's office, I'm just irritating myself further.

"Let me go and speak to her," I demand of Sebastian.

"Nope."

"Why do you get to decide?"

"Because if I didn't, you would be up there yelling at her and making her feel worse than she already does."

"Not fair," I growl, but pissed off that he knows I'd yell at her. Not to make her feel bad, but to let her know how fucking worried I was about her.

He shrugs and goes back to his work.

"Can I go?" Derek ventures.

"Nope."

"Fuck's sake."

"She needs some time on the naughty step. She needs to learn that she can't run off on a whim and make us chase her

207

down and save her from idiot arseholes who want to take her and mate with her. In case you've forgotten, she is *ours*."

"Then we need to fucking step up and show her we are."

"She isn't ready."

"Fuck off!" I roar. "You are being the biggest wazzock on the planet, right now."

"No," he says, throwing his pen down and standing up. He has had enough. I've pushed him, but there's something he isn't telling us, and I want to know what it is. "She doesn't trust us. Until she does. No bite."

He sits down again and picks up his pen.

Well, there it is. And it hurts. It shouldn't after the way we hunted her and stole her, it's no fucking wonder she doesn't trust us.

"I see." I have nothing else to say.

He gives me a grim look which expresses his pain over the matter. We did this all wrong at the wrong fucking time. If we'd reached her earlier, or later, after her heat, we could've done things the right way. It was a clusterfuck, and there is no other word to describe it.

"Is she okay? Her arm..."

"It's hurting her, but Doc gave her some strong painkillers to help her sleep."

"Are we going to tell her what we did?"

"No," Derek says quickly. "Don't tell her."

"Why not? Won't it make her feel safer knowing those wankers are off the streets?"

"I say we tell her," Xander says. He is curled up in the corner of the small sofa, making an odd keening sound every now and again. It's almost like he is pining for her. "Seb?"

He sighs as we all glare at him to make a decision.

"No," Harvey says. "If we tell her that we had them arrested and then arranged for them to have an 'accident' on the way to prison, she won't trust us even more."

"Why? *We* didn't kill them," I grouse, but it's semantics and I know it. I'm just being obtuse and a stubborn fuck. Two of my lesser admirable qualities.

"We stick to the plan," Sebastian says. "They got arrested, we didn't because we were protecting our omega. She has my bite, it's enough for the courts. What happened after they drive out of sight is fuck all to do with us."

"Jesus. Is this really how you do things?" Derek snaps, standing up and running his hand through his hair. "I thought you were good guys, but I'm starting to think leaving my sister with you is a bad idea."

"Sit," Sebastian says in that tone that no one, not even Xander dares to disobey.

Derek doesn't either, and takes his seat again.

"We do what is necessary to protect those we love. Faith is one of them. She may not know it herself yet, but every one of us is completely in love with her. If you want to tear her away from us, you will have a fight on your hands that you will in no way win. Are we clear?"

My gaze goes from Seb to Derek.

"Clear," he grits out.

I relax.

The tension had ratcheted up a few notches and it set the beast inside me on the warpath.

"We need to tread carefully," Seb says.

"She needs to have her arse smacked," I say wickedly, but rein it in, what with her brother sitting a few feet from me.

"I think her broken arm will suffice," Seb says, giving me a look that speaks volumes. He is only saying that because of Derek. He wants to tan her hide as much as I do, but he won't. He is the epitome of self-control when he wants to be. He is the calm before the storm.

Me.

I'm the storm.

"I want to go to her now," Xander says.

He's the fucking tornado that will rip her off her feet.

"Nope."

"Fucking hell, Seb!" I yell, getting agitated again.

"She needs to learn that running, even if it wasn't *away* from us, has consequences."

I lean on the mantlepiece and sigh, staring into the roaring fire. "She will be upset and worried."

"I can guarantee you, she will be flat out."

"Fuckwit," I mutter under my breath.

"Aha!" Seb suddenly exclaims into the morose silence.

"What?"

"An email from my dad. Oh, hell. You're going to want to read this."

As one, the four of us launch ourselves at Seb, gathering around him to read over his shoulder on the laptop screen.

"No fucking way!" Derek shouts. "That can't be right."

"I think we need to tell Faith about this now," I point out.

"No, not yet." Derek spits out. "We don't have anything concrete. I need to go back home and wring that fucker's neck until he fesses up. If he had *anything* to do with my dad's disappearance, I will kill him."

We watch as he storms off and slams out of the house.

"Should we go after him?"

Seb nods towards Harvey, who sighs and follows him.

"I think we need to tell Faith."

"Agreed," he says quietly. "But let's deal with the issue at hand first. There are things the five of us need to discuss, our mating bite only one of them. The sooner we get her to agree to it, the safer she will be."

"Not the way to put it to her."

"Obviously, but you know what I mean. There isn't a single pack in the world that would mess with her once she belongs to the St. James pack."

"I know," I murmur. "She needs to be safe. Did you find out why she left?"

He nods. "I know. I knew halfway to going to find her."

I fist my hand in front of his face with a growl. "And?" He is such a smug fucker.

"Now isn't the time," he mutters when Harvey hauls Derek back into the office.

I grimace at him, but he ignores me. When he is like this, there is nothing in the sea, nor in the air, nor on land that could make him spill the beans.

I will just have to keep guessing until he lets us see her.

## Chapter Forty-Three

Faith

I wake up with a groan, pain is shooting through my arm. I crushed it under me in my drug-induced sleep and now I'm in agony.

"Ow, ow, ow."

I bring it up and cradle it gently, trying to get my bearings.

Oh, yeah. Locked in a room in some Scooby Doo mansion, out in the sticks with four alphas who want to mate with me, give me babies and all my heart desires.

Why aren't I jumping at the chance, again?

"Fuck knows."

Actually, fuck does know. I am fuck, and I know.

It all boils down to exactly what I told Sebastian. Trust issues. I have them and them abducting me, no matter how lovely they have been to me since, has chipped a big crater into the issues I already had. It's going to take me a lot of work to get over it. All of it. But it *is* my work. Not theirs. I hope they understand that.

It's still dark out, but I feel less fuzzy headed, so it must be a lot later than when Sebastian came to talk to me. I glance at the clock and see it's only five o'clock in the morning. I shiver and then freeze when I hear something outside the door.

Drawing in a deep breath, I murmur, "Ocean-breeze." I climb off the bed and go to the door. "Xander?"

"Faith," he croaks out. "I don't have a key; I can't let you out."

"No, it's okay, I don't want you to. I want you all to feel secure that I'm not going anywhere. I wasn't anyway. I was going to come back."

"You wouldn't have made it back if we hadn't found you."

"I know." The guilt floods me and I feel awful. "I hate that I forced you to come and find me and rescue me."

"Forced?" he spits out.

I jump back when I hear a bang on the door, then another. "Xander?"

"Forced." Bang. "Forced." Bang.

"Are you hitting your head on the door?"

"You think we were forced to come and get you. I don't like that word, Faith."

His tone sends an icy chill rippling over my skin. "I'm sorry. I didn't mean..."

"We came because we care about you. All of us. Not just one, or two. *All* of us. I can't say it...not like that. Not like Harvey. I struggle with words."

I drop to my knees and then curl up next to the bottom of the door. I slide my fingers over the thick carpet and wedge them under the door. "You don't need words."

I hear a thud, which I assume is him dropping to his knees as well and then his cool fingers touch mine.

"Faith."

"Yes?"

"Nothing."

"Stay with me?"

"You don't even need to ask."

"I'm sorry for what I put you through. I don't know if Sebastian explained..."

"He didn't."

Great. Of course he didn't try to make it easy for me. Big, fat, annoying alpha. Okay, he is only one of those things. Two at best.

"Are you in any trouble?"

"No."

"I'm sorry. I wasn't running from you. I needed to go to the family planning clinic. That's all. I didn't want to say. I was too shy, and we haven't had that conversation yet about kids and stuff." This was an easy conversation to have with a door between us.

"Oh."

"Do you want kids, Xander?"

"Never thought about it." His short tone tells me he is lying.

"Liar." I call him out. It's the best way with him, with all of them. They respond to directness. Playing games and pissing about will get me absolutely nowhere. It's liberating to speak my mind. I wish I'd been able to do it years ago. The rebel inside me is bursting to come out now.

He snorts. "That's not nice."

"Truth hurts."

"And the hits keep on coming."

"I can't smell lies, but I know you, Xander."

He sighs. "Faith. You are very precious. I am not cut out to raise a child."

"Of course you are. You have more love to give than you think. Your heart is big and beautiful."

"Fuck off," he grouses.

I snicker. "We can table that. I'm not ready for kids yet,

anyway. That was the whole point of the stupid endeavour that I went on."

His silence speaks volumes.

"Do you forgive me?"

"Nothing to forgive. You did what you felt was right for you. You are used to being on your own. You forget that you have four men here who would die for you. A lift into town is nothing, Faith. Please remember that in future."

"Okay," I whisper, tears pricking my eyes. "I don't deserve any of you."

"Stop that right now. I don't do pity parties. Get your act together because you won't get sympathy from me. I don't understand it."

"Ouch."

"Fact."

"Okay."

I smile and oddly feel a thousand times better about everything.

"I'm going to try to get some sleep," I say, stifling a yawn.

"I'll be here." He takes his fingers back, but I keep mine where they are. I have no intention of moving a muscle.

After a few moments, he grips my fingers again and settles down.

* * *

A few hours later, known by the bright, low sun shining through the window, I wake up to a commotion on the other side of the door.

A key turns in the lock and in my newly woken state, I'm too slow to move and when the door opens, I'm pushed along the carpet by a man with great strength behind the door.

"Eek!" I squeal as my fingers get trapped underneath and stop the progress.

"Shit! Faith!" Sebastian exclaims, crouching down and peering around the half-cracked door.

"Oww," I murmur and carefully pull my fingers back.

"What on earth are you doing on the floor?"

"I was sleeping with Xander," I mutter, blowing on my fingers.

Sebastian takes them and blows on them for me, kissing my fingertips. He looks back over his shoulder. "Xander isn't here."

"Oh," I say, disappointed he left me.

"I'm here," he says a moment later, the smell of coffee and toast filling my nostrils.

My stomach lets out a loud, embarrassing growl, which Sebastian does his best to ignore, but I can see by his lips that he is trying not to smile.

He helps me up and I let him without any fuss. He leads me over to the bed and settles me in the cosy warmth. I forget my sore fingers and reach for the coffee, taking a big gulp before I chomp down on the toast, finishing it in four bites.

"More?" I mumble indelicately, putting my hand up in front of my mouth so I don't spray the hot, sexy alphas with soggy toast crumbs.

"On its way," Xander says with a smile. "I didn't leave you. Not really."

"Same as me yesterday."

"You two have spoken about this?" Sebastian asks, his official prime alpha voice in place.

I nod. "Xander didn't forgive me yet," I say, throwing him to the wolves.

"Because there is nothing to forgive!" he exclaims hotly, his cheeks going red when Sebastian gives him a filthy look.

Giving him a smug smile and cheeky raised eyebrow, he huffs.

"Fine, I forgive you."

"Was that so hard?"

"Yes, actually. Because you have made me allude to a problem, but there isn't one. Not as far as I'm concerned."

"She wanted to hear you say it," Sebastian chides him.

He ignores that and me and sits on the floor next to the bed. I reach out and stroke his hair, leaning over to kiss the top of his head. "Thank you."

"Humph."

"Two down, two to go," I murmur.

"Be warned, Ben is in a bit of a mood," Sebastian remarks.

"When is he not?" I giggle.

The two men let out loud guffaws and I know I'm on solid ground with them again. Yes, we still need to have 'the talk', but that will come in its own time.

"Can I see Derek now? I still haven't spoken to him properly since I ran away."

"Yes," Sebastian says. "I'll send him up and we'll leave you two alone."

He gets up to leave, but I grab his hand. He stops and looks down at me with his blue eyes that makes me melt into a pile of goo. "Thank you for everything and thank you for not making a bigger deal out of the pills. I will be ready soon, but things need to be right, first."

He nods slowly. "I hear you. I want things right first too, but before all of that, you need to trust us, one hundred percent, Faith."

"I'm working on it," I murmur.

He lets go of my hand and leaves, with Xander following him. I know he's upset, but I can't go from semi trust to full trust literally overnight. He must know that.

"Sebastian?" I call out.

He stops, but it takes him a few seconds to turn around again.

"I want this. All of this. You four and everything you can give me. Just please give me a minute to sort out this..." I jab my head with my finger a few times.

He softens and smiles. "Minute given."

Then they leave me alone, wondering when the next lot of my fucking food is going to arrive.

# Chapter Forty-Four

Faith

Derek arrives with the rest of my food a few minutes later. He kicks the door open a bit more, and strides in with a tray piled high with food.

"Since when did you eat so much?" he asks, plonking it down on the bed next to me.

"Since I fucking well can. Jesus. A breakfast bowl of spaghetti with a teaspoon of pasta sauce might be in the past, but it also looms in my future if I fuck this up."

"Why would you fuck it up?"

"By doing stupid stuff, like yesterday." I stuff a muffin in my mouth and start to chew. "I don't know how to live like this."

"I know," he says with a sigh. "You've been so messed about, Faith and I'm sorry. I should've done more."

He looks so desolate, I feel bad.

I don't answer because I'm muffin-mouth, so he continues.

"They care about you, love you, even, Faith. I was really not sure about this at the beginning, but they are good guys. They will take care of you."

"Ish fat yur bleshing?" This time, I end up spraying Derek with muffin crumbs.

"Eww," he says, brushing them away. "Gross. Do that to them and you *will* fuck this up. But, yeah. You've got my blessing. Dad will be proud."

I nod and get a bit teary but then what he said, chills my blood and makes me freeze.

"What did you say?"

He smiles and taps the side of his nose. "Can't say too much, so don't even ask, but I think Dad is alive, Faith. I don't know where, but the guys are helping me. We'll find him. I promise."

"WHAT?" I roar, reaching out and grabbing the front of his t-shirt. "You fucking what?"

"Calm down," he says, unwrapping my hand from his shirt. "I know you have a million questions, but I can't answer them right now. You are just going to have to sit tight."

"Sit. Tight?" I grit out. "How long have you known about this?"

"Since the day he died. Well, not exactly. I knew there was something weird going on. I've been investigating. It's all lead to Pete being involved so he could take over Dad's life."

I blink as that hits me square between the eyes. "What?" I ask now, in a lower tone. "What?"

"I know it sounds insane and I didn't want to say anything, but I can't keep it from you anymore. You deserve to know."

"Dad is alive?"

He nods. "But you don't know where?"

He shakes his head.

"How sure are you?" My voice quivers and I clench my hand into a fist so I can keep it together.

"Sure enough to be able to tell you now."

"Fuck. And Pete did this?"

"It looks that way."

"I'm going to fucking KILL HIM!" I thunder, getting off the bed and storming towards the door.

"Whoa," Harvey says, appearing in the doorway, effectively blocking me from going anywhere. "Who are you going to kill?"

"Pete," I growl.

Harvey exchanges a look with Derek, who just shrugs. He sighs and rubs his hand over his face. "We agreed we wouldn't tell her yet."

"Oh no!" I scream, going slightly homicidal and launching myself at Harvey. "You don't get to keep secrets like that from me. Trust? Trust? You want me to fucking trust you?"

"Hang on a minute," Harvey yells at me, to try to get me to listen to him over my shrieking.

"No, *you* hang on a minute! You had no right, none of you." Spinning around, I make a sweeping gesture with my broken arm and end up whacking someone in the chest with it.

"Owww!" I scream, pissed off now.

"Faith," Sebastian says. Being the one I whacked, he seems decidedly calm. "We didn't want to get your hopes up."

"My arm," I squeak with tears pouring out of my eyes.

"Okay, yes. Doctor Fancy-pants is waiting downstairs." He gives me a cautious smile.

"Did he bring his portable x-ray thingie?" I sniff.

"Well, more like an entire x-ray unit, but it's downstairs and waiting for you."

I nod, worn out and in agony. I allow Sebastian to help me down the stairs, while I cradle my arm gingerly.

"I'm sorry we didn't tell you," he whispers into my ear. "We didn't tell you, to protect you."

"That's not fair. I had a right to know, and you can't be mad at me for sneaking out, when you've been keeping a huge secret from me."

"I know," he says, looking down, reasonably chastised for a prime alpha. He's humouring me, I'm sure.

I lose all my fight under the screaming pain in my arm. "Please fix me."

"I'll try my best," he says with a smile, and I lean into him, enjoying his strength as he props me up and leads me down the stairs and long hallway at the bottom, to a previously unseen room, that indeed reveals, an entire x-ray unit.

I sit dutifully and wince when Fancy-pants takes the makeshift cast off, softly crying when he positions it where he needs it. As I sit there, I wonder how much all of this cost Sebastian to arrange. A few grand, he said. Nope. A few hundred grand? More like.

Soon I'm all done and being led over to another area where a friendly looking nurse is preparing my real cast.

"Will you be the first to sign it?" I ask Sebastian with a wan smile.

"Always, baby girl," he murmurs, kissing the top of my head and staying right by my side. "I'm sorry we let this happen to you. If we had been a few seconds earlier…"

I adore him so much in that moment. He didn't blame me by saying, 'if you hadn't gone', but at the same time it makes me feel sad that he's blaming himself.

This situation sucks.

Thinking about other people sucks.

Actually, no it doesn't. It's just this situation.

"I'm sorry for disappearing. I absolutely will not in the future."

"Are you saying there *is* a future?" he asks carefully.

"Yes. A long, beautiful, bright one, if you'll have me."

"Fuck's sake, baby girl. You're going to be the death of me."

I grin up at him and he smiles back, bending down to kiss me on the mouth. He, they, all of them, still owe me a full explanation of what the fuck is going on with my dad, but knowing that he might be alive, and they are trying to find him, is enough for now.

Chapter Forty-Five

Faith

A couple of hours later, all casted up and the pain numbed again, I sit in front of Ben and Harvey with a contrite look on my face, in Sebastian's austere office.

"I'm sorry for being a tit and running off like that. I wasn't thinking about anyone except myself. You must understand that is the way my mind works. It's not an excuse, I'm just explaining the way it is. I've been taking care of myself since Pete the prick started being a knob. I don't want it to be that way anymore. I want to consider you all, I *will* in future. Please forgive me for scaring you, and for making you come and get me."

"Oh, petal," Harvey says, coming to me and kissing the top of my head. "We don't give a fuck that you went out, but it's that you didn't tell us, tried to do it on your own, nearly lost a butt cheek and an eye in the process, got your arm snapped and nearly abducted."

"Nice recap," I murmur. "Thank you for that."

He snickers and I know we're okay. Ben though, he *is* in a mood.

"I don't care about people," he states bluntly.

"Oh." My cheeks blush furiously at that not so nice piece of information.

"I don't. Ask anyone. Okay, maybe these three pillocks, but no one else outside my family. So when you disappeared and we thought the worst, it felt like I was dying inside. It was horrible, absolutely fucking awful, and I don't ever want to feel that way again. I need to be able to trust you, Faith, because if you ever do something like this again, I won't be as forgiving."

"I'm sorry I made you feel that way, Ben. I promise that I won't ever do anything like that again."

He comes to me, wrapping his arms around me, careful of my arm. "I'm beyond pissed off about this," he says stroking my cast. "How am I supposed to tie you to a chair buck naked now?"

I giggle. "DFP said it wasn't that bad. Two weeks in this and then two weeks in a wrist strap thing."

He frowns. "DFP?"

"Doctor Fancy-pants," Sebastian says, his mirth bubbling up so badly, he snorts and then roars with laughter.

"Well, no one ever told me his real name, so I had to make it up," I state huffily.

"St. James," Ben grits out. "He's my dad."

"Noooooooo!" I wail. "Are you joking?"

He shakes his head, a smile playing on his lips.

"Oh, please don't tell him!"

"Oh, I'm telling him. It's your punishment, kitty. He will get a massive crack out of it, so don't worry."

"God," I groan, throwing my head back.

He grasps my chin and tilts my head forward. "Forgiven."

"Thank you."

He kisses me lightly and then lets me go.

"About the reason you left. We need to have a conversation about that."

"I know. The birth control. Look, I do want kids, just not quite yet. Maybe in a year? I hope that's not too long for all of you?" I sit chewing my lip nervously. I've thought about this long and hard. They need a timeline. That's fair and a year isn't that long. I'm sure we will be well settled and happy to start breeding by then.

"The thing is, baby girl, I want to impregnate you now so badly, it makes my dick ache," Sebastian says, his voice, dark and sexy. He almost makes it sound like it turns him on. "Knowing that you didn't get pregnant during your heat, makes me really sad."

"Oh," I mutter. "I'm sorry?" I don't know why I'm apologising.

He shakes his head. "There is nothing we can do about it now, but I'm going to need you to bend on that timeline."

"Uhm."

"I want my baby inside you, Faith. I want to plant my seed and watch it grow. I want to watch your belly blossom with our child. I want to run my hands over the bump. I want to kiss it and make love to you when you are about ready to drop. It's not just a need, baby girl. It's a desire. I want to breed with you, and I want it soon."

"Wow," I whisper. I didn't know this was a thing. He is seriously turned on, going off the bulge in his pants. "I'll think about it."

"Think hard, kitty," Ben says, his tone also sultry and sexy. "We all want what Sebastian does. We want our omega pregnant and popping out babies that we made with you."

"Mmm-hmm." I don't know what else to say. I'm a bit overwhelmed. A baby here and there was my plan, he makes it sound like it's going to be me up the duff for the next several years.

"We love you, Faith," Harvey adds. "We want this more than anything."

I notice that Xander hasn't chimed in yet. He is watching this from over by the door, looking more than tetchy.

"What about you?" I ask him.

He looks startled to be included and straightens up. "You know my thoughts on that already."

"Do they?"

He grimaces at me as the other three men turn to look at him.

I feel bad, but I'm glad the heat has been taken off me for a minute or two. It was getting seriously warm in here with all the talk of breeding.

"Xander?" Sebastian prompts when he doesn't say anything.

"Look, do I want kids? I don't know. How can I be a dad when I can't even look after myself? This is not a conversation I want to have right now. Faith, we've already talked about this."

He turns on his heel and storms out, slamming the door behind him in a very clear sign of stay the fuck away from me.

Three pairs of eyes swivel back to me.

"Dammit, Xander," I mutter under my breath. "Hmm."

"That's about as non-committal as it gets, Faith," Sebastian says.

"I can't give you the answer you want right now. It's all moot until my next heat anyway."

"Well, we can agree on that. But by next quarter, I want you off those pills so I can mate with you properly. Am I making myself clear?"

"That's soon."

"Not soon enough," he snarls and storms out of the office, leaving me a bit shocked by how this conversation ended up.

I look to Ben and Harvey to see if they are feeling the same way, and it's pretty clear, they want this as badly as Sebastian does.

"Can you ask him to come back," I croak out. "I have something to say."

Harvey nods and goes to get him, dragging him back into the office miffed and growling. "What is it?"

"Get something straight on your end," I say, standing up and jabbing my finger in his direction. "No matey, no baby. I will not be some whore you use to pop out your heir and then you throw me out on the street." I know, I *think* I know that's not what would happen, but an omega needs reassurances.

"When have I *ever* given you that impression?" he retorts incredulously.

"Like when you snatched me off the street!" I shriek. Okay, so this is becoming a huge problem that I can't get past. I thought I could, but clearly, I still have issues with it.

He blinks but says nothing.

The room goes silent as the elephant parades around the room, and we all ignore it, stewing in our own thoughts and problems.

He can fix this with one action.

But he doesn't.

And therein lies the problem which throws us into an impasse.

We don't trust each other enough.

# Chapter Forty-Six

Xander

Needing to get away from the situation back in Sebastian's office, I snatch my phone out of pocket and text Derek. He messages straight back with good news. Grimly, I grab a set of keys from the rack and slip outside. The black Bentley is all ready and waiting to go after being washed and cleaned inside, so I click the remote and get in. I start it up and creep as quietly as I can out of the driveway. I don't want anyone to know where I'm going. Not just yet.

They will try to stop me.

There will be tears and recriminations, but I can't sit on this a minute longer when someone is suffering abuse from a deranged prick. I may not know Faith's mum, but I know Faith, and she would want her mother safe. The other alphas would probably take a different approach, but there is only one way to treat a bully and that is to give them something to shit themselves over.

That's me.

I have no intention of letting Pete live, but I'm going to make damn sure he knows terror before he goes on his way down to hell.

After opening the gates, I drive through and close them, turning right and heading out onto the main road.

I like driving. I like cars. I understand how they work. If I had been made to go out and get a job, I probably would've tried to be an engineer. As it happens, I don't get on with ninety-nine-point-nine percent of the population, so for me, working is not an option. Luckily, I have enough in my trust to give me the freedom to stay the fuck away from people and things. I'm just waiting for the day my bitch mother goes to hell and leaves the rest of the trust that is owed to me. But she is clinging to it with her crooked, claw-like hands. I hear she isn't long for this world. Alone, washed up and shunned after what my bastard stepdad did to me, she has sunk into a bottle of vodka and hasn't come up for air.

*Good.*

I hope she rots in it and hurries the fuck up. I need that money to start contributing more to the estate. I won't be a burden to any fucker, not even Sebastian.

Pressing the accelerator down as soon as I get onto the motorway, I head North. The Bentley smoothly eats up the miles and it's not long before I'm nearing the town where Faith used to live. Derek said to meet him at a petrol station on the outskirts of town. I keep my eyes peeled, and spot it as I turn the corner, he said it was on.

I pull in next to a beat-up old Vectra and get out. Derek is leaning against the car, giving me a sceptical look.

"Are you trying to get noticed?" he asks me, raising his eyebrow.

I glance back at the car and shrug. "Is he home?"

"Yep. You sure you want to do this?"

"Couldn't be surer."

He nods, giving me a look of respect and hands over the house keys.

"Does your mum know I'm coming?"

"She knows someone is coming over and she isn't going to get in the way."

"Probably best she doesn't know the details."

"Exactly."

Gripping the keys in my fist, I turn back to the Bentley. "Don't tell Faith. I want to tell her myself."

"Won't say a word."

"Thanks."

I climb back into the car and head the way to the address that Derek sent to my phone, and I input into the Satnav.

A few minutes later, I'm pulling up to a rundown, crappy terraced house, and grimace at it. Poor Faith. She deserves so much more than this life she was living. Climbing out and locking the Bentley – Seb would kill me if it got nicked – I head up to the faded red door with the paint peeling off it and slip the key into the lock. I turn it and enter quietly.

The downstairs is all open plan and I see the frail looking woman by the kitchen sink, doing dishes. She turns to me, and it takes me aback how much Faith looks like her. Or would if this woman wasn't bedraggled and beaten.

She gives me a smile, and then she ignores me and goes back to the dishes.

I drop the keys on the small round table and make my way up the stairs. Derek informed me that Pete spends most of his time watching TV on the bed, in the bedroom. Lazy fucker.

I shove the door open at the end of the hallway, enjoying the look of annoyance on his face that turns to surprise.

"Who the fuck are you?" he growls, hauling his arse off the

bed. He is dressed in a grungy t-shirt and jeans, and he stinks of booze and smoke.

"Me? I'm your worst fucking nightmare."

I bare my teeth and give in to the savage side of myself that rarely gets a chance to come out. I leap forward and land on top of Pete, ready to give him a taste of his own medicine.

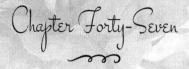

## Chapter Forty-Seven

Sebastian

Not usually one to shy away from awkward situations, this one kind of takes the cake. I never in my wildest dreams thought I would be the one to fight for a family. I thought the omega we chose would be falling over herself in that department. Sure, my need to breed has always been there, simmering under the surface, but as soon as I caught Faith's aroma, it developed into something so much deeper, more erotic and primal. The thought of impregnating her gets my dick so hard, I want to attempt it right now, even though I know it won't happen.

We stare at each other as the grandfather clock ticks away in the corner.

"Fuck's sake," Faith blurts out. "That fucking clock is fucking annoying as shite."

Unexpectedly, I laugh, easing the tension slightly.

"Look," Faith says with a heavy sigh. "We obviously have a bit of a problem here. I don't know what to suggest."

"Me either." I join in with the sighing, but coming to a decision. "I think the only solution is that we have to prove to you how much we care about you and that you will never be thrown out on the street. You hold all the cards, baby girl. We knew we needed you months before you even knew we existed. There is absolutely no way that you should be the one to bend. It needs to be us. I know that in my head. My alpha heart needs to catch up. If by your next heat, you aren't ready, then I won't pressure you, but know, please, Faith, I need you to *know* that not having a family will devastate me, so if you aren't going to give me one, and you are just saying this because you think you should, then I really need to know now."

"Why, so you can throw me out?" she asks coldly.

"No, so I can get used to the idea of not being a father."

Tears pour out of her eyes, and it takes everything I have, not to do the same. She will rip my heart out if she says it's not going to happen.

"Wow," she says, blowing out a breath. "You really want me that much that you'd give up having a family? Are you fucking insane?"

Startled by the question, I look to Ben for help.

He doesn't have any.

Neither does Harvey.

Fucking useless twats.

"Yeah, I guess I must be," I say eventually.

She snorts. "Fucking hell, man. How can I not trust you after that? I've given you a reason to throw me out on my arse and yet you choose me over having a family. That wasn't a test, by the way." She shakes her head. "Well, I suppose it *was* in a way, but I didn't mean it that way. I need to know that *I'm* the most important thing to you, and I guess you think I am. I need that security after everything I've been through."

I daren't even breathe. We are actually making some headway. Ben and Harvey are like stone statues. If they don't move soon, I'll have to go and stick them in the middle of the topiary garden as lawn ornaments.

"You are, and you have it," I whisper, hoping I don't scare her into changing her mind.

She nods slowly and stands up.

Then she walks towards me.

I step closer, anticipating the hug we are going to share, but she stalks straight past me, leaving me wanting and thanking God that I didn't open my arms for her.

My heart is crushed.

I can't even look at the other men.

I turn and watch her leave my office, feeling sick to my stomach.

* * *

I haven't moved a muscle in a few minutes. I can hear Ben take a step forward, but I shake my head, still staring blankly at where Faith left.

I blink when she reappears suddenly. She gives me a shaky smile and holds something up.

It takes me a few seconds to realise what it is.

Her birth control pills.

Watching her closely, she crosses over to the fireplace and throws the three packets into the fire.

"Oh," I breathe out in shock.

She turns with a bright smile.

I reach her in two giant strides, sweeping her off her feet and twirling her around, laughing happily that this hasn't ended in tears.

"Really?" I ask, dropping her lightly to her feet, but keeping hold of her.

235

She nods. "Yeah, really. You made me feel more secure in a few seconds than I ever thought I would be. I *do* want a family with you, Sebastian. And Ben and Harvey and Xander, if he gets over himself long enough to know he will make a great dad."

I snort. "Yeah, I think we need to work on making him more secure as well."

"Well, how about we do the mating now, and then everyone gets what they want?"

"I was fucking hoping you'd say that." I lean down and claim her mouth with mine, twisting my tongue around hers and wishing I could lay her down and ravage her body until my seed implants in her womb. I groan as the pressure of not doing that gets to me. It's not the right time. It will lead to nothing, and she needs to rest after her heat.

"Go and find Xander," I murmur before I kiss her again, losing my soul to this tiny, curvy, sexy, blonde omega and capturing hers at the same time.

"He's gone."

Ben's voice cuts into my happy kissing time.

"What?" I ask, pulling away and looking up. "Where to?"

"I don't know, but we should find him before he does something...Xander-ish."

"Fuck," I mutter and let go of Faith. "Fuck."

I march out of the office, and she follows me. "Stay here," I order her.

"Nope. He responds to me. If he's out there feeling bad because of what I said to him, then I need to help find him and bring him back."

I deliberate for all of two seconds. She's right. Xander responds to her like no other creature on earth. Not even Ben and I can get through to him the way she does.

"Okay," I say, and see her breathe out in relief. "Let's go."

## Chapter Forty-Eight

Faith

We all pile into a Range Rover, the same one that Harvey chucked me into yesterday. The feeling of dread I had then is nothing compared to the apprehension I feel now. Looking outside, the weather is gloomy, like the mood in the car. It starts to rain, and Ben turns on the windscreen wipers. I watch the slow sweep of them across the windscreen as Sebastian hastily checks his phone.

"Anything?" Ben clips out.

"Switched off." Sebastian's reply is just as curt.

"Dammit."

"Do you know where he would go?" I ask tentatively.

"Yeah, there's a few places," Sebastian mutters, only half focused on me.

I decide to remain silent unless I'm spoken to, so I turn my head and look out of the side window. Hunching further into the cream leather interior, I chew my lip in worry. This was *my* doing. I pushed him and he wasn't comfortable, so he disappeared. I feel a sense of overwhelming guilt and I hope that he is okay and coping. He needs me, but I'm the one who hurt him, so I'm not sure how that works. I guess I will have to leave it to him when we find him, take my cues from him, as it were.

After we've swung by a park about fifteen minutes from the Manor with no luck, and I was told to stay in the car, we set off again to another location. This one in the opposite direction and getting further from home.

Home.

The Manor is my home now, I just have to keep remembering that and trying to find my place in it.

Sebastian's phone rings. He snatches it up off the middle console and answers it. "Matt."

I try not to look too interested in the conversation. I desperately don't want any of the alphas to think I'm into him or anything. I never was, but a quick shag in a pub toilet cubicle is still a shag and I think they might be worried about us. I will need to set the record straight about that. Now, obviously, isn't the time for that though.

I chew my lip a bit more, wondering if I've still got that tube of Lypsyl in the bottom of my backpack, when Sebastian hangs up.

"Matt hasn't seen him, but is going to the cemetery, just in case he decides he needs to do something stupid."

*Cemetery?*

Would that be the one where his stepdad is buried?

"Is his dad still alive?" I blurt out and then wish I'd stuck to the memo and kept my mouth shut.

"Yeah," Harvey replies kindly. "But he doesn't see him. Hasn't since the day he left."

"Do you know why he left?"

Harvey shrugs. "He doesn't talk about it, but I don't think he knows. He was only ten."

238

My heart weeps for him. I can picture him, a little Xander, waiting for his dad to come home but he never does.

"How awful."

"Definitely not normal," Sebastian spits out.

I flinch from his tone. I'm not sure if he is having a go at me and my concerns.

"We would never do that to you," Ben states. "So please don't think that."

"I don't," I croak out, but they all know it's a lie.

At least the lie-detector isn't in the car to reprimand me about my stinky lies. That reminds me. I need to ask him what my lies smell like? I'm madly curious, and will probably be a bit grossed out when he informs me they smell like dog crap or whatever.

I jump when my phone rings.

It is stuffed into the back pocket of my old jeans. I really need to get Derek to bring me my stuff. It's not a ton of clothes, but it's more than one pair of jeans and a pair of joggers. I whip it out and see an unrecognised number.

"Hello?" I answer hesitantly.

"Faith." Xander's voice comes down the line, soft and warm.

"Xander! Where are you? We are out looking for you."

Ben swerves and pulls over onto the side of the road. The three alphas turn to look at me, Sebastian making a 'gimme' gesture to the phone.

I shake my head.

He rang *me*.

If he wanted to speak to Sebastian, he'd have rung him.

"Give me that phone," Sebastian grits out, holding his hand out.

"No," I mouth and slap his hand away. "Where are you?" I say into the phone.

"Are you silently fighting with Seb?" he asks instead.

"How did you know?" I give Sebastian an eyeroll, which he grimaces at.

Xander snickers, but then goes serious. "Faith. I need you to listen to me. I'm at your house."

I blink. It takes me a few seconds to realise that he means my old house, not the Manor. "Oh?" My voice goes slightly squeaky. "Uhm..."

"What?" Sebastian hisses. "Where is he?"

I wave my hand to get him to shut up.

"Why are you there?" I ask in my still squeaky voice.

"I've taken care of a problem for you," he states. "Can you meet me here?"

"Yes, yes, of course," I stammer. "I'll tell Ben."

He's hung up before I've even finished speaking.

"Go to my old house. I think Xander has done something..."

"Xander-ish?" Ben asks.

"I'm not really sure what that means, but I guess so. The address is..."

"I know it."

"Oh."

He indicates and sets off, heading towards the motorway.

The car is silent, but not that awkward. I wonder what everyone is thinking about. I'm nervous about what Xander has done. What problem did he take care of? Has he had a word with Pete? Or worse? I vaguely know what he did to his own stepdad. It's not a great leap to imagine what he might've done to mine.

Harvey unclips my seatbelt and I lie down with my head on his lap, holding my broken arm out of the way. He strokes my hair, but we still don't speak. I don't think anyone wants to break the silence and potentially make the unthinkable a reality.

I fall into a quiet doze on Harvey's lap, comfortable and feeling safe on the outside, but my insides are in turmoil.

"He'll be okay," Harvey whispers to me eventually.

"Pete?" I murmur.

He snorts. "No, Xander."

"Oh, fuck. Sorry, I'm half asleep. Yeah, I hope so. Aren't you worried about what he's done to Pete?"

"Are you?"

"Am I awful for saying I hope Xander hurt him?"

"No."

"Not for Pete but for Xander."

"Xander can take care of himself."

"No, he can't."

"He can. He is stronger than he thinks, and he has you."

I smile slowly. "He does."

"He needs you." He leans over and kisses me softly.

"I need him too. I need all of you. I can't wait to reach Xander and bring him home."

"Home," Sebastian murmurs. "I like the sound of that, baby girl."

My smile widens, I know everything is going to be okay. "Me too."

## Chapter Forty-Nine

Harvey

I sit contemplatively stroking Faith's hair as she sleeps. We are nearing the place where she used to live. I have been through almost every possible situation that will greet us when we get there. I just hope that Faith is ready for it. Whatever it is.

We see the Bentley outside a crappy terraced house, and I glance down at Faith. I brush her cheek with the back of my hand, and she stirs.

"Are we there?" she mumbles.

"Yes."

Her eyes snap open and she sits up, looking around and grimacing when she spots the house.

"I don't want any of you to come inside," she mumbles.

"You're not going in there alone."

"Harvey, please," she begs me. "I don't want any of you seeing where I used to live."

I take her hand. "Faith. Please, don't make us send you in

there alone. We don't know what happened. We don't care about where you used to live."

She glances at Seb and Ben, chewing her lip. I know what she's thinking. We grew up a world away from her, but she needs to be reminded of something.

"We are no better than you. They don't think so and I know it. We love you for you, Faith. It doesn't matter to us."

She smiles sadly. "I wish you could've seen the house I grew up in. Much nicer than this dump."

"You can show us one day."

She nods slowly and climbs out of the car.

Seb and Ben follow her quickly, as do I. There is no way she is going into a situation that could be dangerous. I don't even mean that physically, necessarily, but mentally.

She walks up to the door and stops. "Stay here, please," she says to us.

"Not a chance, petal."

I'm about to barge past her to open the door myself, when it swings open to reveal Xander standing there looking like something the cat dragged in.

"Uhm," Faith stammers when she sees his bloodstained t-shirt and mussed up hair.

"You three stay out here," Xander says, taking Faith by the elbow and dragging her inside. He slams the door closed and bolts it, leaving us outside, worried about what's going to happen.

"He won't hurt her," Sebastian says, trying to be reassuring.

"Oh, I know that," I retort. "But what the fuck mess is in there that she is now confronted with on her own?"

"She's not on her own," Ben says quietly. "We have to remember that Xander is one of us."

The simple reminder that we love and trust him calms me

down. I was about to kick the door in, but now I'll stay on this side and put my trust in him.

"Do you think he killed him?" I whisper to the other two alphas.

"If he hasn't, I'm going in there to finish him off," Sebastian growls ferociously.

"Get in line," Ben mutters.

I cross my arms, drumming my fingers in a staccato beat that is irritating, yet soothing at the same time. It's pitch black outside now and we are getting shady looks from some curtain twitchers across the road. Suddenly, everyone seems to be out walking their dog, child, elderly parents so they can sken at us, whispering about what we're doing here.

Drug dealers seems to be winning the poll, the longer we stand out here like mugs.

"Okay, enough," I growl and step forward to kick the door in, my boot connecting with the old door, and breaking the lock easily. Paint chips and wood fly off in all directions. I shove the door open and storm inside, being caught off-guard when I see Xander locked in an embrace with a frail older lady as she cries on his shoulder. Faith is standing by with a smile on her face that she is trying to hide, but it is shining through.

"Everything okay in here?" I growl.

"Perfect," Faith says and beckons me over as Seb and Ben enter the house behind me. "Harvey, this is my mum, Anne. Mum, this is Sebastian, Harvey and Ben."

"Hello," she says, pulling away from Xander and wiping her tears away with a ragged tissue.

We murmur back.

"Come with me," Xander says to us, turning towards the back door, situated on the far side of the downstairs kitchen area.

Exchanging worried looks, we follow Xander outside. He hands me a shovel and indicates the far side of the garden.

"Please tell me we aren't digging a grave," I hiss at him. "Do you know how many people have seen us loitering out here? They are probably watching us now from their back windows."

"Grave's already full," Xander says.

"Jesus. Where?"

He indicates back to the house. "Inside the wall. No one will find him for a while. We need to move Anne out of here, as far away as possible."

I nod slowly and then look at the shovel. Holding it up, I ask, "What the fuck is this for then?" I ask.

"Anne buried a shoebox of cash over in the back corner under the apple tree. Go and dig it up for her."

"Oh," I murmur and head off to do as I'm told, slightly bewildered by events, but rolling with it because Faith seems okay. More than okay. She seemed...free.

I crack on with the task at hand, ramming the spade into the ground and shoving my foot down on it. I'm no stranger to a bit of yard work. My Scottish grandfather used to make me dig his garden up ready for planting in the Spring. And when I say garden, I mean extensive Scottish country estate grounds. 'Idle hands make the devil's work' was his favourite saying. No heir of his was sitting on his arse all day doing fuck all. But I enjoyed it. I start digging and soon, I come across the box. Feeling like a pirate with my buried treasure, I grin and scoop it up out of the ground, only now looking over to see that Ben and Seb are doing the same. Seems Anne had a whole garden full of treasure she was keeping a secret from her arse-hole husband.

I head back to Xander and hand the box over, following him back inside. Xander gives the box to Anne. She gives me a grateful smile and places the box on the small round table. Opening it, her smile widens and then she closes it and hands it to Faith.

"Take this and go," she says. "Live your life the way your father wanted."

"Mum," Faith says, tears brimming her eyes. "Dad…"

"Would want you to do as your mum says," I interrupt her. We can't get this woman's hopes up that her husband is still alive if we never find him.

Faith gives me a filthy look, but she nods and keeps her mouth shut. I understand her need to ease her mother's pain, but now isn't the time. We need her husband in our hands to give to her.

"Go and pack a bag, and let's go," Faith says instead. "Sebastian. Can I have a word please?"

He nods and they go off into a corner, but we all know what she is asking him. He will say yes, and we will all agree that Anne can live in the Manor with us. It's the least we can do for her for giving us the greatest gift on earth. Her daughter, Faith.

## Chapter Fifty

Faith

"I know what you're going to say, and of course your mother is welcome at the Manor," Sebastian says before I can open my mouth to say anything.

"I'll pay for her upkeep until we find my dad," I whisper. "I'll go out and get a job, so we aren't sitting around expecting you to pay for everything."

He sighs. "Oh, Faith. When will you realise that you belong with us? Our omega doesn't have to work to pay for anything. You will be given whatever you need with no strings attached. This is unconditional, baby girl. I wish you would get it through your pretty head."

His smile is almost sad.

"I don't work that way," I start, but he puts his finger over my lips.

"You do now. And while we're at it, there is a shipment of clothes coming in tomorrow. That is what I wanted to tell you when I came looking for you yesterday and found you missing."

I'm horrified. *Mortified,* even. I shake my head. "No. Absolutely not. I'm here now, I can pack up the rest of my stuff and Derek still has some of my things…"

"Faith." He takes my shaking hands. "Stop. I want to do this for you. I want you to feel like the Manor is your home and I want you to have all the things your heart desires. Please, let me give you stuff that makes you happy. I want to see you smile and enjoy them."

I hesitate. As tempted as I am, it's just wrong. "It sounds like you're trying to buy me."

"No, absolutely not. I already have you, don't I?"

The challenge in his alpha tone is unmistakable. There is no way out of this corner I've painted myself into.

"Yes, of course…"

"Then what you are saying makes no sense. I see no reason why you can't accept what I can offer."

"I guess." I look down. I can't help feeling humiliated. He doesn't get it.

"I get it," he says, lifting my chin up. "I'll cancel the order. Let's go and pack your things and ask Derek to bring the rest of your stuff."

I peek up at him. "Really?"

"Really."

"I'm sorry. Maybe one day?"

"Stop apologising, Faith. You have nothing to be sorry for. I'm learning that you are very independent, even though you have a need to be loved and cared for, that independence means a lot to you. I get it."

"Thank you," I say and pull him to me to hold. "You are the kindest man I've ever met."

"Uh-uh, King Dick, remember."

"You're all talk," I pretend-mock him.

He chuckles. "You will never see that side of me unless someone has hurt you. I don't want you to see the bad." His serious tone cuts off the barb I was about to make about his king dong. "And your mother is more than welcome."

"Can I say I think I'm falling in love with you?" I ask tentatively.

His eyes light up which is so sweet, I nearly cry. "Oh, you can say that as often as you like and when you *do* fall in love with me, I will be the happiest alpha in the world."

I cup his face and kiss him softly, but then turn back to the rest of the men and my mum. "I'm going to pack."

"I'll help," Xander says straight away.

I nod, knowing he needs to be near me to seek the reassurances that what he did was okay. It is more than okay. He protected my family from a monster and got him to confess that he arranged for one of the most dangerous gangs of alphas to kidnap my dad. He doesn't know where they took him. Xander believes him. Apparently, he pissed himself and confessed all before Xander had even gotten warmed up. I make my way upstairs and as I pass the small room that Derek used to occupy, I stop. He is in there, fixing up the hole in the partition wall that separates our two rooms. Pressing my lips together, I watch for a minute. The hole is nearly gone and Pete with it.

"We'll pay the rent on this place for six months, just to keep anyone out while he rots," Xander says quietly.

I nod, but don't say anything. I have no words. Taking his hand and giving it a squeeze, I lead him to my room where he gets to work setting out all my clothes and belongings. I wonder where I'm going to put it all, when Matt appears with some boxes.

"Thanks," I say with a smile. "Right on time."

"Let's get you out of this dump," he says and helps Xander fill the boxes.

I watch them for a moment. How did this happen? How did fate hook me up with a one-night stand that led to my ultimate destiny? It's crazy and trying to think about it too much is giving me a headache.

After a while, Matt moves on to help Harvey pack up my mum's stuff, and Xander takes my things downstairs and out to the waiting SUV that Matt drove here. The seats are already flattened for moving all our stuff and that's when it finally, truly hits me.

These alphas would do absolutely anything for me. They *have* done everything for me.

I'm not falling in love with them, I have fallen in love with them.

Truly and completely.

They are my everything, and I will do anything for them in return. I made a big gesture before with Sebastian even though I still had a small doubt in the back of my mind about having babies so soon.

I don't now.

There isn't a single doubt in my mind about what I want.

I want them and I want to be their omega who will give them the family they deserve as soon as I possibly can.

# Chapter Fifty-One

Benjamin

It's been a week since we got Faith home and unpacked. She has settled into the routine of the Manor quite well, although she is still reluctant to allow the maid to do anything for her. The cook, on the other hand, is a whole other story. Faith revels in the delicious meals and it's a joy to see her so happy.

The only dark cloud is that we haven't found her father yet. We will. We will absolutely not stop looking until he is found. Pete sold him out for a fair portion of cash that he did not factor into his ability to spend like an arsehole, and with his lack of common sense that without a job or proper investments, it was going to run out eventually is why they ended up the way they did. The gang has gone underground, but we will find them.

Sebastian will sniff them out, and then they are doomed. Xander is itching to rip them apart for causing Faith so much hurt.

Well, we all are. But some of us prefer to keep it under wraps or find other ways in which to channel the psycho.

Take me, for example. I am naked and currently have Faith tied to a chair, in the middle of her pure white room, mindful of her broken arm and with her full consent, of course. She is blindfolded and buck naked, her legs spread open so that I can see her clit glistening with her slick as this is turning her on and I haven't even started yet. She is a minx. Harvey is sitting on the bed, riveted to this scene in front of him.

"Now then, kitty. You are completely at my mercy. What can I do to you to please myself?"

She whimpers her response. Her lips trembles at the thought that anything could happen. "Anything you want," she purrs.

That sound is music to my ears. I growl softly and drop to my knees in front of her. I flick my tongue over her clit, making her shiver.

"How's that, beautiful?"

"Purrrfect."

"Oh, clever kitty, aren't you? Can I kiss you on that smart mouth?"

She nods.

Instead of placing my lips to hers, I take my cock in my hand and press my tip to her mouth. "Open up like a good girl and lick my cock. I want to feel your filthy tongue slide down my shaft, making me harder for you. Do you want that, kitty?"

She nods and opens her mouth. "Good girl," I murmur, mesmerised by her little pink tongue wrapping around my stiff dick. "That feels so good. You are making me feel so good with your perfectly slutty little mouth, kitty."

Faith lets out another little purr that hardens my cock like iron.

I remove my dick from her mouth and lean over to slide my fingers over her slippery clit and then dip them deep inside her. She wiggles on the chair, bound and unable to escape me. "Come for me, like a good little kitty."

Her breathing is heavy, and she starts to pant. I finger-fuck her deliciously slowly. I press my other thumb down on her clit and rotate as I twist my fingers deep into her.

She moans softly and slick coats my fingers. "Oh, yes, Faith. You are so special, so precious."

Her body shudders as she comes for me, flooding the chair underneath her with her slick.

With a slow smile, I remove my hands from her and indicate to Harvey to join us. His cock is already stiff from watching me with our omega.

"I need you to suck Harvey's cock like a good little girl," I murmur to her, letting my tone soothe her and drop over her like a warm blanket.

Faith opens her mouth and takes Harvey's enormous size between her lips. He groans and throws his head back as Faith gives him a blowjob that looks absolutely heavenly.

"You are so dirty," I growl softly. "A dirty little slut who will do anything I tell her to, aren't you?"

She twitches at my words. They are affecting her deeply and that is what I want. I want her to reach an orgasm without me touching her again. Her clit is already sensitive and ready for more after her first climax, so this should be sinfully easy to do. It thrills me. It excites me beyond anything I have ever felt before. No other sexual encounter has even come close to this. They are all forgotten, never to be thought of again. All I want is Faith. She is my everything.

I turn my head as the door opens quietly and I see Sebastian and Xander there, having received my summons. His face tells me everything I need to know.

They have news.

I nod and step forward to end this before it even got

started so that Faith can learn what they know, but Sebastian's hand on my arm stops me.

He wants me to see this through before we tell her anything. It seems cruel to keep her in the dark, but she is so delectable right now, it doesn't deter me from murmuring, "Everyone is here now, kitty. They are going to line up and fuck your sweet pussy. You are going to service them like a filthy whore, slicking all over their cocks, moaning your pleasure as they ram their dicks into you one after the other, relentlessly, seeking your screams of ecstasy at the same time you beg them for mercy."

Her muffled noise of raw lust makes my cock jerk. My eyes are riveted to her clit again. I want to see her convulse and pulsate. I *need* to see it.

"Step away, Harvey," I instruct quietly. "Let Faith wonder who is going to fuck her first. Who will be the lucky alpha to slide his rock-hard cock into her tight wet pussy?"

"Uhn," she moans, her nipples going tauter.

"When we are all done with your pussy, sweet kitty, we are going to turn you around and ride your perfect arse until we fill that hole up with cum, so that it drips out of you and down the back of your thighs. I'm going to record it and post it on the internet so that everyone can see what a dirty girl you are. I want everyone to see you so full of cum, you can't even keep it inside you. I want them to watch you giving me creampie after creampie, wishing they could fuck you like the pretty whore that you are for us."

"Ah!" she cries, her climax hitting her suddenly.

I groan, my cock twitching like crazy to be inside her responsive pussy. "That's it, kitty. You are so slutty that just words turn you on. You don't even need a man to touch you for your pussy to gush slick all over yourself."

"Fuck," she moans. "Ben, stop. I need you, please take me."

Thank fuck.

I didn't think I could hold on much longer. Sebastian unties her and I pick her up, guiding her straight down onto my rigid cock.

"Fuck, yes," I groan.

She starts to ride me, still blindfolded, clasping her arms around my neck so she can give me a fucking like I've never had before.

"Jesus Christ," I roar as my orgasm is already here and crashing over me, filling her up with cum just like I promised.

She is taken from me, panting and sweating, by Harvey. He has his dick inside her before she can take her next breath. He tears the blindfold from her head, throwing it on the floor, forgotten. She wraps her legs around him tightly, moaning as his monster cock splits her wide open.

"Faith. Sebastian is going to ride your arse while Harvey fucks your pussy. Are you going to enjoy that, sweetheart?"

"Yes," she screams, making me smile. "Fuck, yes, please."

"Good girl."

I crawl onto the bed to sit back and watch as Sebastian pulls the lube that I told him to bring out of his back pocket.

"I will be hard again soon, kitty, needing to claim your pert backside and if Sebastian isn't done by the time I'm ready, then you are going to be in for a double stuffing. Does that sound good, pretty whore?"

"Ah!" she cries out in response to the image I've given her.

Every part of me hopes Seb takes his time with her, because I *need* to see how far we can push her dirty side.

"And before we are finished here, kitty, I need to see if all four of us can fit inside you at the same time."

"Jesus!" she roars and comes in an explosion of slick and screams that resound around the Manor and make me glad we housed her mum in the guest cottage off the kitchen courtyard.

# Chapter Fifty-Two

Faith

Harvey's cock is rubbing right up against my g-spot, and it feels fucking amazing. It feels like one big orgasm waiting to happen. Sebastian has lubed up my rear hole and is positioning me so that he can slide his dick inside. I grip Harvey tighter with my thighs as he lifts me up.

Sebastian guides his cock to the puckered hole and slides in gently.

I gasp, my heart hammering in my chest as he slowly, carefully fills me up. "Yes!" I cry out.

Sandwiched between the two alphas, I'm impaled from both ends on enormous cocks like a dirty whore...and I fucking love every second of it.

"Faith," Sebastian groans. "Fucking hell, yes."

"Harvey, make room for Xander," Ben instructs from the bed.

"Oh my God," I pant. "I can't."

"Yes, you can, and you will. Remember whose little whore you are, kitty."

The sound that escapes my lips is inhuman, wild, savage.

Sebastian slips out of me, and Harvey moves over to the bed. Sebastian lies down and Harvey places me over his cock again. It slides into my back passage as Harvey withdraws. I settle on Sebastian's cock, opening my legs as wide as I can. Xander eases himself into position, his cock gripped in his hand ready for action. He rams it in without any words. We don't need any. This is hedonistic and delicious.

Harvey manoeuvres next to Xander, one leg knelt on the bed, his cock in his hand and squashes it inside my already full pussy.

"Jesus!" I roar as I'm stretched so wide, I feel like I'm going to break.

They start pumping in rhythm, Sebastian plowing me from behind. My head falls back and I'm incapable of speech or thought, only feelings. Overwhelmed with a raw, basic need to please my alphas in any way they want. I will do whatever they want, when they say it with a happy smile on my face. I'm a dirty whore and I don't even care because I'm theirs.

"Bite me," I pant, knowing this is exactly the right time.

After the declaration in Sebastian's office a few days ago, it fell by the wayside with getting my mum settled and other stuff getting in the way.

"Mate with me, please," I beg.

Sebastian growls, his cock buried deep in my arse. The growl is deep and possessive. My skin tingles when I feel his mouth on my neck. He grazes the sensitive skin with his teeth before he bites down on my jugular quickly, harshly, almost as if he can't contain his desire to mate with me.

"Ah!" I cry out as the pain of the deep bite shocks me, but it soon wears off and I cream all over Xander's and Harvey's cocks, shuddering violently in their arms.

Ben shoves his cock into my mouth and fucks it roughly as I'm held in place while their prime alpha mates with me in this decadent setting that couldn't be more perfect if we tried.

With the blood from Sebastian's bite dripping down my neck and over my chest, Xander growls, leaning over to lap up the blood drops before he bites down right over Sebastian's.

"Uhng!" I scream as the pain of one savage bite on top of another hurts me like hell, but I don't care. I want the pain. I need it to know that I've been claimed by them, truly and completely.

Ben withdraws his cock from my mouth and clamps down on the other side of my neck, while Xander still has his teeth biting into my flesh.

"Fuck!" I thunder as another climax hits and slick gushes out of me. "No, no, no!"

I feel hot. Too hot, and when Harvey groans and shoots his load inside me, he knots with a feral grunt, locking not only us together but Xander inside me as well.

"Jesus," Xander pants, releasing me from the bite. "You've sent us into a rut."

"Or you've sent me into heat, you fuckers!" I scream.

"Or both," Sebastian says, followed up with a loud groan as he pulls back enough to still come in my rear passage, but not knot my arse, before Ben releases me from his vicious bite.

"Harvey, can you reach?" I rasp, my voice hoarse with the emotions, the sudden heat, and screaming my lungs out from the pleasure and the pain of this mating.

"I'll try," he snickers and bends down to clamp his mouth over the bite that Ben made.

Bless his Scottish socks, he is gentle and tries not to hurt me, but it does anyway. Not that I care. I am beyond pain now. Only the fuzz of the heat and the pleasure of the mating.

"Yours," I croak and then moan when Xander also knots inside me, and I feel myself tear slightly.

"Sorry, Stawbs, sorry, sorry," he pants, dumping his cum into my too full pussy.

I can't even answer him.

I can't move a single muscle.

I'm officially spent.

My eyes close, but Sebastian whispers in my ear. "You need to return the favour, baby girl."

"Can't."

"Can and have to. I need it."

I force my eyes open to stare into those beautiful blue eyes. He is smiling, full of joy. A third knot in my pussy couldn't even stop me from grabbing him by the back of his neck and baring my teeth. I chomp down good and proper on his neck, wishing he was knotted inside me as well while we did this. But it doesn't matter. All that matters is that we belong to each other now.

"Harder," he pants. "As hard as you can, baby girl."

I do as instructed and tense my jaw up, biting down with all of my waning strength.

"That's it," he pants. "Fuck, yes. Mine." He growls loudly. "Mine."

I release him and purr back. "Yours."

I then turn to the next nearest alpha, Ben, who had his head right next to Sebastian's watching the bite with a lustful interest. "Ready?"

"Born ready for you."

"Fuck you and your sexy words," I retort and then clasp my hand around the back of his neck and bite him as hard as I can.

His growl in response to my bite, thrills me and I produce even more slick around the two knotted cocks stuffed inside my pussy.

I release him at the same time that Harvey's knot goes down and he draws back, making me gasp with the weird suction and feeling my pussy adapt to fit around Xander's knot only.

"Fuck," I moan and grab Harvey when he swims into view.

My mouth is full of blood, but I don't even really taste it. I can't focus on anything except claiming my third mate. I bite him, gently at first, but when he starts to growl at me, I clamp down.

"Better, petal. Mark me as yours."

I do my best and then release him, falling back to the bed with Xander on top of me. I want to lay like this forever, but I make the monumental effort to get up and roll us over. Xander deserves better than a half-hearted bite from an exhausted omega whose pussy is going to need some serious soaking in a warm bath later.

Pulling him up with me, I smile. He returns it, his green eyes full of emotion. "Ready?"

He nods and I lean in to bite him viciously, savagely, thrilling him and his dark soul.

"Fuck, yes!" he shouts out, making me giggle around a mouthful of flesh and blood.

I release him and kiss him, knowing he won't be repulsed by the blood, in fact, if anything, it turns him on even more. Sebastian grips my hair and pulls me away from the kiss, smashing his lips to mine.

"Give me one sec to clean up and then I'm fucking your pussy whether you like it or not," he growls quietly.

My battered pussy winces, but I want it so badly, I almost weep when he pulls away.

Xander's knot releases me, and I roll off him, lying on my back next to him on the bed. I stroke his face and then feel a warm washcloth between my thighs.

Ben.

He is soothing my aches and cleaning up the blood, slick

and cum that is pooling out of me. Readying me up for his prime alpha to mate with me, the way it should be.

Sebastian returns quickly, his cock stiff and ready. He falls on top of me and kisses me, his hands tangling in my hair.

I wrap my legs around him, letting him know it's okay to just dive in there. My heat is in full force now and I'm shattered, but I won't let my alpha, my *mate* down. Not a chance in hell is this omega giving up now.

I lift my hips when he slides inside me with a soft groan.

Muffling the moan that threatens to escape from the burning between my legs, I ignore it and meet his thrusts one by one, harder, faster, needing him to bury himself as deep inside my body as he can get.

"I love you!" I pant as his hips slam against mine.

He stops and stares into my eyes. "Fuck, I love you, Faith. I love you more than I could ever imagine loving anyone. You are mine; I am yours."

"Yes," I rasp and tremble in his arms as I climax fiercely, clutching his cock with my pussy. It tightens inextricably and I groan. It's happening again.

"Jesus," Sebastian pants in my ear as his rampant thrusts die down as my pussy restricts his movement. "Jesus fucking Christ." He groans loudly, which turns into a growl. He knots inside me, firing his seed into my womb and I know. I just know deep down that this is it. Regardless of the barrier the birth control pill has put up, we are creating a baby right now and it feels so right, so pure, I start to cry.

"Baby girl," he pants, my pussy gripping him so tightly he is going a bit red in the face. "What's wrong?"

"Absolutely nothing," I sob my happy tears. "I love you. I love you all." I cast my glance at the three alphas surrounding us, holding out my hands for them. This is something we should all be a part of. Our family. Our beautiful, perfect family.

## Chapter Fifty-Three

Sebastian

Fortunately, Faith's spontaneous heat, along with our rut didn't last as long as a normal one. Within a few days, we were back to business and resuming our search for her father. Now, four weeks later, we have him.

It's been a wild goose chase at times, but we haven't given up. Ben has been relentless in his drive to find answers. He has more blood on his hands than any of us should be comfortable with, but we don't give a fuck. Now, Oliver is found and on his way back to his family.

Ben, Harvey and I are standing just off the driveway, on the luscious green grass on this beautiful, crisp, sunny day, not a cloud in the azure sky, watching our omega play with Xander in the distance. She is running and he is pretending to chase her. They are laughing and it's a gorgeous sight.

"Here's Dad," I say when I see the black Mercedes pull around the circular drive.

We watch as he climbs out and smiles, joining us on the grass.

"Hey, Dad," I say after he slaps me on the shoulder. His version of a hug. "Everything okay?"

"Yes, Oliver is on his way."

I nod and he casts his glance over to Ben. "How's the hand?"

Ben holds up his injured right hand with a smile. "Fine. Dad says it's not broken, just bruised."

"Good, good. I hear the gang member's face is definitely broken." He snickers.

Ben snorts. "You could say that. Pity he told us where to find Oliver before I was done with him."

"Now, now. You know excessive violence isn't the way we do things." He says it, but he doesn't really mean it. It's his official stance.

"Of course," Ben murmurs.

"So, that's Faith," Dad says, folding his hands behind his back and observing our omega running riot over the grass with Xander.

"Sure is," I say reverently.

"I can see why you are so tied in knots over her. She is worthy of the St. James name."

"That and more."

He tilts his head, eyes still on the gallivanting pair. "She has a way with him, doesn't she? It's beautiful to see. I never thought I would see a smile reach his eyes."

"He responds to her in ways that we have never witnessed before. She is remarkable with him. With all of us."

"I'm glad you found her. She is young, but she will give you a good family in time."

Ben, Harvey and I exchange a secretive glance. Faith hasn't confirmed it yet, but we are all fairly sure she conceived during our mating. We are waiting for her to bring it up, even though it is killing me. I want to shout it from the rooftops. We don't know for sure it's mine, but secretly, I think it is. Not that it matters in the long run. Faith has agreed to give us all children and mine will be heir to the St. James pack. Even if she's a girl. I don't care how that will work, but that's the way it is. It has gone down my bloodline for generations and will continue to do so. My father passed the pack to me five years ago and we haven't felt complete until Faith came into our lives. We adore her, would do anything for her and she is finally starting to let us.

"Are you going to tell her the whole story?" Dad asks.

I nod slowly. "We haven't yet decided when, but we will have to tell her that Pete was definitely behind getting Oliver abducted and imprisoned so that he could take over his life. Fucking prick. I can't believe he applied for Oliver's job the day he was declared dead. Arsehole," I growl, "What kind of deluded fucker was he and how jealous he was of Oliver and being passed over by Anne all those years ago when she found her mate in Oliver. It's sick."

"And it's something we are taking very seriously," Dad says. "This type of behaviour in our community is not going to be tolerated. I just hope that Pete turns up so he can face his trial."

We fall silent. We will never speak of what Xander did, what we were all complicit in doing. Pete got what was coming to him. End of story.

"Ah, here's Oliver now," Dad says, gesturing to the Range Rover headed our way.

We hang back.

Faith has spotted the car and is running towards it.

Oliver gets out, he is frail and has been mistreated for many years. But he catches Faith when she flings her arms around him, squealing with delight at seeing her beloved father once more. Anne rushes up to them, a totally different woman to the one we took from that crappy house a few weeks ago.

My heart fills with warmth for them as Derek gets out of the car as well and they embrace as a family for the first time in years.

Faith pulls away from her dad and beckons us over. As one, we surge forward, Xander closer than us and reaching her first.

I hope her dad will be proud of her choices, *us*. It means a lot to me that he accepts us.

"Dad, this is Sebastian," she says, grabbing my hand as I get closer to her.

"We've met," Oliver says with a smirk. "You used to be a little snot-faced kid running riot in your dad's chambers."

"Ugh," I groan, remembering that I was a bit of a tearaway. "Good to see you again, Mr. Halstead."

I hold my hand out, but he grabs it and pulls me to him for a hug my father would never give me. "It's Oliver," he says and squeezes me before he lets go and turns to meet his daughter's other mates.

She smiles secretively at me, and it tells me all I need to know.

She is having our baby.

My heart pounds in my chest and my palms start to sweat.

All I can think of in that moment is that this is the happiest I've ever been, and it can only get better from here.

"I love you," I murmur softly, drawing her to me, inhaling that delicious scent of hers.

"I love you and our family," she replies. "And I can't wait for it to grow bigger and full of even more love."

"Me either."

Ben takes her from me then, gently holding her, needing to be near her. We all do. Harvey can't keep his hands off her either and Xander is closer to her than I ever thought he could get to another person.

It fills my heart with joy, and I know that forever is going to be perfect.

# Epilogue

### Faith

*Three months later*

Wrapping the thin cotton scarf around my neck that smells like all of my alphas, I take a steadying breath and then plaster a smile on my face. Dressed in a white summery dress with big strawberries on it, I shove open the door to the informal sitting room, I find my alphas shooting a game of pool. They look up when I enter, smiling and excited.

"Well?" Sebastian says, racing over with the enthusiasm of a young puppy. "What did he say?"

"Sit," I say, gesturing to the couch.

His face drops into a serious expression and he leads me over to the couch. I sit and they gather around.

"Everything is fine," I say. "More than fine. DFP…" I giggle that I still call him that and Ben snorts. "…got the results back from the amnio, and we're having a boy!" I know that

267

will delight them and I'm not wrong. Cheering and laughter ensues with high-fives and exclamations in a manly manner of prowess and whatnot.

"Also," I interrupt them and hope that they don't go fucking ballistic when I impart my next bit of news. This is the part that makes me nervous. "Don't be angry with me, but I don't like surprises. Never have, after my dad... Anyway, I needed to know on a level that wasn't just curiosity or a need to single any of you out. It goes soul deep. I asked the gynae to do a DNA test at the amniocentesis. Are you mad?" I chew my lip nervously.

I receive four slightly confused looks back.

"Mad? Why would we be mad? We are dying to know," Sebastian says. "None of us wanted to bring it up with you in case you were mad with us."

"Oh," I say, laughing in relief. "Well, the results came back. I was sneaky and got a bit of DNA from all of you. Sebastian. Our baby is the new heir to the St. James pack."

I wait.

Nothing.

I gulp. Is he not happy?

"Jesus," he says, his eyes brimming with tears. "Really?"

I nod, relieved. "Really."

"Fuck, yes!" he roars, jumping up and gesturing rudely to his crotch with both hands in a way that only a man would. I roll my eyes, laughing at his crazy self.

"First alpha down, three to go," Xander whispers in my ear.

I turn to him and cup his face. "I'm so glad you came around. You will make such a loving father. Our babies will be lucky to have you in their lives."

"*I* am the lucky one. I don't deserve to have you love me."

"Fuck off with the pity party. We don't do them here," I say sternly, but also joking at the same time.

He chuckles. "No, we don't. You are right. I should thank my lucky stars that you came into our lives."

"Thank *me*, arsehole," Matt says, joining us. "If I hadn't shagged her that night, you wouldn't be here now."

"Fact," Harvey says. "It's a good thing we like you or you'd be out on your arse looking for another pack."

He snorts. "Oh, please. You know you can't get rid of me that easily."

Running my hands over my tiny bump, I sit back and watch them insult each other with love. We are the perfect pack unit, and I am so excited to see what the future brings. Whatever it is, I know it's going to be epic and absolutely beautiful.

Join my Facebook Group: Sinfully Delicious Romance
Sign up to my newsletter: Eve Newton's News

The second book in this series of RH Omegaverse Standalones is Knot a Tie

**Being privileged and wealthy has its perks, until one day it becomes a liability.** *Being a pampered princess is all well and good until I decide to visit my cousin in London and break down on the side of the road. As I'm waiting for help, I'm hijacked and shoved into the back of an expensive car full of hot alphas.*

# About the Author

Eve is a British novelist with a specialty for delicious romance, with strong female leads, causing her to develop a Reverse Harem Fantasy series, several years ago: The Forever Series.

She lives in the UK, with her husband and five kids, so finding the time to write is short, but definitely sweet. She currently has over fifty book in her catalogue. Eve hopes to release some new and exciting projects in the next couple of years, so stay tuned!

# Also by Eve Newton

https://evenewton.com/links

Printed in Great Britain
by Amazon

82185664R00162